The Goodbye House

WITHDRAWN

The Goodbye House

a novel

LAWRENCE COATES

UNIVERSITY OF NEVADA PRESS
Reno & Las Vegas

WEST WORD FICTION

University of Nevada Press, Reno, Nevada 89557 USA
Copyright © 2015 by Lawrence Coates
All rights reserved
Manufactured in the United States of America
Design by Kathleen Szawiola

Library of Congress Cataloging-in-Publication Data
Coates, Lawrence, 1956–
The goodbye house / Lawrence Coates.
pages ; cm. — (West word fiction)
ISBN 978-0-87417-981-1 (cloth : alk. paper) —
ISBN 978-0-87417-982-8 (e-book)
1. Domestic fiction. I. Title.
PS3553.O153G66 2015
813'.54—dc23
2015014443

The paper used in this book meets the requirements of American
National Standard for Information Sciences—Permanence of Paper
for Printed Library Materials, ANSI/NISO Z39.48-1992 (R2002).
Binding materials were selected for strength and durability.

The first chapter of this book appeared in a slightly different form in
Ascent, a publication of Concordia College, under the title "Temporary
Landscapes." The seventh chapter of this book appeared in a slightly
different form in the *Pacific Review,* a publication of California State
University, San Bernardino, under the title "This Is the Place."

FIRST PRINTING
23 22 21 20 19 18 17 16 15
5 4 3 2 1

. . . • . . .

FOR

Betty and Howard Coates
and Nancy Howell,

AND IN MEMORY OF

Viola and Edwin Kersgard,
Carolyn and Edward Bartlome,
and William Howell

. . . ● . . .

Earth's increase, foison plenty
Barns and garners never empty
Vines with clustering bunches growing
Plants with goodly burthen bowing

Spring come to you at the farthest
In the very end of harvest!
Scarcity and want shall shun you
Ceres' blessing so is on you.
    —*The Tempest*, Act 4, Scene 1

We are such stuff
As dreams are made on.
    —*The Tempest*, Act 4, Scene 1

The Goodbye House

1

SHE REMEMBERED THIS: the time she stepped onto the roof of her childhood home in San José, the time she felt the tilting shingles under her feet as her father held her tiny hand in one of his and kept his other hand broad and strong at the small of her back. Katherine was five, and her brothers, eight and ten, had been throwing a Frisbee across the back lawn while she sat on the cement slab patio and toed the soft grass with her sneakers. "You're too young to play," they'd said. She watched with some resentment the disc spinning back and forth in the lowering sunlight as they all waited to be called in to dinner.

It was the end of August, 1961, and the air in California was still and full, broken only by the distant chirr of power lawnmowers. In a week, her brothers would begin school again, and she would be left behind. Katherine missed her brothers when they were off. Even if they treated her like a pest and left her out of games, she still liked to study what they were doing, plan what she would do one day when she was their age.

The backyard was narrow and completely fenced in by six-foot lengths of cedar running along the property lines, separating it from similar backyards on either side and behind it. As the boys grew bored, they began to throw the Frisbee in elaborate curves out over the fence and back into the yard. They called to Katherine to watch, then spun it up at a steep angle so that it descended right back into their hands. They tried for diving catches, leaping catches, they sprang straight up and grabbed the Frisbee between their legs. Katherine felt a little happier they were at least including her as an audience.

Then her oldest brother tried to curve the Frisbee over the roof, and it caught on the low peak and skidded against the wooden shingles and came to a rest three feet from the gutter. The two boys looked at each other.

"Who's going to tell Dad?" the older one asked.

"*I* didn't do it," the younger one said.

Katherine's oldest brother looked at her, as though considering the possibility of including her in the blame somehow. He looked up at the roof, hoping for a sudden gust of wind. Then he trudged into the house through the sliding glass patio doors.

After a minute, Katherine heard the side door to the garage open and saw her father appear through the gate, carrying a wooden ladder over his shoulder like a heroic fireman. The tips of the ladder were swaddled in cloth fixed with tape, and he laid the ladder gently against the eaves above the stucco siding. Then he scaled it nimbly, bent forward as he stepped from the ladder, and stood up against the sky, high as a tower. He was taller than anyone Katherine had ever seen, and now, on the roof, he looked colossal.

He walked easily over to the Frisbee, tossed it down, then shaded his eyes with a flat hand.

"Hey," he said. "You can see a blimp from here."

There was something special about seeing a blimp in the early sixties. Only a few blimps were in existence, all owned by Goodyear Tires, and unlike airplanes that appeared only as vapor trails, a blimp flew low and lazy and dreamlike. It took up a piece of sky, like a planet you could visit in the future. And it usually had a message, in electric lights across the side. When they saw a blimp, they would all gaze as it floated toward them, and Katherine would wait impatiently for the moment when her father would clear his throat and state, "Here's what it says . . ."

"Is it coming this way?" the older brother asked.

"It's going toward the bay."

"Can we climb up?" the younger brother asked.

Her father hesitated. "Keep one hand on the ladder at all times," he said. "And let me help you over the edge."

Katherine's older brother scrambled up and within seconds was standing next to her father. Her middle brother climbed to the top of the ladder, then waited until her father grasped his hand strongly before he stepped out.

"Don't stand close to the edge," her father warned. "And don't forget you're standing on an incline."

"Daddy," Katherine said.

"You're too small to come up," her older brother said.

Her father looked down at her. She stood next to the ladder, twisting on one foot, hoping to be taken up. She could see her brothers, watching the blimp, and she looked in the same direction, but she could see nothing but empty sky.

Then her father was climbing down. "Promise me you'll be careful," he said. "I don't ever want to see you hurt."

"I promise," she said. It was an easy promise to make. She didn't really believe she could be hurt with her father near her.

He picked her up and placed her on the fourth rung, then climbed up behind her so that his body sheltered her. He helped her to the next rung, then climbed up one himself. Rung by rung, she rose up. Her older brother's head loomed over the edge of the roof. He seemed an obstacle at first, but then he held his right hand out to her. Her middle brother was sitting on the roof as an anchor, holding her older brother's left hand in his. The sky grew larger as she reached the top of the ladder. She took her brother by one hand, while her father held her other hand, and with a step she was on the roof. The wooden shingles crunched and felt oddly fragile, even under her soft-soled Keds.

Her father stood beside her, and she felt utterly safe as they all watched the blimp meander to the north. Katherine could see some lighted lettering on the side, even though it was far away. The lights were flashing on and off and would show up better in the twilight and early evening.

"Here's what it says . . . ," her father said.

They all looked at him.

"It says, 'The Watson family is ready for dinner.'"

Her two brothers objected. Katherine smiled and looked about. The view from high up was new and different. Stretching to the north, to the west, to the east, there lay a plain of roofs, all low-peaked shingled roofs like her own. The roofs extended as far as she could see, humping up and down, an uneven shingle prairie, until the roofs no longer belonged to distinct houses but simply blended in with each other. Here and there, the green crown of a tree broke the line of weathered cedar wood in the still-recent housing tract, and the Coast Range rose to the west. But it was mostly roofs, a landscape of roofs, with a slow blimp floating free above them. Had the person who drew these streets on a map imagined this strange landscape?

She heard the patio door slide open and her mother call that dinner was ready. Then the voice stopped.

"Where is everybody?" her mother asked. "Are you there?"

· · · • · · ·

Now, in the late afternoon, Katherine parked her ten-year-old Saturn in the driveway of the same house. She stood, forty-seven years old, fifteen pounds heavier than when she was twenty, highlights in her blondish hair, dressed in colors of rust and green with long earrings of silver and onyx dangling in the late sun of September, 2003. She took from the car two plastic sacks of groceries and walked to the front porch, concrete with a peeling wooden park bench filled with odd potted plants sheltered by a low overhang. From the eaves, there hung a redwood sign her father had custom-made in Felton that read *Peaceable Isle*.

When she walked in, she still felt that odd sensation of being a teenager again, walking into her old living room. But also the sensation of being her mother. Her mother had always disliked the way the front door opened right onto the living room, with no entry foyer that would allow her to put down her bags, hang up her coat, and not track right over the carpet to get to the kitchen. Katherine found herself displeased in the same way. She walked in with groceries now, not schoolbooks, and just like her mother, she felt oppressed by having to decide what to make for dinner.

Katherine had moved into her father's house ten months earlier, in debt, with a missing husband, with Betty, her disdainful daughter of seventeen, and with Carter, fifteen, becoming secretive and withdrawn. An events planner by profession, in charge of organizing the annual user's conference for BPI, a software firm in Milpitas, but unable to plan for the events in her own life. Her own mother dead when she had been her son's age, absent and therefore eternally wise and silent, always keeping to herself some bit of guidance that would have kept Katherine from error. Her father, a Pearl Harbor veteran, still living in the house that he had bought with a Veterans Administration loan after the war, now eighty and beating back lesions every three weeks with chemotherapy.

When she moved back in with their father, her two older brothers were delighted. One brother was working in story development in Los Angeles. The other was a college professor in Ohio. They had moved on, they were successes, blight had not touched their well-fashioned lives. The national mourning of 2001 they wore lightly, and neither had a child in the army, or nearing eighteen years of age. They had moved on, and they looked back at the house on Catesby Street as old and squat and not the kind of place they would ever live again. And she wondered if her brothers didn't think sometimes that it had all fallen into place rather nicely: her runaway husband, her need for a place to live, their father's need for a caregiver, the tract home that was all paid off with low property taxes. She was the daughter, and she was convenient. And her brothers were off the hook with a clear conscience.

Now she heard her father, Henry, rumble from the sunken den. "By God, who is that in the house?" He was up and walking toward her before she could put down the groceries, wearing one of his bright Hawaiian shirts covered with flowers. He liked wearing Hawaiian shirts, and shirts open at the throat with a silk scarf, and a beret to hide his hair loss. He took her in his arms and hugged her roughly, as he often did. Then he turned her loose and looked at her.

"You're losing too much weight," Henry said. "You're wasting away. Soon there won't be anything left of you."

"Ha," Katherine said. "I feel like a water buffalo." She had been trying to stay a size 8 for years, sometimes coaxing her weight down so that she could fit her clothes and sometimes finding her weight floating up so that half her wardrobe was too tight. When she was thinner, she tended to buy clothes that were brighter in color, cornflower blues and turquoises and aquamarines. When she was forced into the rack of 10s, she found herself buying plainer stuff, beiges and creams and blacks. Her closet looked like a struggle between her aspirations for how she should look and her frequent admissions of defeat.

"You have a secret admirer," Henry said. "Water buffalo or no."

He pointed at a gift-wrapped box on the dining room table. Katherine crossed to the table, picked the box up, shook it. Something shifted inside, heavy and muffled.

"Not a bomb, is it?"

"Hope not."

"This was on the front porch?"

Henry shook his head. "It was right there."

It took Katherine a moment to process what her father had said. "He broke into the house?"

Henry shrugged, nodded. Katherine sat down heavily. She picked up the envelope, the paper thick and textured, and flipped it to look at both sides. Her name was on the front. She slid a finger in and ripped it open. The card slipped out, a romantic card with hearts and flowers and the Eiffel Tower on the front. Inside, it read, "I'll be seeing you in all those old familiar places," and it was signed, "Love, Scott." There was no phone number, no address.

Inside the box was a small, expensive, cut-glass bottle of perfume.

"So he's back," she said. "And this is what he thinks is a good way to get back in touch. Break into the house and leave gifts."

Henry sat down opposite his daughter, at the same table where he had once sat with his wife to talk over what to do. The table had a cloth spread over it because it was old and the finish worn through. It was a solid maple table, the first part of a maple dining room set he and his wife began but never completed. He had never wanted to replace the table. He once thought about refinishing it, but never quite managed to do it.

"What do you think we should do?" he asked.

"I don't know," Katherine said.

She lifted up the bottle of perfume, looked at the label.

"*Passion*," she said. "Incredible."

. . . • . . .

Scott Cochran, Katherine's husband, had run through their money, including retirement accounts, investing in Internet startup companies. It was that time in Silicon Valley. Every day, there were stories about twenty-four-year-olds who had made millions overnight. *The largest legal creation of wealth in history!* Scott read and reread these stories and convinced himself that those kids didn't deserve all that money, certainly not any more than he did. He began to feel old at forty-eight, as though he had been born twenty years too soon, as though the golden opportunity had somehow skipped his generation.

He found his first investment through some cassette tapes he listened to while doing the Stairmaster at the gym. It was an Internet store that would grow through word of mouth. Each store owner would have a portal that would offer name-brand products at rock-bottom prices that could be drop-shipped from a secure location. Name-Brand. Rock-Bottom. Drop-Shipped. Secure. But the real genius was that each store owner could sign up additional store owners. If you had a friend or neighbor who needed a Sony television, you could ask them to buy it through your store at a better price than they could get at Target. You then asked them if they would be interested in owning their own store. As they began to sell things, some small percentage of their profits would come to you. And as they signed up store owners, you would get a percentage of their percentage. If you were in on the ground floor, the profits would soon be tremendous.

With each store you bought, you also received a number of shares in the company. Pre-ipo shares. Scott listened to that on the tape as well. Pre-Initial Public Offering. And when the ipo came through, and each of your shares was suddenly worth thousands, you would read about yourself in the newspaper.

Scott listened to the tape as he worked out, taking one of the machines in the big front windows and wearing classic black Ray Ban Wayfarers so that he would look good from the parking lot.

The phrases *Name Brand, Rock Bottom, Ground Floor, Limitless Potential* hypnotized him. He bought one portal, and then another, since he couldn't buy more shares in the company without buying more portals. Katherine never paid much attention to the financial statements and didn't notice when the balances began to go down. She trusted him for that.

They had moved to a new house in a development called Oak Commons in 1999, where Carter and Betty, their son and daughter, could go to better schools. Betty was beginning high school that year, so it seemed like the right time. The house had a two-story front foyer that opened onto a great room with a fireplace and vaulted ceilings. The master bath, on the ground floor, had a Jacuzzi tub with a garden view, and the bedroom had a walk-in closet large enough to sleep in. They were able to sell their first house for three times what they'd paid for it, and they had a down payment and money to spare. Scott told Katherine they were being smart, could afford it, and deserved it. And she trusted him for that as well.

While waiting for his stores to make good, Scott began to make other investments. There were always tips in chat rooms, and he decided that buying a lot of different recommended stocks was a way to be safe. If even one hit it big, it would make up for dozens of losers.

Then, early in 2002, he was laid off. He had an engineering degree from Chico State, but for many years he had worked on the marketing side of a company that created software to teach people how to use computer programs. The company had been acquiring other firms that sold training software, expanding into online educational products, and reporting record profits. But when clients began to reject the standard three-year license deals and competitors cut prices, it turned out the record profits were an illusion. Sales orders had been booked on products still in development, defective products were returned and the returns never recorded, phony invoices were created by sending orders between fax machines in the same office. The company announced that revenues were down one-third from the previous quarter, and marketing personnel were the first to go.

That same year, Scott and Katherine were hit with a huge tax bill. There were penalties for withdrawing funds from retirement accounts, but Scott had decided that the penalties could be easily paid for with the profits he would be making. He asked for one extension for filling out their income tax, and then another. He spent time at an outplacement firm, posting résumés to Monster, Career Builder, Hot Jobs, and also checking his investments. At the end of each three-month extension, the actual value of the stock he had bought was less.

Scott tried to avoid telling Katherine until he at least had found another job, but a job offer never materialized. His engineering skills were considered out-of-date and his marketing skills tainted. When he finally told her, he said one option was to sell the house. It turned out there were no other options except bankruptcy. They had refinanced once to pay off credit cards and a car loan with home equity, and there wouldn't be much from the house after the bills were settled. And Katherine refused to go into bankruptcy with a man who was so ready to hide the truth from her because he was convinced he knew better.

Scott disappeared soon after the house closed, before Katherine could move forward with a divorce. The studio apartment he'd rented in Cupertino, one small box among many others overlooking a small landscaped commons, was empty after a month. He'd left the house on Catesby Street as a forwarding address, and for months overdue bills for electricity and gas came, red lettering on the envelope stating "2nd Notice" or "Final Notice." Katherine wrote *Not at this address* on the envelopes and left them outside for the letter carrier. Sometimes she wrote *He's not here and I don't give a damn where he is*. Other times, she wrote *If you see him, say hello, he might be in Tangiers*. She was certain he would turn up sooner or later.

· · · • · · ·

Scott had gone back to a barely remembered time of his life, a phase that was over before he even met Katherine. In 1974 he'd enlisted in the navy just in time to aid with the evacuation of Saigon, and after his hitch he put in a year working aboard combat support ships as an able seaman with the Military Sealift Command. He'd been aboard a fleet oiler in the Indian Ocean in 1979, when the Iranian hostage crisis struck, and had spent months servicing aircraft carrier battle groups. Some part of him was disappointed that no action was taken, that he hadn't come back with stories to tell.

The attacks on New York and Washington coincided with his investments dwindling toward zero. After he lost his job, he began to follow the military buildup in the Indian Ocean and the Arabian Sea, the same waters he'd sailed in twenty-three years earlier. He visualized the aircraft carrier battle groups converging on the region and wondered if the same great names were there that had been there in 1979: the *Kittyhawk*, the *Nimitz*, the *Enterprise*. And he visualized the fleet oilers, like the ship he'd sailed on, standing off over the horizon, ready to rendezvous at dusk to fill a carrier's vast tanks with jet fuel, while fighter jets swarmed overhead to provide cover.

The war in Afghanistan resolved itself quickly, according to reports. But the war in Iraq, foretold by newspapers and magazines and network news, was just ahead when he had to admit to Katherine how much money he had lost, how much they owed, what a mess he'd made of things. He was broke and living in a one-bedroom apartment. He was unemployed. He saw the age of fifty looming, a narrow doorway to a narrower corridor. He was still seeking a life of consequence. And he found a website for the Military Sealift Command (MSC). With battle groups in the Indian Ocean indefinitely, he knew there would be a need for experienced seamen.

· · · • · · ·

Katherine received the first letter from Scott soon after the war began. Then they came weekly. Scott's letters described the long hours of work, the nights when they stayed at the refueling rigs until dawn with an aircraft carrier to port and a destroyer to starboard. They described the empty sea between refuelings, the kinds of routine maintenance he was always occupied with, slushing the rigging, chipping rust and painting with red lead and a top coat. They described the sunsets over the Indian Ocean, and how bright the stars were at night, and the sound of the ship's wake as it spread out from the stern.

Katherine wrote him back and told him that he should under no circumstances consider himself welcome to stay at her father's house. It wasn't his home. She wrote that she hoped he would stay safe and settle somewhere nearby when he came back, so that he could stay involved with the children. Money was also a problem, since her father had to keep most of his funds for his own medical expenses, and she'd like to be able to help with college for the kids.

His letters back didn't acknowledge her letters at all. He told of watching a helicopter hover over the ship's flight deck, forward of the bridge, and lower canvas bags of mail and pick up bags of outgoing mail. And he told of his hope, as he watched, that the mail contained a letter from her. He didn't mention that she'd written him that he wouldn't be welcome. It was infuriating.

Then, in August, the letters stopped. A week went by without a letter, and then another week. Carter was getting ready to begin high school, seeming a little adrift since they'd had to move. Betty had graduated and moved to Aptos, living with her boyfriend in a house owned by his parents, waiting tables at a small Szechwan restaurant on West Cliff Drive. Henry had his chemotherapy sessions. Katherine didn't notice that weeks had gone by without a letter until the month turned and she stopped to wonder if he was well. The news coverage of the war rarely showed ships, but she thought she would have heard if a support ship had sunk. She watched CNN several nights in a row, but the news from the Middle East was contradictory and confusing and didn't tell her anything about the man she was still technically married to.

After a few days, she forgot to wonder about him. A phone call would come, sooner or later, and he would be over his big adventure, and they would settle some things.

· · · • · · ·

Most afternoons when he felt well, Henry had lunch with a regular group in the Garden Spot Café at the Blue Skies Bowl, a bowling alley surrounded on one side by subdivisions and tract homes and on the other side by the Western Horizons Shopping Mall. The Blue Skies Bowl was built in the early sixties, the name chosen to appeal both to those "Blue Sky" families moving to San José to be part of the aerospace industry and to those older residents who remembered the Irving Berlin song from the Bing Crosby movie. After four decades, the bowling alley was slated for demolition, to be replaced by townhouses and condominiums, and the regulars at the café had not yet decided where they would gather once it was gone.

In the café, Henry had a reuben or a hot pastrami sandwich, bad for his heart, he knew, but since his prostate was going to kill him first, it didn't matter much. The group he met there were all of an age more or less, some city workers, some in real estate, one who had managed the produce section at a Safeway. They were veterans—all had served overseas during World War II. They weren't the sort who joined the Veterans of Foreign Wars or the American Legion, but they held that time in common, and though they didn't discuss it among themselves, a number of them gave talks about the war through a Veterans in the Schools program.

Henry's prostate cancer wasn't the first in the group and probably wouldn't be the last. A man who liked a dirty joke, Al Dayton, told them all that it was the pissing that first let him know he had a problem, the pissing and the backaches that weren't just the routine. And when he was ready to go in for the radical surgery, he looked down and sang "Thanks for the memories," like Bob Hope.

Henry found the gift box of perfume one afternoon when he came back from the Garden Spot. He knew it wouldn't have been hard for Scott to see that nobody was home. He kept his Buick LeSabre in the driveway, since the garage was filled with things he'd never thrown away, and he drove the few blocks to the bowling alley. When he was younger, he had enjoyed the walk, but the chemotherapy left his feet swollen and tingling, like a thousand small knives were cutting into the soles. Neuropathy, he was told. And so he began to wear oversized slippers with rubber bottoms, and he drove to the café. Anyone could see that the driveway was empty during the day, anybody could see when the house was vacant.

. . . • . . .

Katherine had thought about support groups when Scott left, but she decided against it. There were probably support groups for women whose husbands had blown all their money on Internet stocks. She was sure of it. But there wouldn't be support groups for women whose husbands had run off to sea at the age of forty-eight. Pretending they were twenty-five again. That's not normal. Running away to sea. The whole thing seemed archaic.

When two days passed since the perfume was left, and Scott didn't try to contact her like a normal human being, she decided to try to catch him in the house. Perhaps they could talk to each other like adults. Her father insisted that she take him with her, and so she left work at noon and met him at the Garden Spot. She liked seeing her father sitting at the same round table in a vinyl-lined booth in the corner. He always seemed perfectly content there, happy that his little haven hadn't yet changed, happy to meet old friends, even if the talk was no longer about problems with business or the kids and now centered on doctors and medical bills and retirement accounts.

Henry stood up when Katherine came in. "See?" he said. "I told you an attractive young woman was picking me up today."

The other men laughed and asked Katherine to sit down, join them, have a cup of coffee, but she told them next time, when she wasn't so busy.

They left together in his Buick. Henry still liked to be the one driving. When they went in for his chemo treatments, he drove to the oncology unit and they took his car, even though they both knew that she would be driving back after he'd had the shunt in his chest hooked up for three hours.

They saw an old green Plymouth Fury in front of the house.

"Look at that beater car," Henry said. "You think he's driving that?"

"I don't know, Dad," Katherine said. "But I guess I'll find out." She flipped down the sun visor and looked at her hair in the mirror and grimaced.

When she moved back into the house, she had to adjust to opening the front door. During the years of living on her own, and then with Scott, she had evolved from just walking in as though she still lived there, to giving a quick knock and then walking in, to ringing the doorbell and waiting for her father to let her in. After moving back, it took her some time to be able to simply open the door. At first she felt some reluctance about it—she didn't want to admit that, yes, she had moved back home at the age of forty-seven and those other houses and apartments she'd lived in were only temporary. But after months of unloading groceries or walking in with two briefcases and bracing the screen door open with her hip while she fumbled with her keys, her resistance vanished with the press of the everyday.

Now, absurdly, she knocked three times before turning the key, as though Scott had some rights over the house she was entering. She patted her hair once more and opened the door.

· · · • · · ·

Scott had been at sea longer than he'd expected. Baghdad fell in May, and he thought that the aircraft carriers and their battle groups would soon head for their home ports, and his own ship would make the long voyage back to Subic Bay, in the PI, and he could get paid off and back home. But after May, the carrier groups stayed in the region, circling around, and he heard they were still flying sorties day and night. And his ship stayed in the area too, having its own massive tanks refilled by a commercial tanker out at sea. The only land they saw in months was the coast of Oman, which looked like a giant sand dune to Scott. They sailed east out of the Arabian Sea only after another oiler came out to relieve them. The nearest he'd been to Iraq was hundreds of miles south. The war continued on without him, without the promised end.

The first thing Scott did after he flew in to San Francisco was buy a car. He knew his credit was short. He didn't have a bank account. He had no place to live. But he had six months' wages, almost twenty thousand dollars, in cash in a pouch hung around his neck. He picked the Plymouth Fury because it was the biggest thing on the lot. It reminded him of something his father would have owned, with a hood that stretched out long in front of the windshield, sharp lines and square corners, a roar from the V8 when he turned the key that the dealer couldn't guarantee was not due to a faulty muffler. The vinyl top had peeled, and the metal underneath showed rust, but the air-conditioning worked, and the radio was tuned to KNBR, the San Francisco Giants station, and the utter rightness of sitting in a big car listening to the pregame show in late September sold him.

Scott's insurance had expired, but the dealer arranged to sell him two weeks' worth of coverage through the Internet, so he could get off the lot and have something until he got settled. Then he took off on Highway 101 and headed toward the Santa Clara Valley, San José, home.

He checked into the El Rancho Motel, about ten miles from where Katherine was living with her father. The El Rancho was one of a few old motels, built along freeways in the fifties in California, that had survived into the age of franchises and centralized registration systems. He took a room on the second floor, paying for a week in cash. The room had heavy plastic drapes covering a single window, a sheet-metal box that controlled both the heat and the air-conditioning, a lowboy chest of drawers, a twenty-three-inch TV, and a king-size bed.

Scott had only a large duffel bag for luggage, and he threw it onto the lowboy, kicked off his shoes, and fell back into bed. He breathed in and out deeply, softly, trying to feel he was at a homecoming, trying to feel he had accomplished something, trying to feel he was in control.

The following afternoon, he drove by the house on Catesby Street. The driveway was empty, though he noticed one oil spot that looked fresh. Katherine probably still hadn't repaired the oil leak in her Saturn. The blinds were drawn, and the aluminum-frame windows were cracked open. That told him the house was probably empty. The lawn was a little ragged, and the rose bushes along the side of the house were growing tall and awkward, with spindly sprays of faded blossoms hanging down, and the other shrubs needed pruning. There was work he could do.

Next to his father-in-law's house, someone had bought two of the old ranch houses from the original subdivision and razed them and was erecting a two-story house in their place. This had happened since he left. The house was already framed up and sided, and it pushed out close to the property lines on both sides with a steep-pitched roof towering over everything else on the street. Scott looked at it as he drove by slowly, wondered about the square footage, the number of bathrooms, the number of bedrooms. But he had no doubt, he was looking at a multimillion-dollar house. Once a house was grand enough to deserve that title, any further precision about the actual price seemed superfluous.

At the end of the block, he turned the Fury around and cruised back by his father-in-law's house. He envisioned a house even larger than the one being built rising from the land. And he thought that if the old slab house could be torn down, or if a fire should strike it, it could be worth a fortune. A fortune.

Scott left for an hour and came by one more time close to five. A Buick LeSabre was in the driveway—his father-in-law was home. Scott looked at his watch. He knew his father-in-law's habits, and he knew he had been at the Garden Spot all afternoon.

The next day, Scott parked the Fury right in front of the house, so that anyone who saw him would think he had nothing to hide. A narrow walkway alongside the garage where the garbage can sat led to a gate into the fenced backyard. A single-paned aluminum-sash window opened from the sunken den onto the cement slab patio. It was simple to jimmy the screen—the aluminum bent easily, and he would reshape and reinstall it before he left. He grasped the window frame and hoisted himself up, ducked his head through, and put a foot down on a black sofa before stepping onto the floor.

The house was weirdly quiet. He had been in his father-in-law's house many times, but never alone. He took two steps, then stopped. His steps seemed loud, loud enough for someone outside to hear him, and he sat down on the edge of a step and took off his shoes. In his stocking feet, he made a round of the house, crouching down near any windows that faced the street. He saw that Henry remained in the master bedroom. His wife's room held objects he knew from their own room together. A wooden tree that held bracelets and necklaces, a frame screwed to the wall with earrings hanging from it, three bottles of perfume, a small lamp shaped like a tulip. There was nothing from Betty. She must have moved out, as Katherine said in one of her letters.

He wondered whether Katherine slept in the upper or lower bunk bed. Both of them were neatly made with bedspreads that probably dated from the time she'd lived here as a girl, purple chenille with a fringe of small dangling balls. He lifted a corner of the bedspread on the top bunk carefully and saw that there were no sheets underneath. The bottom bunk had sheets, and Scott smiled, pleased with himself. He sat down on the edge of the bed, and swung his feet onto it, and lay still.

He felt the house breathing all about him. The stillness that earlier had seemed weird and threatening now felt warm, enveloping. He didn't feel like a sneak or a thief. He felt like he was right where he belonged. He felt he could go to sleep peacefully here, and peacefully awake.

His watch beeped, and he opened his eyes. He had set the timer to remind him when he had an hour left before he had to go. He made the bed carefully, so that the bedspread was arranged identically to the one on the upper bunk, and he went into his son's room.

There was a twin bed on one side of the room and a cheap computer desk in the corner. Nothing on the walls except a poster with a saying by Chief Seattle that he remembered from Carter's room in their old house. He looked in the closet and didn't see anything that would let him know what his son had been thinking or feeling while he had been gone. Just jeans, T-shirts, a windbreaker, sweatshirts. One sports coat that he wore to church, with a clip-on tie attached to the lapel. Scott made a mental note to teach Carter to knot a real tie as soon as possible.

He looked at the computer on the desk, a bulky Dell in black plastic. There might be more of Carter's mind in the computer than anywhere else.

He looked at his watch. Then he tiptoed back to the den, put his shoes on, and replaced the screen, pushing it back into shape. He left by the back door, walked back out to his Fury, and drove back to the El Rancho.

The next day, Scott entered the house the same way. He went to Katherine's bed and lay down for a half hour. Then he went into his son's room and turned on his computer. As the screen brightened, he got down on his knees and looked at the back of the computer tower. They still had dial-up Internet service. At their house in Oak Commons, they had always upgraded to the fastest possible service as soon as it was available. For the kids. Was this a measure of how Carter was suffering? Slow and outdated Internet service?

He clicked on Explorer to look at the favorites, what was bookmarked, what sites had been recently visited. There were a couple of sites related to Shakespeare. A school project. Scott nodded approvingly. He opened up Word and looked at the documents Carter had recently written. One on *The Tempest* had been saved last night, probably still in progress.

He began to search through other documents on the hard drive. He didn't admit it, but he was looking for something about himself. Some kind of journal, a letter never sent. He was searching for the profile he formed in his son's imaginative horizon, the dark cutout figure of the absent. He wanted to know he was missed, and he wanted to know exactly how he was missed, the quality of his son's regret for his departure. He felt he didn't know his son very well, felt he had only fulfilled the external forms and ceremonies of being a father. If he knew how his son missed him, he might know how his son needed him to be.

When his watch beeped again, he had found nothing, and he had to shut the computer down. On his way out, he stopped where keys hung from a row of hooks and found a ring with a number of similar keys. One fit the back door, and he took it with him. He could make a copy and return it before anyone noticed.

Scott continued in this half-life for several weeks, occupying during the day the space his family would occupy at night. He came every two or three days after replacing the key, so that his car wouldn't become too conspicuous. He grew comfortable with the routine. The house changed about him as he spent time in its rooms, mellowed into a warm, familiar place. He left his Fury, walked around the back, opened the door, kicked off his shoes. He glanced at the books on his father-in-law's desk in the den, looked at the catalogs and magazines that had come in the mail since his last visit. He peeked inside the refrigerator, always pretending to himself that he might want a snack of some kind, always pretending that he wasn't really hungry.

He circled back continuously to his wife's bed and his son's computer. In other places, the bad moments could suddenly rear up, force themselves before him with their awful presentness: the way he'd managed to lose money, the way he'd been laid off, the way he felt when he received the tax bill and knew that he couldn't hide anything from Katherine. But he found, when he lay in the lower bunk, where Katherine had slept a few hours earlier, his mind quieted.

At his son's computer, he felt more urgency. He was continually hunting for how Carter felt about him. He read school papers Carter had written six months ago. He visited the websites Carter had been on. He tried logging onto his son's email a number of times, thinking that somehow he would guess the password. But it all remained obscure to him. He wanted to find something magical, like a golden key in a children's fairy tale, which would let him into the tower. So that when he saw Carter again, they could share a perfect understanding.

On a hutch by the dining room table, there was always a stack of unopened mail addressed to Katherine. Offers to open new credit card accounts, offers to transfer balances, envelopes full of coupons, bulk mailers promising to help you lose weight, promising a face cream that made wrinkles disappear, promising an herbal supplement that would cure the terrifying diseases that threatened you. There were statements from credit cards, unopened bills. Scott began to rifle through the envelopes on every visit, shaking his head when he found the same unopened statements in the pile after three days. This had always driven him crazy about Katherine. He didn't understand why she couldn't just open up junk mail right away, glance at it, and toss it. He didn't understand why she couldn't just open up a credit card statement when it came, instead of waiting, as though the amount due was going to go down if she let it ripen a bit.

After three weeks, he found in the pile a bank statement addressed to himself, forwarded from the address in Oak Commons. He had finally opened a bank account and deposited the thousands of dollars in cash he'd been carrying, and he'd used the Oak Commons address since it was the address on his driver's license and passport. In Katherine's hand, he saw "Not at this address" scrawled. He pocketed the envelope. He was at this address, even though she didn't know it yet. He wondered if she would notice the missing envelope and found himself hoping she would.

Two days later, he found a credit card statement of hers that had been opened but remained in the pile. Carefully, he slid the statement out of the envelope and scrutinized it. He saw where she had shopped last month, the kinds of things she had spent money on. Clothes for herself, clothes for Carter, school supplies, new tires for the Saturn, gasoline. It all added up.

Then he saw that last month, she had paid only the minimum on the balance. That was crazy. She had never been good at managing credit. That was something else that had always frustrated him. They were going to have to sit down and talk over how to manage money. He found himself beginning a conversation with her right there, completely convincing her of the need to pay off balances every month, the foolishness of considering clothing "an investment," the vicious cycle that the credit card companies were sucking her into. The responses he imagined from her tended to be questions he was able to answer, and she never brought up the fact that he'd cashed out their retirement accounts. The entire conversation was very satisfactory. So satisfactory that he promised to pay part of her balance if she would change her ways. And he wrote down the payment address and her account number.

Her obvious need for him made him feel like he was already part of the household again. They had just been having such crazy schedules that they had hardly seen each other. But that was something they could work on, spending more time together. Quality time.

When he left, he forgot about paying her bill and instead drove to Macy's to buy perfume. A woman about Katherine's age was behind the counter, and he told her that the perfume was a gift for his wife, that he gave it to her only on special occasions, like their anniversary. She misunderstood and thought that their anniversary was coming up, and he found it easy to go along with her mistake, so easy to talk about their twenty-third anniversary, two children (teenagers, you know), a cozy house. As he talked, it all sounded right and good, and he loved the approving smiles she lavished on him. When he left, she said, "She's gonna love it," and even though he had been telling lies, he believed the salesperson was speaking the truth.

The next day, he left the perfume, gift-wrapped, on the dining table. Something was going to happen now. He was sure of it.

· · · • · · ·

After Katherine knocked, she opened the door. The living room was empty. She glanced at the kitchen and down into the den, but he wasn't there. She had expected him to be waiting for her. What else could the perfume have meant but a desire to meet? And the knocks on the door were a way to alert him, so that he'd be standing, ready to talk.

But he wasn't standing, ready to talk, and as she paused in the kitchen, she grew furious. Everything about the way Scott was going about this was so typical. He could never be open and up front about anything. He always expected things to fall into place, expected Katherine to fill in the gaps in their relationship, and then he turned passive and whiny when something went wrong. He hadn't told her about their money troubles up front because he thought she'd just know somehow. He avoided agreeing to a divorce because he would rather have things work out, and then he disappeared after losing his job without telling her that he was leaving. When she was young, that attitude that something magical would happen for them was enchanting, but now it just pissed her off. And his bright idea of breaking into her father's house was just a way to provoke her into recognizing his presence and his right to be here instead of being an adult, a man, and taking some goddamned initiative.

She stalked into Carter's room. Nothing. Then she looked into her bedroom.

Incredible. He was sleeping on top of the bedspread of her bunk. As she stood in the doorway, he stirred but didn't open his eyes. She had seen this face in this attitude thousands of times over the years. It occurred to her that she had seen this face asleep more than she would ever see any other face in her life, more than either of her children, more than any new love she might find. This face would stay at the gates of her dreams. It was still a handsome face, sharp black eyebrows and a straight nose and a jawline that somehow evaded the sagging fleshy wattle that came to men in their forties. And his body seemed tauter, as though some months at sea had tanned him like leather.

Then she thought of his card—*I'll be seeing you in all those old familiar places*—and here he was, in that most familiar place, without even bothering to ask, without even bothering to say hello first. It was too much.

She snatched the pillow from the upper bunk and hit him across the face with it. He sat up, startled, and she smacked him again.

Sitting outside in the Buick, Henry witnessed a miraculous sight. There was his son-in-law, bursting out the front door and running with his arms raised about his head. Followed by his daughter, splendid in her anger, raging after him with a pillow in both hands. When he slowed to try to speak, she whaled away at him, buffeting him about the shoulders, until he finally broke into a run for the Fury. He locked the doors and started the car with a smoky roar while she beat upon the driver's side window. As the Fury pulled away, she raised both arms, like a goddess rampant and triumphant.

2

SOME WEEKS BEFORE his father reappeared, Carter began attending Montalvo High School. Because of the move to his grandfather's house, he came with no group of friends from middle school, no circle he could eat lunch with, and he felt like an outsider. All the people from his middle school went to Oak Commons High School across town, a newer school surrounded by newer houses, and even though they promised to keep up with each other, the separation began almost as soon as Carter left.

Montalvo High had been built in 1960, after the first subdivisions had sprung up in the old orchards and the first baby boomers were approaching high school age. The school spread out broad and low amid the subdivisions, one-story buildings separated by open walks and cement planters, no enclosed hallways because of the mild weather. The buildings all had generous eaves that covered banks of school lockers, and most classrooms were entered directly from the exterior. One central plaza, with tables and benches, was open to the sky.

Carter had the sense, at his new school, that everyone knew exactly how to *be* except for him. Everyone knew how to dress, how to talk, how to hang out, except for him. There were groups of students who looked alike, some with leather and silver rivets and piercings, others with baggy pants and skateboards, who formed their own closed circles. The Hispanic kids tended to cluster together in one part of the plaza, as did the black kids and the Indian kids. From the outside, they all looked to have a social ease and knowing that he thought he would never have.

Carter was more than six feet tall, but he tried to hide it by slouching. He wasn't proud of his body because he was so thin, and he compensated by wearing loose, oversize sweatshirts that flapped about him. He wasn't happy with his face, either. He had a beakish nose that seemed even larger than it was because of his severe cheekbones and long jaw. He didn't think his face was one that could be loved.

He kept hidden the disappearance of his father at his new school. It was too weird, and he already felt weird enough. Divorce, separation, those were known categories he could fit into. There were plenty of kids his age who could talk knowledgeably about custody arrangements, the complications of having two bedrooms, the kind of takeout food favored by one parent over another. But nobody had ever said anything about having a father who appeared only as handwritten letters from a ship in the Arabian Sea.

The war in Iraq was six months old then, and though it had seemed over at one point, it had risen again, metamorphosed into a new and murderous shape. Carter found the war was talked about differently at Montalvo High School than at Oak Commons Middle School. Everyone at Oak Commons, it seemed, and everyone at his church, had been against the war. Carter had joined in an antiwar march in the weeks leading up to the war and a noontime peace rally at the school. He felt good to be surrounded by people who felt as he did, comforted. And he didn't mention his father shipping out to anyone. He was embarrassed to have a father who not only was prowar, but who had actually gone off to join it.

It was different at Montalvo. Many students had older brothers and sisters in the military, some of whom had been part of the drive to Baghdad. Those students, both boys and girls, had a photograph of a marine or soldier taped inside their locker doors, the kind of portrait taken at the end of boot camp, when a young man or woman is newly minted a warrior. The photos were of young men mostly, their faces shaved and unlined and achingly young, holding their chins high above the severe collar of the blue marine dress uniform, the white hat with the eagle and the globe always seeming a bit too large for them, a bit of a burden to hold up. The students with photos in their lockers were prowar—they couldn't imagine being otherwise.

Carter didn't know how to talk with them. Among the people of his church, the deaths that occurred on a daily basis were proof that the war had been a mistake, whereas among those students at Montalvo, the deaths were a reason for rage, a reason to keep fighting. So Carter kept silent at his new school. He was fifteen, and he didn't feel confident enough to speak up unless he knew that he would be agreed with.

· · · • · · ·

As the second anniversary of 9/11 came up, all of Carter's old friends at Oak Commons High planned to wear antiwar T-shirts. Someone had discovered a website advocating that students wear a public display of protest, and they emailed Carter to get him to participate at Montalvo. Carter emailed back that he didn't think anyone at his new school was going to do that. Not everyone was prowar, but a lot of people were, and he thought they would be hostile. His friends emailed back that it was going to be big, that a lot of people at a lot of high schools were going to do it. If he showed up wearing a T-shirt, he would find others who were wearing T-shirts too, and then he would know who was cool. Carter knew almost nobody at his new school, and he didn't want to lose his friends from his old school, so he agreed to do it.

Carter walked to school that day, wearing a loose chamois shirt open over his T-shirt. He arrived fifteen minutes before first period and walked around the plaza past the various social groups that were beginning to form. Each group had its own corner staked out. He sneaked looks at people, tried to spot anyone else wearing a shirt in protest of the war. Nobody was. In front of the Drama Building, a couple of picnic benches were set up, and Cal Baker and Jeffrey Thomas, both seniors, were lounging back and waiting for the first bell. Cal was one of the good-looking boys, with short brown hair that had a natural wave and perfect features. Jeffrey was short, but massive. His arms and thighs were enormous, and his body was thick and solid. He lifted weights daily, and it was rumored he took steroids. Neither of them wore anything that referred to the war.

Carter raised a hand in greeting, and the two boys nodded. " 'Sup?" said Jeffrey.

"Not much." Carter hunched his shoulders so that the chamois shirt draped over his T-shirt, covering his slogan.

The first short period was homeroom, and the day began with the Pledge of Allegiance. In middle school, everyone stood for the pledge. In high school, everyone had been too cool to stand and simply sat and allowed the pledge to be read over the PA system. But at Montalvo High School, after 9/11, students began standing again and were still doing it when Carter began there. Especially on the anniversary of the attack, everyone would stand.

The classroom flag was tiny, about the size of a piece of binder paper, and it hung from a thin black dowel canted out from the wall near the clock. When the round speaker began to crackle, Mr. Elliott, an English teacher, stood and faced it, and the class did as well. Carter stood straight, and his shirt fell open. Two girls on either side noticed what his shirt said, and their eyes widened. Then, in the middle of the pledge, Mr. Elliott glanced his way.

"Peace!" he blurted.

Everyone turned to look. Carter took the chamois shirt off and stood with his T-shirt exposed. He tried to act casual, as though he was not taking off his shirt for any special reason, but he felt his heart ring in his chest.

Above them, the school secretary's voice asked for a moment of silence in memory of September 11th before the announcements.

The pathways between the buildings, asphalt and pebbled concrete, were always crowded between classes. The sheet-metal locker doors opened and slammed shut under the eaves as students switched books and binders between classes, and talk filled the open space. Many students, even while they were talking, checked cell phones for text messages or thumbed in quick messages themselves. Carter put his chamois shirt back on, but he didn't make an effort to hide the slogan. In the center of the plaza, where students walked rapidly in both directions, he saw some faces recognize the shirt, register surprise. Then he was past them, on his way to chemistry. He looked for other shirts, or some sign of his friends' idea that a war protest had spread, but he saw nothing.

Between chemistry and English, in the flow of students, someone punched Carter in the chest. Stunned, Carter stopped while people kept walking past him. He looked around to see if someone was looking at him, was claiming credit for the blow, but there was no one. Whoever had thrown the punch had continued walking. Just a quick sneaky fist square at the sternum, no eye contact, no explanation. It was as though the crowd as a whole had struck at him.

Between English and algebra class, it happened again. A punch from nowhere, given in a crowd, stiff enough to stop Carter where he stood. He rubbed his chest, feeling the soreness. Again between third and fourth periods, even though he was watching, someone hit the same spot, a fist from the disapproving crowd. It happened once more, just before lunch, and he went down on one knee as the students marched about him. One of the janitors, a short man with iron-gray hair and a permanent scowl on his face from a career of dealing with the garbage of teenagers, saw Carter go down. He went to him and helped him up and, without a word, walked him to the main office.

After a half hour, Carter went in to see his counselor, Mr. Geoffrey Hartmann. Mr. Hartmann arranged his office as much as possible to resemble that of an Oxford don or an Ivy League professor. He wore tweed jackets and had his diplomas framed and on the wall, along with a fading photograph of a rugby side he'd played on in college. He kept several pipes in a pipe rack and a vintage Boston Coarse Cut tobacco tin on the shelf behind him, and even though smoking had long been forbidden indoors, a faintly sweet scent of pipe tobacco hung in the office. Whenever he signed anything, he used a fountain pen and a rocker blotter with a mahogany handle. He told himself that these touches, these accoutrements, were to inspire his students to go to college, but they were really the little ways he compensated for a disappointing career.

Carter sat down in one of two bow-back chairs placed at angles in front of the desk while Mr. Hartmann leaned back and perused his file. Carter sat straight, so that the slogan on his T-shirt was plainly visible. He had decided that he was being persecuted for his beliefs, suffering for his beliefs. And that felt like a good thing. If he was suffering, that meant that his beliefs were true, they meant something. Jesus suffered for his beliefs too. And Gandhi.

Mr. Hartmann creaked his chair forward and laid the file flat on the desktop and tapped it significantly with his index finger. "You came from Oak Commons Middle School," he said. "You must have moved."

"Yes."

"Any problems adjusting?"

Carter had been to a therapist a couple of times after his father moved out. His mother's insurance policy provided for ten visits with a mental health professional per year, and she had made him go without ever going herself. The therapist had asked the same question, to get the conversation started, and then wanted to prescribe an antidepressant. After the second visit, Carter decided he didn't like her. She seemed to think she knew all about him, and Mr. Hartmann seemed to think he knew all about him as well.

"I'm fine," Carter said. "I just like to show my beliefs."

"Well. We all have our beliefs. But if those beliefs upset others, they might be kept private."

"But there's freedom of speech, isn't there?"

"Of course. But in a civilized society, we learn to respect that others have opinions as well. And it's best, if we're to keep functioning, to avoid incitement."

"So you think it's my fault." Carter crossed his arms in front of his chest.

"Of course not."

"I know what you're saying. I'm gifted in English. You think I've got family trauma, and that's the real reason I wore this shirt on 9/11. You don't think I'm *sincere*."

"Listen. Carter."

Mr. Hartmann leaned forward, the leather elbow patches on his jacket propped on his desktop. He tried to sound as earnest and understanding as possible.

"There are students here who have close family members in Iraq right now, though nobody has lost anyone yet, thank God. I believe you have strong feelings too. But you can't wear clothing that's disruptive. Those are the rules."

"If my dad was in Iraq, I could wear whatever I wanted?"

Mr. Hartmann hesitated. He doubted whether Carter's father was in Iraq, but he saw the boy ready to pounce.

"No," he said at last.

"It's the same rules for everyone?"

"Yes. That's fair, isn't it?"

"What if I wore the shirt like civil disobedience? Like Gandhi?"

"Then you would probably end up right back in this office."

"Like Gandhi would."

Mr. Hartmann let Carter go after he agreed to keep his chamois shirt buttoned the rest of the day. Carter wouldn't promise never to wear a protest shirt again, because he didn't want to give up his freedom of speech, and Mr. Hartmann finally said that as long as he understood that there were consequences, he could make his own choices.

It was near the end of lunch period when Carter was finally released. The plaza was bright and hot, and nobody was walking across it. Students had all gathered in the small areas they had claimed as their own, with friends and books and iPods and cell phones, waiting for the bell to announce the first afternoon class. Carter walked across the plaza toward the Drama Building, feeling watched. He had his chamois shirt buttoned, but he walked erect, not slouching. He felt as though Mr. Hartmann's warnings had made him grander and more important than before.

In the first afternoon class, the teacher tried to lead a discussion about the terrorist attacks and what they meant for the country. She and others at the school had downloaded lesson plans from websites, and a lot of the emphasis was on letting students express their feelings and making sure that they felt safe in school. The discussion didn't touch on the war in Iraq, though the teacher, a young woman who was already thinking about a real estate license as a way to escape teaching in the public schools the rest of her life, invited the class to write about the troops in the last ten minutes of class. Carter kept silent for the entire period, enjoying the feeling that others might be waiting for him to make a statement. The last class of the day was Spanish, and they spent the entire period drilling on the irregular verb *tener*.

As soon as he left the school grounds, Carter opened the shirt and let the slogan show while he walked toward home. Some seniors drove to and from school, but Carter only had a learner's permit, and his mother was not anxious for him to get his license because of the insurance costs. He was getting driving lessons from his grandfather, but there was never a fixed date at which he'd take his driving test. To get home, he had to walk from the high school to Prospector Street, a commercial strip with gas stations and strip malls. He couldn't take a more direct route because an expressway lay between the school and his grandfather's house. Prospector intersected with Saratoga Avenue, which ran between the Western Horizons shopping center and the Blue Skies Bowl, and Country Lane Road led into the subdivision just beyond the bowling alley.

Before he got to Prospector Street, a purple car sped toward him with the windows rolled down, and three older boys inside shouted at him. He couldn't understand the words, something "Terrorist," but they were yelling and pointing at him, and he hunched his shoulders as though a rock had been thrown at him.

Then the purple car was past, and he was untouched. He looked up and down the busy street. It was like a long chute, the road channeled between tall stucco walls that marked the edges of sub-divisions. There were two lanes going each direction and left-turn channels where there was an entry road into the housing. The sidewalk was squeezed between the road and the tall walls. More cars passed him, disregarded him, and after a moment he continued walking.

On the other side of the center strip, the purple car drove past him. The boys in the car saw that he had noticed them, pointed at him. He turned his head. The car made a U-turn at the first break and sped up toward him again. Carter waited. On the other side of the stucco walls were green backyards, but the walls were ten feet tall. He heard the yelling, and the car swerved toward him and made him jump back.

Then the car was past again. He recognized the make, a purple Hyundai, a Tiburon. He watched it go all the way to Prospector Street and turn left. There were several hundred yards to Prospector, and he began to walk quickly and decided to button his shirt. He would feel safer near the businesses, where there were other people around.

Prospector Street was lined with steel lamp poles and creosote-soaked telephone poles that smelled on hot sunny days, and the sidewalk was discontinuous, appearing in front of a fast-food franchise and then disappearing in front of gas stations and used-car lots. Carter never saw anyone else walking along it, as he did. The cars passed close as he walked and made the air thick and heated, and the only people he saw were clerks, standing outside their small businesses, smoking a cigarette until a car pulled into the narrow parking lot in front of them.

He was in front of a Rotten Robbie's gas station when the purple Tiburon reappeared. He saw it coming, but there was nowhere for him to go. He angled across the asphalt, close to the open glass doors of Mrs. Robbie's Food Shop, the tiny convenience store that stood back from the gas pumps.

The Tiburon pulled into the parking lot alongside the store and jerked to a halt, and three boys piled out. They were students at the high school who all had older brothers in the military and who ganged together because of it. K. J., the driver, had a brother with the Fourth Infantry Division in Iraq. Mitch's brother was on a destroyer in the Arabian Sea, and Brownie's brother was in the Marines, though currently based in South Korea, which seemed kind of lame, so they didn't talk about it.

K. J. was short and wiry and always in motion, too impatient to be good in school, though he knew he was smarter than his teachers thought. Acne scarred, not tall enough or strong enough or fast enough to be in sports, he had been one of the kids without a place until his brother overseas finally gave him something to feel special about. He claimed that he was going to join up too, after high school, and serve right alongside his brother. *Tip of the spear*, he said, *tip of the spear*, and he talked knowingly about the situation on the ground in Baqubah. And other students nodded with a respect he had never known.

His brother had left the car with K. J. and told him to use it until he came back, and having a car made him feel larger, tougher. His brother had also left him a leather aviator jacket that he wore all the time, though it was a little oversized for him.

When Brownie told K. J. about the new kid, he felt that the kid was taking something from him by wearing a T-shirt against the war. K. J. already hated students like Carter, the well-behaved kids, the ones who tested well, the ones in the fast classes. He resented them. He thought they must have been brought up in an atmosphere of safety, a bubble of privilege in which they thought they could say anything. And he thought this new kid might need to have his ass kicked.

The three boys formed a knot around Carter, blocking off the doorway to the business.

"Hey!" K. J. bounced on the balls of his feet, grinning and manic. "I gotta question for you."

"Yeah?" Carter stopped.

"When did you stop being a fag?"

"Never," Carter said.

"You never stopped? That means you must still be one." K. J. laughed, and the boys behind him punched each other.

"I mean I never was one."

"Maybe you're just a big pussy instead," Mitch said.

"You don't know me," Carter said.

"Open your shirt," K. J. said. "I want to read what it says."

"What if I don't want to?"

"What if we make you?"

Carter looked around. The clerk behind the counter was talking on a cell phone. And if he had glanced through the glass windows, he would just have seen four high school kids and wondered if they were going to come in to try to buy cigarettes with fake ID. On the street, the cars passed ignorantly by.

"You know what it says already."

"Come on," K. J. said. "Aren't you proud of it?"

"Yes, I am."

"So?"

"Okay." Carter unbuttoned his shirt, and K. J. leaned in and made a show of studying it carefully, the acne scars reddish across his pale face.

"Looks to me like it says, 'I am a pussy terrorist.' What's it look like to you, Brownie?"

"That's it," Brownie said.

"Isn't that what it says?" K. J. asked Carter.

"No."

"Mitch thinks so. And Brownie thinks so. Looks like you're out-voted."

"Okay."

"Okay what?"

"Okay, I'm outvoted."

"So what does your shirt say?"

"You know," Carter said, "they persecuted Gandhi for what he said too."

"Yeah," K. J. said. "But you're not him."

"Can I go now?"

"Is anybody stopping you?"

Nobody moved, so Carter had to walk around the three boys.

They waited until he was a dozen yards away, with his back turned, opposite the Dumpster alley. Then they rushed him, grabbed him on each side, and stumbled him toward the Dumpster. Carter flailed away with his legs, his arms pinned. Two boys hoisted him up, half into the Dumpster, and dropped him.

"Let's bail," K. J. yelled.

By the time Carter pushed himself out, the doors were slamming on the purple Tiburon.

He brushed himself off and watched the car screech its tires out of the parking lot. The smell of garbage was in his nose.

3

KATHERINE THOUGHT about telling Carter that his father was back, but the whole episode seemed too absurd. She knew Carter would have questions about Scott, and she would be unable to answer any of them. *Your father has been breaking into the house and sleeping in my bed. No, I didn't really get a chance to ask how he was. No, we didn't really talk about getting back together. No, he didn't really ask about you. I chased him away with a pillow before he could. Otherwise, I'm sure he would have, honey.*

It was easier for her to decide that Scott would soon be back in touch in a normal way. Carter would find out then and never have to know that he had broken into the house. It would save Scott some embarrassment.

. . . . ● . . .

After wearing the shirt and finding no one else doing the same, after being thrown into the Dumpster, Carter didn't tell anyone. At first, he had felt a kind of pride in being singled out because of his beliefs, but it soon turned into shame. He couldn't imagine repeating the story to anyone and being proud of the way it had ended. He couldn't imagine how to make it sound like being thrown halfway into a Dumpster made him come out on top. It could only sound humiliating. For a fifteen-year-old in a new high school, the notion of suffering for one's beliefs didn't keep its appeal for long.

He couldn't tell his grandfather, or his mother, or even Reverend Nancy at the church who had called this an evil war. Any one of them might decide to contact the school, call the principal, and use the institution to punish the three boys. If that happened, Carter would be sunk. The story would get around school, and he would be the boy who got thrown in the garbage forever. Famous!

And no matter what happened to the three boys, he knew they would get him back some way.

He began to brood on revenge fantasies of his own, heroic scenarios. He vowed to wear an antiwar T-shirt again, once a month. And he saw himself inspiring others to wear antiwar slogans too, a group of them, and they would all drive down Prospector Street like a convoy and sweep purple Tiburons from the road. Or he saw himself in a car, finding one of the three—K. J., the ringleader— alone in an alley, helpless as he stomped on the accelerator. K. J., scared of him, at his mercy.

In the weeks after the 9/11 anniversary, Carter found himself gravitating toward the Drama Building. The groups there were not stringent about whom they would accept. He didn't have to dress or look a certain way. There were girls who wore red or green berets and matching capes, a few of the black-leather girls, some boys with smooth faces and dark eyes and petulant lips. And there were others who were there because they didn't fit in anywhere else and found they were praised if they could sing or play an instrument or memorize lines and enunciate.

Carter's gift was his voice, his clear and effortless tenor. When he spoke, even though his tone was in the upper registers, there was a weight and depth to it, so that his words penetrated. And his singing voice, with a slight vibrato, had been treasured by choir directors since elementary school. He joined the choir at Montalvo High, but the praise he got for his voice didn't seem to make up for the lack he saw in himself when he looked in a mirror and studied his funny nose and ears and scrawny elongated frame.

The voice teacher, Mrs. McCarthy, was severe and demanding. She wore starched white or cream blouses, always with a bow at the throat, and dark skirts, and she stood at the piano during class with her right index finger in the air and her left finger hammering the note she was seeking. She wanted him to be her special student, but he felt that she would be a teacher who would set hurdles for him, each one higher than the previous one, and that he would never be able to feel he had accomplished anything. The fragility he felt after his father left made him keep up his guard around her.

He wasn't ready to give anyone too much power over his sense of well-being.

The drama teacher was unlike anyone he had ever known. Her name was Carolyn Cotts, though everyone, including her students, called her by her nickname, Nu, a letter from the Greek alphabet. She was sixty, with the lined face that told her years, but she was as lithe as a girl, which she attributed to yoga and body work. She wore her red hair long, either loose or gathered into a soft rope along her shoulders, and she dressed eccentrically, sometimes showing up in jeans, sandals, and a smock, sometimes in a cotton peasant dress with a variegated handwoven shawl of her own making, and sometimes all in black, with a black turtleneck and barrette and black skirt and hose.

The classes were all held in the theater. Oak Commons High, where Carter thought he was going to attend, had a new theater with banks of fixed and upholstered chairs rising around a thrust stage. At Montalvo, the theater building was forty years old, with a straight proscenium arch and a large open space filled with folding chairs during performances. Yet there was a sign hanging over the stage that bravely named it "The Theater of California." Students had painted the sign in gold and blue after Nu told them that the name California came from a novel written by Ordoñez de Montalvo, in whose honor their school was named.

The classes in drama were comforting for Carter. The students who had been together in theater in middle school took their cue from Nu and welcomed him in, and the juniors and seniors weren't threatened by him. He felt less self-conscious of his looks in drama, because Nu always said that there were roles for all, the theater contains multitudes—kings and clowns and lovers and monsters, all have a place on the stage.

From the beginning of class, they were reading Shakespeare because Nu had written a grant to a local foundation for one of their shows and had proposed they put on *The Tempest*. In class, Carter didn't usually read the leading roles, Macbeth or Henry V or Othello. His high tenor voice and physical awkwardness fit him for comic roles, those who are tricked and befuddled, like Andrew

Aguecheek. He memorized lines easily, but Nu pushed him and everyone to have less recitation in his delivery and make each line sound more like it was being coined and spoken for the first time by a living and breathing human being.

"Make it new," she repeated. That phrase, from the modernists, was the origin of her nickname.

In one of Nu's classes, she had them work with makeup techniques, and he was paired up with a girl who wore a nose ring and dyed her hair black and had the funny name Blossom Haven. She explained once by saying that her mother was an old hippie. They now lived alone, she said, just the two of them, and her mother was still kind of a hippie, but had learned enough about massage therapy and Reiki to make the rent every month. Blossom Haven didn't like to act, but she loved the technical side of theater, the lighting and the sets and the costumes and makeup. She said she wanted to be a best boy someday, so that when the credits rolled at the end of a movie, people would see: "Best Boy—Blossom Haven."

Nu went to each pair and gave directions as to what face they should put on the other. Some she directed to make very old, with lines on the forehead, crow's feet at the corners of the eyes. Others she directed to make look like cavemen, with beetling brows and shadowed eyes. When she came to Carter, she paused.

"Make him a drunk," she said. "Make that beautiful Roman nose red as a cherry."

Carter leaned back and watched Blossom Haven's face as she studied him and then the makeup kit beside her. She took a container of pancake from the box, moistened a sponge, and began to smooth the base onto his face. She blended in a lighter shade of pancake onto his cheekbones, to make them stand out, and then worked in spots of rouge to make the skin florid. Similarly on the nose, she first used foundation to emphasize the bone structure, then worked in red to give the broken-veined impression of a drinker, and she rimmed the bottom of his eyes with a special red eyeliner.

The feel of her hands was calm and firm, and her face was calm as she worked. She didn't interact with him. She looked at his face as a canvas. But he thought he felt connection and care in her touch. He had been shy when she talked about her single mother, unwilling to contribute when others offered takes on the strange and alien ways of their parents. He wasn't sure if he fit into the category of having a single mother or not, and he kept quiet. Now he wished he had spoken, to give them something in common.

Before the end of class, Nu had everyone walk across stage and improvise a character based on their makeup. The elderly hobbled about, and the cavemen grunted. One girl made up as a twenties flapper shimmied up to a boy made up as a sheikh. Carter was the only drunk, and he swayed his lanky body across the stage in an unsteady totter, seeming out of balance before just catching himself to take one more step. He stopped and took out a handkerchief with exaggerated delicacy, and then he honked his nose into it, and the class laughed.

He looked for Blossom Haven after class, before the next period started, but she seemed to have vanished. The open plaza, broken with square cement planters, was busy with students walking to their next class, talking with friends, texting on their cells. He ducked back into the Drama Building and looked at the empty chairs. Then he walked across to the exit on the far side of the building, where the heavy metal door was propped open with a brick, and pushed through to the scruffy untended area behind the building, a dozen feet of rocky ground between the building and a chain-link fence that marked the edge of the school grounds. Beyond the fence, a row of tall spruce trees gave the space a feeling of privacy.

Blossom Haven wasn't there, but Nu was, leaning against the wall and smoking a cigarette. She smoked between every class, sometimes joined by students. She didn't encourage them to smoke, but she said she wouldn't be a hypocrite either, and she made everyone pick up their butts and scuff out their ashes so that the maintenance crew wouldn't bust them. She smiled a welcome to Carter and didn't look surprised to see him, even though he was not a smoker and not one of the regulars behind the building.

"I can't give you a cigarette," she said. "I have some ethics."

"I . . ." Carter looked around, even though it was obvious Nu was alone. "That's all right."

"Are you going to audition for the play?" Nu's voice was low and husky, a smoker's voice. "Next week?"

"I don't know."

"I wish you would." Nu blew smoke down from the corner of her mouth away from Carter. She waved a hand in front of her. "Watch out. Secondhand smoke is worse than smoking."

Carter waved a hand in front of his face as well. Nu laughed and took another drag.

"And you don't want to audition because . . ."

"Well. Like. I don't think I'm ready. Like, everyone else knows each other already, and I'm all new, we moved here from Oak Commons since my dad left last year, and I don't know anyone here from middle school." He began to tell her about moving into his grandfather's house, and his grandfather's chronic cancer, his sister leaving and telling him "Escape or die," his mother trying to act like everything was normal, and how weird it all felt. He said to Nu the things he wanted to say to Blossom Haven, to grow the feeling that they had something in common. "I just feel like a freak here," he said.

Nu had stubbed out her cigarette into a small portable ashtray and slid the metal cover back over it. She had been teaching for many years, and she knew when and how to listen. When he finished, she put an arm around his shoulders and looked into his eyes.

"When I see you in class, like I saw you today, I see a big fat joy. Big fat joy. Nothing freaky about that."

"And I'm not, you know, like Cal."

Nu knew what he meant by that. She had heard it many times. It was common enough in high school. Cal was the handsome boy, and everyone else fell short. She had a stock answer, one that a director had given her once when she realized that she had a long face, a little horsey in the way her small mouth was dominated by her flat cheeks.

"In the Globe," she said, "there's room for all."

Carter knew, whenever Nu said *Globe* in that tone of voice, she was referring to Shakespeare's theater, the Globe Theatre, on the banks of the Thames.

The second bell rang. She gave his shoulder a squeeze. "You're late for class," she said. "See you at auditions."

Carter felt relieved that he had finally told someone about his father, his mother, his grandfather. He'd felt like he'd had a big sign on his forehead saying, "Don't make friends with this one. Too weird." Telling Nu would make it easier to talk about them with the others. Maybe with Blossom Haven.

· · · • · · ·

For the first round of auditions, all the boys were to memorize Prospero's speech, from act 5, where he vows to break his staff and drown his book after he has regained his dukedom and brought about a marriage between his daughter, Miranda, and the son of the king of Naples. Carter practiced it in the backyard, walking from the cement slab patio to the lawn and speaking to the cedar fences. There was one corner of the backyard that had been a vegetable garden, with four tomato cages still standing at odd angles, now overgrown with weeds, and Carter addressed them as though the elves and fairies at Prospero's command were dwelling within and ready to spring forth.

As Carter strutted around the backyard, playing Prospero, his grandfather Henry sat in one of the patio chairs with a copy of the play open in his lap. Henry still felt heavy-bodied from a treatment a week earlier, but being with Carter eased him. When he found out that the big play of the fall was going to be *The Tempest*, and that Carter was going to audition for it, he picked up an old leather-bound edition of Shakespeare that had belonged to his own father and read it through. It seemed to him, more than anything, a play about a father trying to see that his daughter found happiness. The enchanted island of the play could be anywhere a father tried to help his children—like his own house, where in 1950 he'd hung the redwood sign from the front porch that read *Peaceable Isle*, to distinguish it from those islands he'd seen in the Pacific war, green and bloodsoaked.

Henry had never done with the backyard what he might have. Others on the block had long since replaced the cement slab with a redwood deck, or a roofed greenhouse, and had landscaped the back lawn into small oases, with garden seats and trellises and water features. He had left it the same patch of fescue and crab-grass as when he bought the house—at first because his young chil-dren could play on it, then, after his wife died, because he had lost the desire to change it. Only the rosebushes, trellised to the back wall, and the small rectangle of vegetable garden showed an effort to cultivate the space. His Peaceable Isle. A poor sort of enchanted island for a Prospero to rule over.

"I have bedimmed the noontide sun, called forth . . ." Carter paused. "Called forth . . ."

"The mutinous winds," Henry said.

"The mutinous winds. Thanks, Grandpa."

Henry had never done this for his own children. His two sons were distant now, and visited rarely, and he had never been one to chat on the telephone just to stay in touch. That had been his wife's role. He had let her be the one to keep the family close and to orga-nize their social life. He thought now that his sons had both been closer to their mother than to him, and he wondered if they would have moved so far away if she had lived.

Mary Katherine's death in 1973 still seemed like a cheat to him. She'd been beginning to move to the next stage of her life, with the two boys in college and Katherine in high school. She was always the joiner, the one who wanted to be involved in something larger. She'd left behind the PTSA and the school board and was looking into joining the League of Women's Voters. And on the way back from an evening meeting, she was killed on the freeway by a wrong-way driver. The police never discovered why the other driver was going the wrong way or even where he had gotten on the freeway. A mystery. Impossible to make sense of.

Henry never got the chance to see her age, never got to see her hair silver, and her eyes brighten through crow's feet, and her voice gain an elder scratch. When he looked at himself in the mir-ror now, bald, even his eyebrows and eyelashes missing, she was the only woman he could imagine beside him, and he wondered what she would think, still youthful and beautiful as he remembered her, beside an old hulk like him. It was a stupid thought, he knew, because she would have aged as well. But he imagined her young at his side, and the bright colors he wore, the silk scarf around his neck, the French beret, were all to look younger beside the conjured face of his wife.

"And deeper than did ever plummet sound," Carter said, "I'll drown my book."

Henry applauded as Carter bowed.

· · · ● · · ·

When Katherine leaned in to Carter's room in the evenings, to listen to her son murmur low the lines, he inevitably noticed her and stopped.

"Mom, I'm *con*centrating. This is important. This matters."

Katherine didn't know exactly when it happened, but Carter had stopped confiding in her. It wasn't when Scott had disappeared and when they had moved to Catesby Street. It had begun happening earlier, more gradually, as her son had carved out a private space for himself. But she noticed it more now. He had become more inward, took himself so seriously. It scared her that he took himself so seriously, because it left him so vulnerable to the bruises and hurts of the world. He didn't talk about school, about his classes or the people he was meeting, and she thought he was hiding things from her. He'd had friends at the old middle school, but even though he claimed they were still friends through email and IMs, he didn't see them anymore. And she blamed herself because those friends might have been a cushion against the difficult changes, though she usually remembered to blame Scott too for the situation they were in.

Katherine had a habit of foreseeing catastrophe. She could envision her airplane falling from the sky, her car ablaze, her son's bicycle wrapped around the front of a truck. And she invented connections between the present and the future to keep catastrophe at bay. She would tell herself, when driving on the freeway, that if she could just get safely to the next overpass, she would reach her destination without crashing. Or if she felt a small earth-quake and there was no damage, that meant she and her family were safe from all other earthquakes for six months. Six months seemed like a reasonable amount of time to expect.

Now she found herself making the same kind of deal for her son. She was happy he was concentrating on drama class, if it gave him a center. And she told herself that if he just got a part in this play, it would mean he would be safe from all harm for the rest of the school year. The auditions were held the first week in October, just days after she had chased Scott from the house. He hadn't yet tried to get back in touch, and she still hadn't told Carter that he was back. She didn't want to upset him until he had a part for himself.

· · · · ● · · ·

Nu made the auditions as genuine and professional as possible. The drama room was dark, and a pool of light, a hot spot, was marked on the stage with an *X* of masking tape. Each student walked out to the hot spot and heard Nu's voice rise from the obscurity.

"So what are you going to do for us today?"

One by one, Carter saw the other boys recite Prospero's speech. Some stumbled over the language—some spoke well but were reciting rather than speaking as a character. Sometimes, Nu asked a student to repeat a line with a different inflection and intention. Cal spoke beautifully, as did a student named Francisco Vallejo, who wore his jet-black hair slicked back and had a small black chin beard.

When Carter was called, he stepped out onto the stage and into the bright light. The light would have kept him from seeing much of the audience even if it weren't darkened, but he could hear the students breathing while they waited. Nu asked him to start, and he breathed deeply.

Ye elves of hills, brooks, standing lakes, and groves.

He tried to speak in a lower range of voice than normal. He had noticed that the students who sounded best had deep voices, and he wanted to sound like them. He wanted to sound as though he could genuinely create storms, throw lightning bolts, cause earthquakes, raise the dead.

He found himself running out of breath before the end of lines, having to run words together and then gulp in air. It was not as he had practiced. He didn't forget any lines, but he began to rush toward the end, just wanting to get offstage.

Then Nu's voice floated up, cutting him off.

"Carter?"

Carter stopped, tried to look toward the voice.

"Start over again," Nu said. "And I want you to speak as though you don't believe a word you're saying, as though you find the whole idea of being able to 'bedim the sun at noon' somewhat ludicrous."

"Ludicrous?"

"Funny. Something to make sport of."

"Okay." Carter closed his eyes for a moment. Then he began the speech again in his own high tenor voice. He pranced lightly through the lines, making some of the most serious declarations into doubtful statements or questions. He heard some giggles, and when he came to the line about calling forth the mutinous winds, he turned his back to the audience and stuck out his buttocks and made a loud farting noise. There was laughter as he finished, and he made an exaggerated, loose-jointed bow.

"Thank you," Nu said, as she said at the end of everyone's audition.

· · · • · · ·

Carter walked to school the next day, wearing again the T-shirt with the anti-war slogan underneath his chamois shirt. Three weeks had passed since he'd worn it, and it was October, and he had vowed that he would wear the shirt again. Even though nobody had heard the vow but him, it seemed terribly important to him that he fulfill it. He didn't want to be the kind of person who took vows and then broke them. Prospero took a vow and had to leave his magic island, but it led to a happy ending for his daughter, Miranda. It was important to Carter that he do the same. He wasn't sure if there would be a reaction to his shirt this time, and in some way he wanted nobody to notice. That way, he could fulfill his vow but still fit in.

In homeroom that morning, when they stood up for the Pledge of Allegiance, Mr. Elliott glanced his way. Carter hadn't taken off his chamois shirt, but it had fallen open enough for the slogan to be visible.

"Bush," Mr. Elliott blurted, and the rest of the class turned to stare.

Carter was sent down to the counselor's office, and Mr. Hartmann again tried to explain the limits on speech within the sphere of the high school. Just as you couldn't shout "Fire" in a crowded theater, you couldn't use disruptive speech in school. But Carter wasn't persuaded. Yelling "Fire" was banned only if it was a lie. If it were true, it wouldn't be illegal. And the words on his T-shirt were true.

Mr. Hartmann, seeing that rhetorical suasion wasn't working, finally told him that the next time he wore a disruptive shirt, he would be sent home and his parents informed. And he told him to just sit outside the office for the rest of the period, until the bell rang.

On his way to algebra, Carter saw a group of students outside the Drama Building, talking, waving their hands in the air, jumping up and down, and he thought the cast list must have been posted. He wanted to cross the plaza, to find out if he'd been chosen, if his name was beside one of those on the list of Dramatis Personae in the front of the book, but he didn't want to be late to a class after already being in the office once.

He stopped at his locker, under the broad eaves of one of the buildings. Then he joined the busy flow of students filtering by each other, turning into classrooms. As he was walking, he heard a voice at his side.

"You're pissing me off, Cochran."

Carter looked to his left and found that K. J. was walking beside him in his leather jacket, shadowed by Brownie wearing a black hoodie that hid his face. K. J. spoke out of the corner of his mouth, keeping his eyes forward, not looking at Carter.

"You must like getting your ass kicked."

"Hey, freedom of speech," Carter said.

"People are *dying* for your *freedom*," K. J. hissed. Then they passed him by, walking swiftly. Neither of them diverted their eyes or gave any hint that Carter had been addressing them.

"Freedom of speech," Carter said again to their departing backs. The second bell rang, and they were gone.

After algebra, Carter walked swiftly across the grounds to the Drama Building. Outside, Cal and Jeffrey and some other boys were talking at one of the picnic tables. When Cal saw Carter approaching, he hailed him.

"What ho, Trinculo!"

"Trinculo is reeling ripe," Jeffrey added. Carter heard him and began to walk like a drunk, exaggerating the ungainliness of his long, skinny frame.

He'd been given the part of the court jester, Trinculo, who forms part of an absurd conspiracy with Caliban and Stephano to take over the island. Jeffrey, the weight lifter, would play Caliban. Nu had cast Cal as Ferdinand, the young lover of Miranda. And Francisco was given the part of Prospero.

Inside the Drama Building, the girls had gathered, talking over the casting. The social groupings around the theater still generally fell along gender lines. Windy Donne, who had large beautiful eyes and long hair, had been given the role of Miranda. Ariel, the spirit, was given to Sharan Lowenthal, a musically gifted student who could sing and play the flute. Girls were also cast as figures in the masque, Iris, Ceres, Juno, the reapers, the nymphs.

Carter walked to the bulletin board outside Nu's office. He wanted to see the cast list posted, just to be certain. It was a single sheet of paper, with the word *Players* centered at the top. And there was his name, the tenth down, opposite Trinculo.

The girls nodded to him and went back to talking. He didn't see Blossom Haven's name anywhere on the cast list, but he knew she would be working tech. He could tell Nu was in her office because he smelled the fresh and strong espresso, and he wanted to see her. He wanted to thank her, but more, he wanted to hear her praise him further, hear in her voice how he deserved the role.

He hesitated near the door, and Windy Donne caught him with her eyes and shook her head.

"She likes to just be left alone after she casts a play," Windy said in a low voice. "You can't blame her. Too many hurt egos."

Carter went back outside, to where the boys were gathered. They were loud and raucous, shouting out lines from the play and improvising. When one spoke, another would cry, *This is a scurvy tune!* Prospero's line *You'd be king o' the isle, sirrah?* was revised to *You'd be king o' the Drama Building, sirrah?* or *You'd be king o' the high school, sirrah?*

Carter sat with them and laughed, but he didn't join in. They were already a group, and every jibe and joke reinforced their membership in the group. They had a history together Carter didn't yet share. He thought he might, through the course of the play, grow comfortable with them and be one of the jokers and laughers, but he felt safer holding back, observing, waiting for a cue from them before joining in.

After being cast, he kept his shirt buttoned, so that nobody could see the slogan. He was happy and didn't want anyone to ruin it. Nobody had deliberately shouldered into him in the plaza, or hit him, and he hadn't run into K. J. again. But he still had the walk home, along the same route, and the glow of having been given a part, and being recognized as a player, suddenly lessened.

He looked for the purple Tiburon as he set out. When he didn't see it, he unbuttoned his shirt. He walked on the left-hand side of the street, so that a car couldn't cruise up behind him, but he still kept glancing over his shoulder. He didn't pay any attention to the Plymouth Fury that drove past him once, circled around, and then parked ahead of him at the corner of Prospector and Saratoga Avenue.

In the days since Katherine drove him from the house, Scott brooded in the El Rancho Motel. As she was chasing him out, she was yelling at him what he should do. He should call her, like any normal person would do, they should meet and talk, he should get back in contact with his son and daughter.

Scott had been paid off his ship almost a month ago. He still had a month before the Military Sealift Command would want him to ship out again. After a couple of days, he took the Fury out and traced the route he knew Carter would have to follow as he walked home, and he began to cruise around the high school when classes ended, hoping to find his son. He thought he could talk to him. He thought Carter would appreciate that he'd gone to help with the war effort, even though Katherine hadn't.

In truth, the role Scott played at sea was little changed from the work he'd done in 1979 during the Iranian hostage crisis. He again sailed on a fleet oiler, a ship that refueled navy ships at sea. Every few days, near sunset, an aircraft carrier pulled alongside the oiler, and they steamed together on parallel courses a hundred feet apart. The carrier shot projectiles with light nylon cord attached over the deck of the oiler. The cords were then bent to lines that carried heavy cables from the oiler back to the carrier. The cables were put under tension by massive hydraulic rams, and then large hoses were sent across via the cables, and fuel was pumped. At dawn the carrier broke away smoothly and picked up speed, leaving the slow, wide oiler in its wake.

Scott worked under a rig captain at the number-three rig. He faked out line that would carry the cable across, manned the sound-powered phones that put the rig in direct communication with the carrier, helped at the windlass that brought the lines back, and secured the rig. There was no adventure to it. The rig captain didn't want adventure. He wanted to follow the procedure, to make refueling as routine as possible, just another part of the job.

Scott wasn't planning on telling his son just how menial his role really was and how far he'd been from any real danger. He didn't see any reasons to get into details when he first saw him. He'd been near Iraq, and he thought Carter should appreciate that much, anyway.

On the third day of cruising between the high school and the subdivision, Scott spied Carter walking down Prospector Street. His son looked taller and even thinner than when he'd left, walking with a nylon messenger bag slung over one shoulder, walking a little hunched as though he were afraid of something. Scott thought that he'd have to get Carter going on some weight training, to get him to stand up straight and muscle up. Maybe some supplements, too, to build up lean muscle mass. That was something they could do together.

He looked down critically at his own gut. Not bad, but not great. The physical work he'd done at sea hadn't been nearly enough to make up for the bacon and cheese omelets for breakfast, spaghetti for lunch, beef or pork with gravy for dinner that the ship's cooks laid out every day, the heavy and filling food that the crew demanded. Some of the young guys, twenty years younger than him, had been able to work on deck all day and then go down to the ship's small weight room and pump the weight machines. Scott found himself in that middle age, young enough to think still about working out and sculpting his body, but feeling an indefinable heaviness at the end of every day that kept him seated and reading the paperbacks handed back and forth among the crew.

He took the Fury around and parked it near the corner of Prospector and Saratoga, and he watched Carter walking toward him on the sidewalk, about a hundred yards away. He wished he had a better car. He wished he had a new Mustang convertible, red with a black ragtop, something that would say clearly that he was a father who was successful now, not the father who had lost everything. As Carter approached, he sucked in his belly and opened the door.

He had imagined opening his arms, sharing a hug with his son, almost man-to-man now. But as he stood up, and Carter stopped in shock, he read the message on the T-shirt.

"Why are you wearing that shirt?"

Scott might have understood, if he had reflected, that this was not the best way to say hello to his son.

"Dad?" Carter stared. His father seemed to have sprung like a jack-in-the-box from an old beater car and was standing in his way, black Ray Bans covering his eyes.

"That shirt. They let you wear that to school?"

"What?"

"They shouldn't. It's disrespectful. Did you see a counselor? You should have seen a counselor. I know what a counselor would say. He'd say it's disrespectful."

"Dad, where did you come from?"

"Your mother didn't tell you I was back?"

"No."

"She doesn't want you to know. That figures. She doesn't want me to come and straighten things out. Look at you. Do you think you're accomplishing anything by wearing that shirt? I can answer that for you. No. You're not accomplishing anything by wearing that shirt."

"I accomplish things," Carter said. He was thinking about the part in the play, but he decided not to mention it. He decided his father would just shit on it.

"I've been in Iraq," Scott said. Not technically true, but true in spirit. "How do you think it makes me feel to come back and see my son wearing that? Did you think of that? Did you think of me?"

"But you weren't here."

"So if I'm not here, I don't matter? I was in Iraq!"

"I don't care where you were," Carter said. "You weren't *here*."

"Well, I'm here now."

"Well, thanks for nothing."

Carter noticed the purple Tiburon cruise past them as he spoke. Stares. A pointed finger. Then the Tiburon turned and disappeared down Saratoga Avenue. He had forgotten about them. Now he wondered if talking with his father had held him up just enough for them to spot him.

"I've got to get home," he said.

"I'll give you a ride," Scott said. "Hop in."

Carter hesitated. A ride would keep him safe for today. But he didn't want his father to show up from nowhere and become his protector. He felt better not depending on his father.

"No thanks, Dad. I'd rather walk."

"Wait." Scott reached for his wallet and pulled out two hundred-dollar bills and held them toward Carter. "Here. Something for now. You need some walking-around money, don't you?"

Again, Carter hesitated. In truth, even though his father had been blustering, Carter understood he had a choice in how much to let him in. And he saw neediness in the way his father reached his hand toward him, sweetened with two hundred dollars. More than he needed the money, his father needed him to take it.

He took the bills and folded them up and put them in his shirt pocket. His father pulled a book of matches out of his pocket. "Here. This is where I'm staying."

Carter looked at the matchbook. On the cover was a line drawing of the El Rancho Motel and its address and phone number.

"Okay," he said.

Scott smiled as Carter walked down Prospector. "I'm back," he called after him. He watched until his son had turned on to the commercial strip of Saratoga Avenue, then got into his Fury. The engine sounded huge as he turned it on. He waited for a moment and then turned to shadow his son back to the subdivision.

Scott felt like a failure most of the time. He could never stop comparing himself to others his age or younger who had gotten more than him, who had risen up to some level of success and ease that was always just out of his reach. He used the phrase "Got it made" with deep envy and resentment. Speaking of someone else, he would say, "Well, he's got it made" or "He's got his ticket punched," and mean that the other person was really undeserving and there was or must be something crooked behind it all. At the very least, those others were no more deserving than himself.

His sister in particular drove him crazy. She had graduated from Chico State two years after him with a degree in English, while he had slaved away at engineering. After college, she had taken some time off, to have kids, and let her husband, a high school teacher, support them. Then she began selling cosmetics for Mary Kay, and found she had a knack for it, and was soon the regional sales leader. She was making twice what Scott had ever made, lived in a beautiful house in Gilroy with a pool and a hot tub in the backyard, still married to her dopey husband even though his salary was pathetic. While Scott was getting laid off, she was getting bonuses.

Scott's mother lived in Las Vegas with another guy who had it made, married him only three months after meeting him. He ran self-actualization seminars, designed to help people create life-success plans for themselves. He ran them in conference rooms at the MGM Grand, and they were always booked full. He even had a few individual clients, poker players competing in the big tournaments, who paid him thousands of dollars. He guessed his mother had it made too, since she married somebody rolling in dough.

Even when he'd had a job, he always felt like he was just keeping up, never really breaking free of the crowd. Trading up in houses was a mistake, but he had convinced himself that they deserved it, that being surrounded by all that success would make them a success as well. And that first mistake led to his investment mistakes, each mistake an attempt to make up for the previous one, each mistake one more lunge at having it made, at getting his own ticket punched.

On good days, he could talk himself into believing that shipping out and doing the same job he'd done when he was twenty-three was a good thing. He could tell himself that he was part of something larger than just himself, part of a great national mission. He could forget the wearing physical labor, the eighty-hour work-weeks out at sea, the deep fatigue he felt that he hadn't felt in 1979. On bad days, he wondered what he was going to do next, whether shipping out again in December was as good as it was going to get.

If Katherine and Carter had admired what he'd done, it would be easier not to feel like such a loser. He had already thought about Henry's house, how many hundreds of thousands of dollars it must be worth, what kind of a home equity loan it could bring, what they could do with that money. Maybe tear down the house and build a palace that his sister would envy.

All impossible, unless he got Katherine back.

He decided, on balance, that this was a good day, despite the antiwar T-shirt he'd found Carter wearing. Carter had taken the money, after all. He would use it for himself. He would start to think well of the old man. And that would be an opening. He wondered what it would be like if he really stayed on as an able seaman. With a snug house waiting for him between ships, a loving Katherine welcoming him back from the sea, and being pampered and cherished and fussed over, like the Gloucester fishermen in

Winslow Homer's paintings must have been. If he couldn't find a job back in Silicon Valley, would that be so bad?

He cruised slowly down Prospector Street until he caught sight of Carter, the thin frame, the light curly hair. Carter was walking against the traffic, in front of the strip malls, and Scott watched him across four lanes of traffic, with a large center-divide island separating the two streams of cars. When he drew a little ahead, he pulled the Fury into a McDonald's parking lot and watched his son walk.

From a distance, he saw three boys emerge from a purple car in a parking lot and step onto the sidewalk in front of his son. He saw Carter hesitate. Two of the boys were big, but a shorter kid wearing a leather jacket was doing the talking, hyped up, dancing around, almost jumping. Carter was talking back to them, it seemed, but Scott could see that this was some kind of confrontation.

Carter tried to walk forward, but the two big boys blocked his path. He tried to walk around them. He didn't break into a run or try to dodge them. Scott was cheered, seeing his son's maturity, seeing him not act like a scared kid.

Then leather jacket said something, and the two big boys rushed Carter, picked him up under the shoulders, and pushed him backward into a Dumpster. They laughed and ran back to the purple car. Carter pushed himself out and brushed himself off.

Scott turned the key on the Fury, and the V8 engine roared as he backed up and then pulled out of the parking lot into traffic. The purple car was already heading in the opposite direction, and Scott pulled into the left lane and cranked his wheel left and bounced his car over the traffic island, fishtailing across two lanes before straightening out and accelerating.

The purple car was a long block and a half ahead of him. He saw it pass under a traffic light, not moving much above the speed limit, and he stepped on the gas to beat the light. It turned yellow just as he entered the intersection. Ahead, he saw the purple car turn right, off the commercial strip, into a residential section.

Scott turned the Fury after the car, but didn't see it ahead of him. The streets in this subdivision were a perfect grid, all straight lines forming right angles with each other, and the houses were smaller than the ones around Catesby Street, stucco ranch houses of a thousand square feet or less. Scott slowed his car and cruised past the first block, looking left or right. Nothing.

He let the Fury idle forward. The houses here were all nearly identical, with picture windows and one-car garages and a front door withdrawn behind a square of lawn and some shrubs. The grid of streets had created a kind of uniformity, so that no place was distinct from any other place.

He thought, for the purple car to have disappeared so quickly, that it must have turned at the second or third block. He followed a hunch and turned left at the third block, and he sped past the houses, pausing at each intersection to look both ways.

He spotted the car after five minutes. It was stopped in front of a house on a street to the right, and one of the big boys had gotten out and was standing beside it. The car took off before he caught up with it, and he began to follow it. There were two boys in the car now, and Scott could see their heads going back and forth, talking. The boy in the passenger seat turned and looked at Scott, then turned back and said something to the boy driving.

The purple car turned right. Scott turned the Fury right, following. The purple car turned left at the next block. Scott turned left. The houses they passed were all the same stucco, painted blue and green and red, with ficus or jacaranda trees in the front strip, sometimes some shrubs under the picture windows, sometimes with shiny Astroturf replacing the front lawn beside the driveway.

The purple car sped up, going to forty miles an hour through the residential streets. Scott accelerated to keep up with them.

The car turned left, skidding its tires. Scott had to slow down to make the turn with his big boat of a car.

He found the purple car stopped in the middle of the street, halfway down the block. As he pulled up, the kid in the oversize leather jacket got out of the driver's side of the car.

The kid stood there, thin with black jeans, his legs spread. Maybe seventeen years old, his face sneering and creased with acne.

"Hey, asshole. What the fuck you following me for?"

He began to walk toward the Fury.

"Hey, asshole."

Scott stepped on the accelerator. The car leaped at the leather jacket.

"Hey!" The kid dove to his left.

Scott felt the bump as one fender clipped the kid's legs and spun him around.

He kept driving. In his rearview mirror, he saw the kid on the ground, his friend out of the purple car and kneeling beside him.

He turned right and sped up. If he kept going, he thought, he would come to another edge of this grid and break free.

4

KATHERINE HAD WORKED for BPI, Batch Processing, Inc., for twelve years. The company specialized in software that analyzed batch manufacturing—any process that took raw material at one end and created a finished product or products at the other end. Crude oil cracked and refined into gasoline and other products was a batch process. Raw whole grains milled and ground and baked into cornflakes was another batch process. BPI's software could retrieve and record data at many stages of the process, to find problems that were cropping up and to uncover hidden inefficiencies that could be addressed. In the past few years, BPI had made it possible to view data on any process in real time on the Internet, so that the functioning of many plants anywhere in the world could be supervised from one location.

The chemical engineers strolled the carpeted halls in khakis and golf shirts, badges dangling from their belt loops, relatively normal. The programmers were more eccentric. One programmer kept a large rock on his desk next to his computer. He said that when he felt stuck, he looked at the rock and said, "The rock is doing its job. Now you do yours." Another programmer, Ron Newbury, once brought a pet sugar glider to work one day in a canvas bag he kept hanging around his neck. He claimed that the animal had to get used to his smell. At lunchtime, when he opened the bag to show everyone, a small mammal with large liquid eyes and stripes down its back leaped onto the desk. Ron lifted it onto his shirt and began to stroke it, and it peed.

Katherine was neither engineer nor programmer. She had the title of events planner, and she was in charge of organizing the annual users' conference for BPI clients, held every March in Monterey. Her year usually had a lull in April and May, then grew steadily busier as she distributed publicity by emails, met with sales reps to make sure they would emphasize the conference to clients, met with engineers and programmers about the topics of various presentations, with the CEO and the vice presidents about plenary sessions. She had to arrange food services and entertainment, and a few favored clients were always comped at Pebble Beach Golf Links.

She worked in a broad, U-shaped desk space that she shared with two others employees, Rajni Thekkiam, a twenty-five-year-old from Bangalore, and Heber Grimshaw, a little older than thirty, who kept his hair short and neatly parted and wore a suit and tie to work every day except on casual Fridays.

Katherine compared herself to Rajni and wished she could eat the way Rajni did and not gain weight. She envied the way her coworker always had matching accessories, scarves that went perfectly with her blouse and her greenish eyes, and pendants and earrings that tied every ensemble together. Her own clothing choices always seemed less coordinated, drabber, older. But she liked talking with Rajni about hair, and purses, and shoes. Rajni always seemed to know where there were great bargains to be had, special clearance sales, early-bird pricing, consignment shops with designer clothes. And even though Katherine never had time to run out to the places Rajni mentioned, she liked talking about them. It made her feel that she was not really in a different age and different time of life, that she hadn't really changed much since her early thirties.

Sometimes, Katherine fantasized that if she had never married Scott, she would still be twenty-five. It was that decision that had made her age, and if she hadn't made it, she would still be the same age as Rajni, an age of infinite possibilities. She would be making decisions about nothing of consequence, and her life would be as light as tiramisu after an Italian dinner, light as a new handbag at the mall, light as an initial email sent through a dating service. Then she thought about Betty and Carter, Carter's curly hair that haloed his pale face and Betty's sardonic remarks that Katherine couldn't live without, and she would feel guilty for imagining them absent from the world.

Rajni was also a gossip, and she would wait until Heber was away to talk about him. She said she would never date him, because they worked so close together, but that she'd heard from other women. He would date them, but at some point, he'd just draw back. It might be because he was raised a Mormon, and so he didn't really know how to be around women, but she wondered if he was really gay and didn't know it, like that character in *Angels in America*. He was a Mormon too.

Heber's job, which he was coordinating with Katherine, was developing webinars, seminars on the systems-control software that could be offered on the Web. His job required him to know much more about programming than Katherine, and she wondered if he wasn't eventually going to make her job obsolete, if someday there would be no need for companies to send employees to Monterey once a year for training and presentations, if it would all be done online. Already, in the past two years, she had noticed the number of conference attendees level off, even though the number of companies using the software had increased. She wondered if she would end up working under Heber someday.

The fact that she'd had to take a vacation day every three weeks to get her father to chemo had been noticed, and it would be noticed more just before the users' conference. Even though she was not taking any other kind of vacation, her boss, whom they called the Colonel, had made a note in her personnel file that too many "personal days" could begin to affect employee performance. They called him the Colonel only behind his back. He had been a career army officer, but in fact had only made lieutenant colonel and had to retire when he was passed over for promotion. Some of his demand for efficiency, Katherine and Rajni thought, was because he was compensating for the fact he'd never made general.

Heber had been able to cover for her several times while she was with her father, since he helped on the users' conference during crunch time, and she was grateful for that, even while she felt somewhat threatened by him. She thought that her company was still sexist—90 percent of the programmers were men, and all the founders were men—and she was afraid that if the position required less personal interaction, less F2F as the Colonel put it, less "feeling stuff," the woman could be the one squeezed out. And as nice as Heber seemed, Boy Scout nice, she didn't want to let him take over her responsibilities any more than necessary.

· · · · ● · · ·

After work that day, unaware that Scott had tracked down Carter, she pulled into her father's driveway—her driveway too, she declared to herself—and stayed in her car. There was something comforting and cradling about that driver's seat, that place where she sat and nobody else ever did, despite the Saturn's oil leak. It was a place that had stayed with her, that she had been able to depend on for the past ten years.

She began to talk to her mother, as she did from time to time. She told her mother that she wasn't completely secure in her job, Scott had been laid off, she could be too, and then where would they be? She asked her what she thought of having Carter take Dad to chemo. Carter had his learner's permit, and he could drive accompanied by her father, and she didn't think it mattered if her father was weakened by the chemo on the way back. It might be good for Carter. He could feel responsible, more grown up, he could feel she trusted him. As she talked to her mother, she gradually began playing in her head the conversation she would have with Carter. She would present it as a favor he could do for her, as a concrete way to help his grandfather. He would understand what she was asking and feel proud to be able to help. He would begin to mope less, and be less moody, and help around the house. He would become a model son!

Her mother never really answered Katherine. She had died so suddenly, at a time when Katherine was acting sullen and withdrawn, thinking that she had nothing to learn from her. Katherine had missed out on maturing and learning to appreciate her mother, missed out on drawing closer to her when she went to college, got married, had children. There was no fund of experience and good advice that Katherine could remember and draw on to bring her own distant children close again.

Katherine felt her mother only as a warm presence, wishing her well, though unable to warn her or guide her. But one thing her mother had said haunted her—*You'll do better than me.* She'd said it once in passing, a thing parents say reflexively to their children, but it came back to Katherine now that she was again living with her father. How had she done better?

She opened the back door of the Saturn and grabbed a cardboard file box filled with demo CDs and résumés of some possible entertainers for the conference, and she walked to the front door.

"By God." Katherine heard her father's voice boom when she walked in the door. "By God, who is that coming in?"

"Stay put, Dad, I'll come over."

But Henry had already stood up from his desk in the sunken den, shambling toward her like a friendly bear, walking tenderly in oversize slippers that eased the spiked pain in the soles of his feet. He was still a big man, even shrunken from cancer, and he took Katherine in his arms and hugged her. Then he let her loose and looked at her.

"You're losing too much weight," he said. "Your growth is stunted. You need to have more sex, girl, if you're to survive at all."

Katherine knew her part to play in this. She tapped his arm, as though embarrassed. "You didn't follow your own advice. You didn't remarry after Mom."

"And look at me," he said. "It's a wonder I've survived the last thirty years."

"You're surviving," Katherine said. She walked over to the kitchen and opened the refrigerator door and stared at the bright space. For a moment, she couldn't remember why she had opened the refrigerator. The shelves were full of labeled jars and bottles and foods shrouded in plastic bags or Tupperware, but she couldn't think why she was looking or what she was looking for. Then she thought of dinner and stared again at the shelves, but nothing came to her. She gaped at the shelves full of food, thinking something must be there for a dinner. She would be perfectly happy with a bowl of cereal, and everyone else ought to be as well. A bowl of cereal, or nothing. Just announce we're having *nothing* for dinner.

Henry followed her into the galley kitchen, not a separate room but a narrow bay with a sink beneath a window that looked out on the street.

"I'll treat us to takeout tonight," he said, as though he could read her mind.

"Lord be praised."

Katherine closed the door of the refrigerator and leaned back against it, as though shutting the cover of an unpleasant book.

"I wanted to talk to you before I asked Carter, Dad. What do you think if he took you to chemo? You could drive there, and he could drive you back. It would be a big help to me."

"Good by me," Henry said.

"Is Carter home?"

"Sort of."

"What's that mean?"

"It means he came home and went into his room and shut the door," Henry said.

"Any reason?"

"Nothing he wanted to share with his grandfather."

"I wonder if he didn't get a part in that play."

"Maybe not."

Katherine sighed. "I wanted that for him."

"Maybe you should tell him you've seen Scott."

"What good would that do?"

"If he knew his father was acting like a nutcase," Henry said, "he might be easier on you."

Katherine squeezed her father's arm, then walked through the living room to the hall that led to the bedrooms. The door to Carter's room was a blank face. She walked up to it, thought about knocking, decided against it. He would come out soon enough, and she didn't want him to come out already armored with resentment. She touched her fingers to the wood of the hollow door, as though she would be able to feel the warm heart of her son through the door. Then she went back to the dining room, hoisted her file box to the table.

While his mother leaned toward the door, Carter was talking quietly on his cell phone to Betty in Aptos. He had never been very close to his sister. She was older by three years, and she treated having a younger brother as an embarrassment, said that she was happy at least that she never had to be in high school with him. And she was a rule breaker, always willing to try something new for the experience, and he was a goody-goody in her mind. But he didn't know whom else to call about seeing their father.

She told him that she hadn't seen him yet, though it was probably only a matter of time before he tracked her down.

"God, that will be great. DAD will show up at the restaurant where I'm working and want to have a heart-to-heart. As though we ever talked before he lost all the money and bailed. Know what I'll tell him if he shows up?"

"What?" Carter was talking while lying on top of his bed, with his knees tucked up and the phone cradled by his head.

"'Sorry, Dad. I'm busy peeling shrimp.' Does Mom know he's here?"

"I don't know."

"So what did he want?"

"I don't know that either. He started yelling at me. And then he gave me two hundred dollars."

Betty hooted. "That's Dad. Great with the interpersonal relationships. What did he yell at you about?"

"What my shirt said."

"What did it say?"

Carter told her.

"Really? And he saw it?" A note of respect came into her voice. "That's awesome."

"He said it was disrespectful."

Betty snorted. "Look, it's obvious he's trying to buy back your love. It's because he knows how much he fucked everything up."

"So should I keep the money?" Carter uncurled from the bed and sat up.

"What, are you crazy? Does this run in the family? OF COURSE keep the money. Just because he gave it to you doesn't mean he's bought anything."

"Maybe I should give it to Mom."

"NO. She fucked up too, by being clueless. The best thing you can do is wait it out until you finish high school and then get out like I did. And the more money you can stash away, the better. Two hundred bucks is nothing."

"Okay."

"Remember what I told you. Escape or die."

"Right."

"What kind of car was Dad driving? I want to be able to spot it."

"One of those old boats with a vinyl roof? Green, with black vinyl. But the vinyl was peeling, and you could see the metal starting to rust underneath it."

"God, what a loser."

After they hung up, Carter logged on to his computer to see if anyone had messaged him. Nobody had. He felt very alone. He had thought, for a second, of telling Betty about the boys who had jumped him again, after she seemed impressed by his wearing the shirt. But she might think that the vow he made was just stupid. She was good at making him feel stupid and making him feel that whatever happened to him was because he just wasn't savvy about the world.

He couldn't tell her, or the boys at school who were starting to act friendly. He couldn't tell his mother or grandfather.

He looked at the computer screen again, screen-save mode now, with nature scenes fading in and out. There was no one in that box he could tell.

He didn't want to tell his mother the good news, either, about getting a part in the play. He could let her know that his life was harder now than it had been before, but he didn't want to allow her to think that his life was getting better. In his opinion, it wasn't.

He walked out of his room and into the hallway. The house was so small that any movement out of his room immediately put him into his mother's sphere, and he now spent more time with the door closed than he ever had in their house in Oak Commons. He found his mother at the dining room table with some papers from the cardboard file box spread out. Maybe his sister was right. She did look clueless. A pair of reading glasses was sliding down her nose, and her hair was bunched up where she grabbed it with her fist while she read.

After a moment, she looked up. "Hi, sweetie," she said.

He looked at her without speaking.

She glanced at the kitchen, suddenly feeling guilty. But why should she? Why couldn't she just say that *nothing* was for dinner?

"Grandpa is going to pick up something at the Pho Garden for us," she said. "Does that sound good?"

"Sure."

"Here. Have a seat." She cleared away several stacks of file folders and patted the chair beside her.

Carter sat down, stiff and unwilling.

"I wanted to tell you," she said. "I saw your father a few days ago."

Carter's first impulse was to tell her that he'd seen his father too, that afternoon, and that he'd already been belittled by him. And then he'd been thrown into a Dumpster again. But he heard Betty saying that their mother was clueless, and he decided to keep it all to himself.

"How is he?" he asked.

"Well . . . he hasn't quite gotten settled," Katherine said. "He still feels in between things. I think he'd like to be here, with us. But I don't think that's a good idea. Right now."

"No. It's not a good idea," Carter said.

"But it makes things hard on me, not having him around. And that's where you can be a big help."

"How?"

"It's getting hard for me to take time off of work to take your grandfather to chemo," she said. "So I was wondering if you could go with him. He could drive there, and you could drive back. It would be like an extra driving lesson for you."

Carter thought Betty would approve of how he was handling the situation. This offer took him by surprise, and he liked it. He liked anything that let him drive more often. But he wasn't ready to show it. Better to make it seem like some favor he was doing for her.

"Will I have to miss school?" he asked.

"Just once in a while. You won't mind that so much, will you?"

"I don't know. I got a part in the play, you know." He presented it to her now as something that made his time important, that made her request more of a burden.

"No, I didn't know that." Katherine brightened. "Will taking your grandpa be too much?"

"No. I don't think so. The rehearsals are at night. I might need a ride sometimes, though, since I can't drive myself yet."

"Of course," she said. "I can always take you."

· · · • · · ·

Two days later, Henry Watson, Pearl Harbor survivor aboard the USS *Phoenix* and veteran of the Battle of Leyte Gulf, walked down the hallway from the master bedroom, dressed in a green terry-cloth bathrobe and flannel pajamas. In the kitchen, he poured himself a cup of coffee from the half-empty pot his daughter had left for him. Eight A.M. He rolled back down the hall and paused in front of Carter's door. When he heard no sound of stirring, he pounded the door with a fist.

"Now reveille, reveille, reveille. Heave out and trice up. Drop your cocks and grab your socks. The uniform of the day is dress blues. Inspection at Oh Nine Hundred Hours. Now reveille."

He took his coffee back to the kitchen and added a teaspoon of sugar. He used to drink coffee black, but he found as he grew older that it tasted better with a little sweetness added. He sipped it and looked out the kitchen window to the street where he had lived the past five decades, the same landscape, tiny and familiar. He sipped his coffee. Another chemo day.

Henry was diagnosed in 1998 and by 2003 was a medical miracle. It was only because he was in fine health that they used an aggressive regimen to try to stop the cancer. He had his prostate removed, and his testicles taken, and chemotherapy. He was a large man, six foot three and two hundred solid pounds, but he felt his whole body slacken from the cancer and the chemicals and the hormones. His shoulders grew thinner, and he grew more of a gut and a sag of flesh under his chin.

After chemotherapy they found that the cancer had migrated to his liver. This was a very rare occurrence. His kind of cancer usually went to the bones first. He went back on chemo to shrink the new lesions, and a surgeon burned them off and told him he was cancer free, but he never really believed it, and the lesions came back. After a different regimen of chemotherapy, the lesions shrunk to nondetectable size, but when he was taken off chemo again, the dark spots returned to his scan, numerous and deadly.

Then he began chemotherapy just to be able to live with his cancer, not to cure it. His oncologist had no idea how long it would last. He was an ongoing experiment. Every third week, they poured poison into him through a shunt near his heart, putting him flat on his back for days. At first, he could eat nothing. After a day, potato soup was the only thing that tasted good to him. Then he was able to eat some white chicken. Gradually, he rose from the dead and was able to walk, think, laugh, until the next round. Every three weeks, another near-death experience and another resurrection.

Year by year, Henry felt his grasp of the visible world slipping. The tidy house, his Peaceable Isle, had gradually gotten away from him. He no longer had the strength to clear gutters, trim shrubbery, paint, fix, maintain. It was all deteriorating, and he couldn't raise his hands and bring it back into order. He cherished the return of his daughter, but she brought sorrow and longing with her, beyond his powers. And he could not legislate his grandson's chaotic feelings into happiness, despite trying to do things with him that he hadn't with his two sons. His chemotherapy every three weeks gave him at best a tenuous control over his own body, and he felt at any treatment the cancer could escape, erupt into something winged and clawed. He knew what the next step would be if this regimen failed. Some new and harsher treatment that poisoned him like a rat and might not work and then abandoning therapy for a few gorgeous months of good feeling before failing utterly.

He heard Carter moving about, heard the hollow bedroom door open and the bathroom door close as his grandson scurried across the hall to take a shower. Before his treatment, they were going together for a Veterans in the Schools presentation. Henry had volunteered after being talked into it by two friends from the Garden Spot. They told him he should talk to kids about what Pearl Harbor was like. There weren't that many survivors around anymore, and if he didn't share his stories, they'd be forgotten. His two friends had been going to schools and talking about their time in the war for years, but requests had gone way up since 9/11.

Henry wasn't one of those who talked about his time at war as the greatest adventure of his life. Sometimes, he felt as though he had lived his life inside of a dream, though he was not the dreamer. The war was waiting for him at the end of childhood, the childish games he had thoughtlessly played grown into monstrous reality. And he had walked from his life at war into his life postwar with little reflection, as if he were not truly the agent of his actions, but only a figure moved in concert with millions of others, moved within the obscure designs of some larger dream. The family waiting for him, the landscape of homes waiting for him, it wasn't something he himself had created. He sometimes was aware of being in a dream, as the mind of a dreamer is sometimes aware, but he could not move completely outside of the dream, to glimpse it whole.

Henry had a cousin his own age, a Lutheran minister, an author of some note, who wrote in a book that the contentments of family were a foretaste of heaven. But his cousin had never married, and Henry himself could never accept the simple answer that he was living inside the design of God, not after the many and anonymous deaths of the war, not after the singular and intimate death of his Mary Katherine.

Henry had never talked about Pearl Harbor with any of his grandchildren. It wasn't one of the medley of family stories that were passed around and repeated over and over, their repetition forming part of the identity they shared. But now, he hoped that if Carter heard him talk to the schoolkids about the war, he might grasp some plausible narrative of his family's past, an appreciation of the house where they were all living, that might lead him to soften his resentment. A story Carter could believe in, even if it was one that Henry himself found lacking.

Henry dressed up to visit the school. A nice pair of tan slacks, a light wool sports coat, and an Oxford shirt open at the throat where he tied a bright colored scarf. When he agreed to give the talk, he looked over the clothes he used to wear to work. None of them fit. He had gained weight, softened and fallen, because of the cancer and the surgery and the hormonal treatment that followed. When he went to Mosher's, a men's store where he'd been buying clothes since the fifties, he joked with the salesman that what he really needed was a training bra. They shared a sympathetic laugh, and the salesman found him a constructed coat with enough of a shoulder pad to give him back some of his outer shape.

He still wore a beret. He thought without it, he looked like a turkey buzzard, bald head perching on a bald neck, no eyebrows, no eyelashes, just slack naked skin, mottled with spots. The scarf and the beret were a defense against the signs of his condition, an attempt to control at least how others saw him, though futile, he knew, against the condition itself.

Midmorning, Carter drove the Buick under Henry's direction into the parking lot of the James D. Phelan Elementary School, a public school located near the new and prosperous developments financed by dot-com money that curled into the foothills above Cupertino and Los Altos. The lines of parking places beside the school were separated by thin strips of dirt and grass rimmed by cement curbs and punctuated by spindly young trees held straight by wooden stakes and rubber hose. Carter bumped the left tire gently against the curb, put the car in park, set the brake, and turned off the ignition, while Henry nodded at each step. Carter wore his normal school jeans and a sweatshirt—he wanted to show he was not making any special effort.

They walked through doors of heavy glass framed by thick metal and entered a bright, open atrium. The principal had his secretary watching, and when he heard that his guest had arrived, he rose and walked with a stately air to greet him.

"I want to thank you for coming today, Mr. Watson." He took Henry's hand in his own.

"You're welcome," Henry said.

"I'm proud to shake the hand of a Pearl Harbor veteran." The principal had worn a blue suit with a flag lapel pin in honor of Henry's visit. He was African American, and he took care to observe the proper forms and customs in all things. He had learned that being dignified and reserved kept others—white people—from feeling uncomfortable around him, and he learned the lesson so well that it became his normal affect.

When the principal signed the school up for the Veterans in the Schools program, he thought of his father, also a World War II veteran, dead too young. After the war, his father had used the GI Bill to buy a house in East Palo Alto, called East even though oddly it was actually north of Palo Alto. East Palo Alto, E.P.A., a poor and unincorporated area that was redlined by bankers and brokers and the only place in the area where his father could get a mortgage because he was black. His father held on to that house the rest of his life and raised a family there. He had been a mechanic for the US Army Air Corps and fought in no famous battles, but the principal thought that he was as much a hero as any veteran.

The principal himself was a veteran of Vietnam, a Ranger, a lurp. When he came home to California and found no honor for what he'd done, he tried to forget the past. He took a degree from San José State, became a teacher, rose to be principal. Yet he noted that the Veterans in the Schools rarely if ever included vets from Vietnam, and he thought cynically that heroes are chosen by the times, not by the deeds, and that the ambiguities of Vietnam did not suit the country's mood.

But he did not like to act out of bitterness, and none of this history was the fault of the elderly man who was giving up his time to visit the class. He wanted the visit to be a success and the students to find inspiration. That was his job—that was the expectation.

He turned to Carter. "And this is . . ."

"My grandson, Carter."

"I'm glad you came. You must be proud having a Pearl Harbor vet as a grandfather."

Carter grunted.

The principal led them down a hallway illuminated with long banks of fluorescent lights and floored with green speckled linoleum tile. It was quiet, but muffled sounds pushed out as they passed the closed classroom doors. The principal explained that they would be meeting Miss Anderson's class of fifth graders, and that she had been preparing the students for his visit.

He paused in front of one heavy door in a green metal frame and leaned in. It was perfectly quiet.

"You should go in first," he whispered to Henry.

Henry lifted his beret and ran a hand over his smooth head. He still sometimes unconsciously went to pat down his hair, finding then that it was gone.

He replaced his beret at what he hoped was a jaunty angle and pushed open the door.

A chorus of young voices greeted him. "Thank you, Mr. Watson."

The children sprang to their feet, all dressed in red, white, and blue. Miss Anderson had the idea to honor their visiting veteran by asking every child to wear some combination of blue pants and white shirt or red blouse, or striped red and white shirt. She was a young second-year teacher, and she supported the troops, and she intended to show it. She herself was dressed in a blue wool skirt and white blouse and used a flag pin to hold a red scarf in place. The classroom had also been decorated with crepe streamers in red, white, and blue, hanging like bunting along the walls and swinging from the light fixtures in arcs above the children's heads. The bright colors were cartoonish, like the interior of an ice cream parlor.

Miss Anderson introduced herself to Henry and led him to a chair she called the seat of honor in front of the blackboard. Some students had chalked the words *Pearl Harbor Veteran* in big block letters above the chair, so that when he sat down the letters arced above his head. The principal stood near the teacher's desk, but Carter remained slouched against the wall beside the door, thin and uninterested.

The children were of many heritages, with parents who came from all over the world, and they stared at Henry—a large white man in a boxy suit coat, no hair and no eyebrows to soften the large nose, fleshy fallen throat gathered up in a scarf. He looked funny, different from the adults they saw every day, who were all quick and busy and connected. He looked like he was from another time, an exhibit that took its place under the sign identifying its importance.

Henry shifted uncomfortably, and Miss Anderson began by having the class recite facts about Pearl Harbor. She asked questions, and they sang out the memorized answers. What was the date of the attack? December 7, 1941. What time did the attack begin? Seven fifty A.M. How long did the attack last? One hundred ten minutes. How many Americans lost their lives? Two thousand four hundred and three. What American ship was damaged the worst? The *Arizona*. Who was president? Franklin Delano Roosevelt. What did he do after Pearl Harbor? Declared war on Japan. What did he call Pearl Harbor in his speech? A date which will live in infamy.

The young piping voices were a little muddied on the last two answers, but Miss Anderson turned to Henry for his approval, and he nodded. The principal also nodded, and Miss Anderson read that as approval for how she was running the classroom.

"Now Mr. Watson is going to share some of his own memories of that day," Miss Anderson said. "He was on a ship called the *Phoenix* and stayed in the navy until the end of the war."

Henry stood up. A rough map of Pearl Harbor was sketched out on the chalkboard, and he began by drawing a line where the battleships were anchored near Ford Island and then placing an X where the *Phoenix* had been tied up, to the northeast. He told how he had been eating breakfast on the mess deck when he heard the call to General Quarters, and the first explosions began. General Quarters, he explained, meant that everyone in the crew had to be at battle stations—engine crews, gunners, damage control, everyone. His station was on the port bridge wing, ready to take bearings to fix the ship's position once they got under way. He was wearing a big helmet over a sound-powered phone set, so he could talk to the chart room.

It took a little time to light off the ship's engines, but his ship's antiaircraft guns were going before they got under way. His own row of ships was not heavily targeted, but they were trying to get moving so that they wouldn't be sitting ducks. From the bridge, he could see explosions and fire coming from the battleships, and he remembered seeing the masts of the *Oklahoma* slowly tilting as the big ship turned turtle.

Henry drew an arrow over the place where his ship had been anchored. He said part of the second wave of Japanese planes came very near his ship, but passed over to strafe targets on Ford Island. There were more explosions from Battleship Row, but it was lucky for the country that aircraft carriers like the *Enterprise* weren't in port when the attack came.

"I just remember how beautiful Oahu was that morning. Beautiful green island floating in a blue sea, looking like paradise. And in a moment it was filled with death. We did our duty. That's all it came down to. We did our duty, that day and the years that followed, hoping we could see the end of the war and come home again."

The principal walked to Henry's side. "Here's what you have to remember. Henry Watson, and all the other men and women who served with him, did what their country asked them to do. They sacrificed their youth and sometimes their lives. And we should thank them all. So let's say 'thank you' together."

"Thank you," the children chorused.

The principal nodded, thinking that some small part of that thanks might be directed toward his own father. It was a private thought, and he would not share it.

"Now, do you have any questions?" he asked.

Several of the children raised their hands. They had written out questions ahead of time, and Miss Anderson called on them one by one. How old were you when you joined the navy? What medals did you get? What did you do when you heard the war was over?

Henry answered the questions one by one, smiling at the questioners sitting at their half-size desks. He paused a bit when one girl asked him why he'd joined the navy. He knew that he might be expected to say that he joined because of patriotism, but in truth he joined because he wanted to leave a home where his stepfather didn't have much use for him. So he avoided the real question and said that he'd joined the navy because he'd always liked the ocean.

Then one boy asked Henry if he had ever been scared, and he said he had been, many times. "Everyone was scared at some point or other," he said.

He glanced at Carter, still leaning against the wall in the rear of the classroom, gazing at the ceiling, as though bored. None of the talk seemed to have broken through the moody circle he'd drawn around himself.

Henry looked at his watch, stood up. "I'm sorry, but we're going to have to leave early. Medical appointment."

Miss Anderson was confused, but she responded as she thought the principal would like. "Well, let's give Mr. Watson one more big thank-you for coming. Class?"

"Thank you, Mr. Watson," they sang.

Back in the Buick, Carter drove without knowing where they were going, but happy to be out of the school. He thought the whole thing was really about the Iraq War, and he didn't like it.

He knew they were hours early for the appointment, but he followed the route toward the hospital until Henry told him to take Saratoga Road. In the years before the freeway system was built, it was common for roadways to be named after their destinations.

"So where are we going, Grandpa?" he asked.

"Someplace I've had your mother take me before chemo, when she's had the time. You'll get a chance to practice driving on curves."

At Saratoga the road narrowed as it went through the old downtown. Saratoga was at the edge of the valley, not a thoroughfare, and it had retained some of its old distinctive shape around the town square. The blacksmith shop was now a French restaurant, and the five-and-dime was an antique store and the old brick bank was now a cozy bar and grill, but the building facades had been preserved and ornate green streetlamps and benches and planters lined the sidewalks.

Past the town, the road climbed along Saratoga Creek. The landscape steepened, and the road hugged the hillside and curved sharply around tall stands of second-growth redwoods, and they passed signs for Boy Scout camps and a Lutheran retreat and old health resorts. Carter had never driven such a twisty road, and he fought the car around the turns, entered them too fast and then oversteered coming out of them, putting the tires over the double yellow line before regaining the right side of the road. The redwood trees sprang up repeatedly, seemingly right in his path, and meant another jerk to the left or right.

"Good practice," Henry said.

"Sure," Carter said.

"Just slow down going into a turn and accelerate out of it."

"Okay." Carter was hunched over the wheel and gripping it with both hands.

At a sign for a vineyard, Henry said, "Turn right here."

Carter cautiously turned the Buick onto a side road, and they climbed out of the steep creek bed and broke onto a broad slanting hilltop. The road ran between blocks of vineyard, rows of vines with the ragged look of being recently harvested and not yet pruned. Below the road, the blocks of vineyard ended in sloping grassland and scrub oak. Above, the cultivated land adjoined the old redwood forest.

The winery building was designed to look vaguely European. After parking, they entered through an iron gateway into a small courtyard with grapevines climbing trellises along the walls and a round fountain playing at the center. French doors opened beyond the courtyard and led to the tasting room, a broad, airy space decorated with blond woods and bright chandeliers. A long row of tall windows out the back of the tasting room overlooked a broad terrace and gave views of the Santa Clara Valley. In summer, all the windows would be open, but in October they were closed.

Carrie Yamamoto, standing behind the counter, felt bored as soon as Henry shambled in, followed by Carter. Two more tourists, she thought. She had a business degree from Santa Clara, and she'd thought that working for a vineyard would be exciting, but she spent only half of each day dealing with sales reps and distributors. The other half was spent managing the tasting room, a job that brought no respect from the winemaker, who called it Disneyland. He was always bragging that he'd been in the doctoral program in enology at Davis and then quit, because the best didn't finish their degrees, they went out and did the work, the real work of making wine.

The winemaker. He was in his thirties and liked to make her feel small before he hit on her. She always turned him down politely because she couldn't afford to alienate him. But she knew his type—Asiaphiles, noodle chasers, the kind of guy who would say he only dated Asian women and expect you to take it as a compliment. She sometimes wondered if that's why he gave her the job, so that he could hit on her.

Even though she already wanted to get out for the day, she straightened up as the two approached. She knew that being successful with the tasting room was her ticket to rise, to land those events with sommeliers from fine restaurants, to build up her own network and her own credentials. And then she could move on, drive her Miata to a new job, a better job, and leave that winemaker far behind.

She saw the boy was too young to drink, but she didn't think he would ask. It was in groups that someone underage tried to get a glass of wine, usually a nineteen-year-old sophomore from Stanford with a twenty-two-year-old boyfriend.

"Can I help you?" she asked.

Henry rubbed the small white fringe of beard at his chin, the only facial hair that returned after his treatments. "Pouring any sparkling wines?"

"Our blanc de noirs. Or we have a special cuvée, vintage 1999."

"The blanc de noirs will be fine."

She uncapped the heavy bottle and poured a flute full for him. The wine held a pale tinge of red, and small bubbles climbed vertically up the sides of the glass. He requested a Calistoga for Carter, also in a flute, and he paid her. Then they walked together onto the terrace and sat at a cast-iron café table and looked out at the valley.

When they had time, Henry had come to this vineyard with Katherine before going in for chemo. To savor the taste of wine, before the treatment again wrested away all pleasure in taste. To enjoy the landscape, the belvedere, designed to offer a sense of ease and fulfillment and mastery. It was pretend, make-believe, but it allowed him to beguile the sense of death stalking and get through another treatment and rise again. It helped him retain that sense of control now escaping him.

He'd had the foolish hope that Katherine and Carter—and Betty, don't forget—moving into his house would effect a kind of restoration. All would come to his Peaceable Isle and find their happiness, and he would feel what he'd felt when his wife was young and alive and his children with him. Now he felt he could conjure happiness for no one. Carter was in his life intimately now, more intimately than his own sons, perhaps, who had never taken him to treatment, never seen him wrecked in the aftermath. But that intimacy would bring no remedy for Carter's own moody retreat, which Henry could only feel but not alter.

Carter was looking skeptically at the champagne flute full of mineral water, at the sandstone walls and slate terrace. "This is kind of fake-o," he said.

Henry sipped his blanc de noirs. "The wine is real. You're real. I'm real."

"Yeah." Carter was unconvinced. "That Pearl Harbor talk was pretty fake-o too, wasn't it."

"It was," Henry admitted. "Listen, I'll tell you something real about Pearl Harbor, something that doesn't get into the stories people want to hear. We got the *Phoenix* under way, and we had our guns firing into the sky at all those planes, the loudest noise you could think of. And the battleships were burning, big clouds of black smoke, and water was covered with oil and some of it was on fire, right on top of the water, and your mouth tasted like diesel. And there were some bodies in the water as well, young men not much older than you. We got out of the harbor, looking for enemy ships or subs. The attack was over then, but we didn't know that.

"But here's the funny thing that sticks in my memory. I never got breakfast that morning. The attack started just as I was sitting down on the mess deck. And we didn't eat until around ten at night, when we were out at sea and standing down from General Quarters. The ship was dark. That meant that all the porthole covers were dogged down, and you couldn't even light a cigarette on any weather deck. But I stood in line, and I got a cup of hot coffee and a sandwich, and it was the best thing I ever ate. It was delicious. Because I was so hungry. And because I could have died that day. That's the real thing."

Carter nodded. "What kind of sandwich?" he asked.

"Fried Spam and onion."

"Best thing ever?"

"Best thing ever. Here."

Henry took Carter's flute, spilled out the water, and filled it with half his sparkling wine.

"A toast," he said. "To the best thing ever."

"I don't know what mine is yet," Carter said.

"Yours is still coming," Henry said. "You've got a lot of time. Believe that. Okay?"

"Okay."

They touched glasses and drank. The valley below them spread out in tan and black and green, stitched with expressways, platted with tract housing and office parks and malls, home to a million and more.

Henry decided to drive down the hill and to the oncology clinic, because of the sharpness of the road and the half glass of wine Carter had drunk. He wheeled the Buick out of the parking lot in front of the tasting room and drove back through the blocks of harvested grapes to the road along Saratoga Creek.

The car, even in Henry's hands, didn't seem to be under control. He found himself taking turns too wide and braking to bring his car back into his lane, then unwittingly speeding up again before the next curve. Points of the road led straight off into the ravine before doubling back at the last instant, and the stands of redwoods sprang up from nowhere.

"Watch out, Grandpa," he heard Carter say.

The turns were coming faster than he expected, and he looked for the gentling of the slope and the broadening of the valley that would tell him they were close to Saratoga. He leaned forward, over the steering wheel. The road was hazy, as though his tires were barely in contact with the pavement. He thought that if he could just get back to the level, he would be fine.

He turned the wheel to the left, and his tires screeched. He was going too fast. But the town had to be close. He was sure of it.

"Grandpa . . ."

A car leaped in his way. A yellow car, enormous, filling his windshield.

He cut the tires hard right. A horn blared. Air bags exploded all around them.

5

KATHERINE HEARD about the wreck at work and had to leave an in-box of email full of inquiries about travel, hotel and conference registration, seminar schedules, special dietary needs, visas post 9/11, and odd questions about golf. (Did they rent Big Berthas at Spanish Bay? Who knew?) She told Rajni she would be back as soon as she could. Heber asked what was wrong, and Katherine laughed.

"I'm just going crazy, that's all," she said.

"Is there anything I can do to help?" he asked.

Katherine laughed again.

She drove to the emergency room at the Community Hospital in Los Gatos. On the way, she talked with Carter on her cell and found out that neither of them had more than a few bruises, though a few bruises for an eighty-year-old man like her father might be more than a few bruises for a fifteen-year-old. She was relieved, in a way, that her father had been driving and not her son. It wouldn't make insurance rates for Carter astronomical in a year or two, and he'd been having such a hard time she didn't want him to feel guilty about not having gotten his grandfather to chemo safely. She wanted him to feel good about being able to help out. But she was exasperated by the fact that they had gone to the winery at all. What was her father thinking? Now he had missed his appointment, and the Buick was totaled, and she would have to take him herself tomorrow and miss another day of work, because there was no way they were going to postpone his treatment. She remembered the last time he had tried to go off chemo and went six weeks between checkups. The lesions had multiplied, and his PSA shot up, and the oncologist had put him in for a treatment that very day.

She couldn't stay angry with her father, though, when she picked them up and he looked so sheepish, both about going to the winery and about deciding to drive himself. She took them home and ordered a pizza. After they ate, and she had her father settled, she drove Carter to the high school for drama rehearsal. Carter told her he thought he could get a ride home, but she told him to call her if he couldn't. It would be dark, and late, and she'd had enough emergencies for one day. Then she went back to work.

The office building was dark, and she had to tap in a security code on a shiny metallic keypad to let herself in. She turned the fluorescent lights on above the bay of workspaces she shared with Rajni and Heber, and she clicked on her mouse to wake up her computer. There was a sticky note attached to the side of the screen in Rajni's hand, saying that the Colonel had been by to ask about her and didn't seem pleased that she was gone.

Katherine sat down and looked despondently at the scene that appeared on her computer screen, two white beach chairs in the shade of a grass hut overlooking a tropical lagoon. In truth, she liked her job. All the months of planning coming to fruition in a single long weekend, when people from around the country and the world gathered to learn about the software and exchange ideas and take something back that would make their jobs and their businesses better and more efficient. The company had been small when she was hired, only thirty employees, but even then the president and company owner told her that they would never stop improving their software, there would be continuous progress, and so a continuous need to educate and inform. She liked feeling part of that. Continuous progress. It reminded her of what she heard about Disneyland when she was young: Disneyland will never be finished—anything is possible in Disneyland. During conference weekend, she was constantly busy with one crisis or another, always on her Blackberry, running from place to place. But afterward, she was able to reflect on what she'd brought together and feel a real satisfaction.

On her desk, Katherine kept photographs of Betty and Carter, one of her father in his beret and a Hawaiian shirt, and an old photo of her mother at Christmas, a scalloped-edged print taken with a Brownie camera in which the russet and gold of her dress and the decorations had blurred and deepened with time. She looked at the photos, then reached into the second drawer where she kept a small hand mirror. She looked like hell. She looked exhausted. Her makeup was trashed. Her hair was chopped into layers, and her stylist wouldn't let her grow it out. It would be a bad-hair year before she got it looking like she wanted it.

She put down the mirror. It would be stupid to fix her makeup when the rest of the building was dark and deserted. She looked around, even though she knew she was alone, then reached behind herself and unsnapped her bra and shimmied out of it by pulling her arms back in through the sleeves of her blouse. Then she breathed in and out deeply and attacked the work at hand. She hoped that Carter wouldn't need a ride home later, since she wanted to get all caught up, especially with the Colonel breathing down her neck and the need to take her father to chemo tomorrow.

At ten o'clock, she stood up and stretched. She had a book with the title *Desk Yoga*, and she always intended to read it and incorporate the simple stretches into her day, but she never did. She only stretched when she'd been working too long and was trying to ignore that her lower back was killing her. She checked her Blackberry to make sure that it had been on and that she hadn't missed any messages from her son, and she ran her thumb gently down the side of the device. Even though she worked for a software company, there seemed to be something magical about the technology, something that needed tending and attention to work properly.

No word, no messages. She wished she had told him to call her when he had gotten home. She thought about calling him, but wasn't sure if that would be too overbearing and show that she didn't have any confidence in him.

Yoga. She opened the book and stood with her hands in prayer position before her and then lifted them up and bent over at the waist and let her upper body hang. This was supposed to be relaxing, but as she was bending, she noticed her bra hanging over the back of her chair, and she made a mental note not to leave it hanging there when she left, and then she became self-conscious about bending over without a bra on when she was alone in the building.

She tried to empty her mind of all thought. *Be where you're at, because you're already there,* the book advised. But the thoughts kept intruding, and it wasn't relaxing at all, and finally she thought about making herself a cup of coffee.

At the end of the long space that had been cut into cubicles and bays were a sink and counter and refrigerator and several coffee-makers, an espresso maker, and electric kettles for the tea drink-ers. In the freezer, coffee of various kinds was stowed, all in metal-lic bags rolled tightly shut. Those who drank Peet's claimed it was far superior to Starbucks, and one person bought only LaVazza for espresso and refused to drink anything else. Katherine found Peet's coffee too intense, and she used a mix of half-caffeinated Lightnotes, but she didn't like to admit it since it sounded wimpy. She packed the cup of the espresso maker full and twisted it into place. It was the fastest cup of coffee, and she needed a good jolt.

Three hours of work, and she was only half caught up. And time off tomorrow again to take her father in. She didn't want another note in her file from the Colonel before annual performance reviews. She had been with this company for a long time, but she didn't feel indispensable, like Ron Newbury with his pet mammals in small cloth sacks around his neck, and the other men, so many men, who said things like *Code hard, Rage in* PHP, *Don't be a Douche-grammer.* And seniority hadn't saved Scott, had it? The last time she had been to see a dentist was before she'd moved back in with her father, because she didn't want to take time off from work, and sometimes she thought all her teeth would fall out. One tooth had broken two years ago, a high point on a molar around a deep sil-ver filling that dated from her teens, and she'd needed a crown. Now she expected that the teeth around her other fillings would crack, and she wouldn't have time or money to get them fixed, and she would become a crack-toothed hag with hair that wouldn't grow out.

She poured her coffee, dumped the grounds, walked back to her desk. Her screen saver was on, and she spent a moment watching the images of paradise cycle through. Then she looked at Heber's desk, tidy and straightened up. He'd left no loose ends at the end of the day. A copy of *The 7 Habits of Highly Effective People* was upright beside a dictionary, and it looked somewhat worn in the spine, with a few Post-it Notes of different colors sticking up from it, as though he actually consulted it. An enigmatic photo, the one that made Rajni think he was gay, was the only photo on the desk. He looked twenty years old, and he stood beside another young man the same age. They were in Toledo, Ohio, in front of the Toledo Museum of Art, and they were both wearing black pants and white shirts, with a plastic nameplate above their left pockets. They were not touching, did not have an arm around each other's shoulder— rather, they looked sober and serious, the wait until the camera shutter opened and closed an obvious strain. Heber told Katherine, when she asked, that it was a photo from his Mormon mission, but when she said *Oh, you're Mormon,* he said no, he wasn't, and smiled without explaining anything.

Heber wasn't Mormon, but he didn't drink coffee, or diet Coke like some in the office. A homely jar of Postum was on his desk, a "roasted grain beverage," the kind of thing Katherine associated only with aged aunties and hairnets. She picked up the jar, then put it down. She knew she wasn't being highly effective. She was being nosy. She picked up Heber's copy of *7 Habits* and opened it to one of the pages he had bookmarked, about the "Time Management Matrix."

Amazingly, she discovered that the book advocated spending more time on relationships, on building production capacity, and less time on crises and deadlines. Spend more time in Quadrant Three (planning and building relationships), and you'll spend less time in Quadrant One (immediate crises). She felt like she spent *all* her time on crises. She sat down and began leafing through the book, stopping at places Heber had underlined. It all sounded like good advice.

She took the book to the copier and photocopied a blank weekly schedule. There was a section for Weekly Priorities, and she spent time thinking about what she needed to accomplish during the week, rather than simply reacting to the load of emails requesting an immediate response. The list made her feel calmer.

Near midnight, she shut down her computer and left on the desk for herself a plan for the rest of the week, one even Stephen Covey himself would approve of. If she could manage to get her father to cancer treatment, and her son to drama rehearsals, and make sure her husband wasn't going to break into the house or do something else crazy and stupid, maybe she would be highly effective, at last. She gathered up her purse and her coat, remembered her bra, and looked at the schedule. On impulse, she wrote **Research Divorce** in bold letters at the top of her Weekly Priorities.

At home, the space where the Buick was normally parked in the driveway looked blank and lonesome, and Katherine suddenly felt sad about the car. Her father had owned it for ten years, only putting a couple of thousand miles a year on it recently, and it made him happy. She wondered it if would be the last car he ever owned. It was parked now in the side lot of a gas station until it could be hauled off to a junkyard. From her childhood, she could still remember the jingle *Wouldn't you really rather have a Buick . . . this year?* And her father, in his retirement, had finally moved up to Buick.

She pulled her Saturn in where she normally did, still leaving the Buick's normal space free, in case it should reappear during the night. *This year.* This was the year, the jingle promised, that you could reward yourself, purchase an outward sign of the success and well-being you had arrived at. And the jingle said nothing of the wreck that age and time made of any sense of wellness.

She was quiet inside the house, peeked in at Carter sleeping faceup, mouth parted. She knew his many postures of rest and peace. He was asleep and safe, she could see, and she was glad she hadn't insisted he call her when he arrived home. Whatever bruises he had from the car crash weren't keeping him from sleeping.

She cracked the door to her father's room and heard him snoring. This also she had grown to recognize as rest and peace. She had told him not to wait up for her, but she was afraid he would anyway. Even as she behaved motherly toward him, he still behaved fatherly toward her. And maybe he had the right, since she was sleeping in the same room she had slept in as a little girl. Nobody was going to sing, *Wouldn't you really rather have a Saturn . . . this year?* She went to sleep thinking about being highly effective, thinking about drinking Postum and having mastery over all the obstinate tasks that presented themselves to her, thinking about driving Highway 1 along Big Sur, the driving effortless as bird flight.

· · · • · · ·

The next morning, as she stared out the small window above the kitchen sink, she noticed something odd about the driveway, but she couldn't figure out what it was. The coffeemaker gurgled out its first pot of the morning, and Katherine didn't feel awake. She felt thick and stunted, and she was still in her bathrobe since she was taking her father to chemo instead of going to the office. Something about the morning sunlight, the bewildering brilliance.

Carter was out of the shower, but she didn't have to hurry this morning. She hated having to coordinate bathroom time with her son. She'd hated it when she was growing up in this house with her two brothers, and she hated it even more now. It embarrassed both of them, and it was a step backward from the house in Oak Commons, which had a full bath with the first-floor master bedroom, separate tub and shower, and two full baths for the bedrooms upstairs. That crazy house that could have put them all in bankruptcy.

Henry blustered out of his bedroom, also in a bathrobe and carpet slippers. "Can a man get a cup of coffee in this joint?" he growled as he rounded into the kitchen.

Katherine slipped the pot from the maker and poured coffee into two of the odd assortment of mugs that crowded one shelf of the cabinet. This morning she ended up with one that advertised a serotonin uptake inhibitor, a mug her father must have snagged at a doctor's office.

Henry put a spoonful of sugar into his mug, while Katherine drank hers black. She had been worried about getting fat in her teens and decided that she was going to learn to drink coffee without sugar or cream, and now, at forty-seven, she still drank it that way and she still worried about getting fat.

Henry sipped his coffee. "By God, you've got a good hand in the kitchen. Where would I be without you?"

"Thanks, Dad." Katherine looked back out the windows distractedly.

"What are you looking at?"

"Nothing," she said. "Just the funny sunlight."

"Hmmm." The galley kitchen was so narrow that he had to lean past her to look out the window. "Well, either my Buick has come back to life, or there's another car with a hell of a Simonizing job parked in its place."

"What?"

Katherine belted her bathrobe tightly around her and walked out the front door, followed by Henry in his bathrobe. Several seconds later, Carter stood behind them, also in his bathrobe, with his hair still wet.

The Fury had been detailed by an expert. Its dark-green paint gleamed with a depth that invited them forward to caress it—the tires had been blacked and the interior conditioned so that the old vinyl seats shone like buttery leather. Any sign that it had hit a seventeen-year-old boy and run over his leg was, no doubt, cleaned away.

"That's Scott's car," Katherine said. She approached it slowly, like it was a snake, half-expecting to find Scott sleeping in the backseat. He wasn't breaking in—now he would start sleeping in their driveway. But the car was empty. She walked around it, studied it from all angles, rapped on the trunk to hear that it was hollow and didn't contain a dead body. The doors were unlocked, and an envelope lay on the front seat.

Carter still hadn't let on that he'd seen his father two days ago. But he wondered if this was one more attempt to buy back his love, like his sister said. And this one was more interesting than two hundred dollars. The car didn't look so bad if he was going to get to drive it.

He leaned in the passenger-side window. "There are keys in the ignition," he said. "Mom? You gonna read what's in the envelope?"

"Sure." She opened the car door, which swung silently on greased hinges. It was a cheap envelope, tan colored to make it look like expensive stationery, with an address preprinted in the upper left-hand corner. The El Rancho Motel, off Highway 101. A small drawing of a mission bell hanging from an adobe arch was beside the address.

"Is this where he's been staying?" she asked aloud. The envelope was addressed to her and licked shut, as though Scott was afraid of someone else reading their private correspondence. She ripped it open and began reading aloud.

"My Dear Katherine:

"I know it's not quite time for you to welcome me back. It's been difficult. I haven't adjusted to normal life very well, since being at sea. Everything seems different from when I went away, even though it's the same and it's me who is different. And so, I haven't proven myself worthy of you yet. But I will, if you'll just have patience and wait for me. I'm going away again, for a little while, but I will be back on my feet in no time. Meanwhile, I'll stay in touch.

"I'm leaving the car in case Carter can use it, so he doesn't have to walk back and forth to school. Insurance is all paid on it through the end of December, so anyone can drive it. And I left the signed pink slip in the glove compartment, in case something happens to me and I can't come back.

"All my love, your husband, Scott."

As she read the letter, Katherine's voice grew louder, until she was nearly shouting the last lines. Her neck grew red, and then her face flushed. She felt like her head was going to explode. It probably would have been impossible to write a letter more perfectly crafted to piss her off. The sense of self-pity. Blaming forces beyond his control. Pleading for sympathy. Guilt-tripping. Expecting her to be the forever-forgiving, forever-welcoming maternal figure. Trying to make her fear for his safety.

She paused.

Carter and Henry stared at her, as her face turned the color of a brick.

"Jesus Fucking Christ," she said. "Why doesn't he just show up with his arm in a sling and a bandage around his head and limp around playing a fife? Why doesn't he just say he's suffering from PTSD and that he needs our help to be able to heal? Why doesn't he just blame California for not having scrap-metal drives, and war-bond campaigns, and food rationing?"

"Mom," Carter went.

"Not a word about me. Not a word about what I've been doing while he's been gone. Not one word about two teenagers and no savings and no house."

"Mom . . ."

"You know what I'd like to do with this car? I'd like to take it to Devil's Slide and put a brick on the gas pedal and run it over the cliff! *In case something happens to me.* He can kiss my ass!"

"Mom, everyone can hear you."

"Good! Let 'em know what a self-centered bastard my husband was."

Henry had walked over and put an arm over her shoulder and was walking her back into the house. Three people in bathrobes in the front yard on a Tuesday morning wasn't a normal sight on Catesby Street, especially when one was shouting obscenities.

Carter reached into the Fury and snagged the keys. "Mom? I had an idea."

"What?" She turned toward him. "Pour gasoline on the car and throw in a match?"

"Do you need to go to work today?"

"I worked until midnight last night, and I've got a Priorities List a mile long."

"Why don't you go? I can take Grandpa in Dad's car. Just like we planned to do yesterday."

"You think I'd let you drive that?"

"Why not?"

"Because . . ."

Katherine couldn't think of a reason, other than that it came from Scott. And if they used it, it would mean that they actually needed it, and Scott had been helpful. And then she would owe some gratitude to Scott.

Carter began circling the Fury, running his hands over its sharp, squared-off fenders. "This thing is so old, it's cool."

"It's so old, it doesn't have air bags," Katherine said. "That might have saved your life."

"He drives carefully," Henry said. "I'm the one who wrecked the car yesterday."

"You're ganging up on me." Katherine watched Carter admiring the car, suddenly a much more normal fifteen-year-old in love with horsepower and independence. It should have been that his father taught him to drive, took him to the DMV, and finally, maybe, bought him a car. Something large and safe would have been good. Instead, her husband abandoned a Fury in their driveway. But here was her son, acting as though it was all normal and appropriate, all wonderful that a car had appeared, wonderful to grow up and learn to drive even though his father was absent.

Even when he wasn't trying to, it was easy for her son to make her feel guilty, easy for him to make her want to say, "Yes, if it will make it up to you. Yes, if it will make you feel better."

"Why did he leave the car?" she asked aloud. "I don't get it."

"Just say I can take Grandpa, Mom. I can do it."

"I know you can, sweetie," she said. "Okay. You take Grandpa. But don't get the idea that the car is yours, no matter what the letter said. I'm going to track down your father and have a talk with him."

Henry looked at his watch. "If you're going to go to work, you'd better get changed. You're still in your bathrobe."

"What a stupid car. I'll bet it gets twelve miles a gallon." She turned and marched into the house.

At the office, she launched directly into the tasks she had left from the night before, feeling a surge of power and mastery. She was finishing the schedule for the first day of the conference, checking off the AV requirements for each presentation, when the Colonel arrived on his rounds. He began by telling her he was happy to see her at work, insinuating that she had been absent too long. He expected her to be defensive, but she completely disarmed him by being easy and casual and even a little flirtatious. He blushed a little when she told him that the regimental stripes on his tie looked sharp and that red and blue were good colors for him. He left without even asking for details about where she was at with her work, thinking that anyone who could speak that confidently must be on top of things.

Rajni looked at her admiringly after he left. "You're feeling good," she said.

"I'm faking it," Katherine said. "Things are all screwed up and confused."

"You ought to fake it more often then," she said. "Keep him out of your hair."

At quarter to twelve, feeling that she had earned an early lunch through her baffling of the Colonel, she drove to the Borders Bookstore and Café at the McCarthy Ranch Shopping Center. McCarthy Ranch was an open-air shopping center nestled alongside a large freeway interchange. It had once been a pear orchard, and now the large stores had facades recalling the outlines of rustic barns, with gambrel roofs sheathed in corrugated metal. Like a ghost of the orchard, anonymous trees that aspired one day to bring shade were spaced out in canted squares amid the parking places, and little islands of decorative grasses and irises sat at the end of the lanes.

Katherine liked the café for a light lunch, and she liked the bookstore. She treated it like a library where you could eat, frequently taking the time to look up information in books that she wouldn't buy unless it was very important. If the bookstore was big enough, a superstore, the information was easier to come by than through Google, and the process of looking was more pleasant besides.

When she was settled at a café table outside, looking up at the golden pear that marked the entrance to the shopping center, she called Betty in Aptos. Her daughter never called her. Since she'd moved in with her boyfriend, into a beach house owned by his parents, she seemingly had no need for advice or guidance or counsel from her mother. Katherine always had to call her, and she had the feeling that Betty treated the calls as a duty she had to fulfill. Katherine didn't want the calls to seem like she was checking up on her daughter. She wanted them to be a way to share some warmth and love, maybe friendship. But Betty's attitude made it clear that she needed friendship as little as she needed advice. She had made decisions and she was in control, and when she spoke with her mother she affected an air of knowingness that Katherine put up with because she didn't know how to break through it.

Katherine had talked with Betty briefly yesterday to tell her about the accident with the Buick. She heard Betty register a bit of surprise when she heard Katherine's voice again, but as soon as Katherine asked if she had seen her father, Betty sighed. "Now what's he done?" she asked.

Katherine told her about his latest move: leaving the car in the driveway. As she described the note he left, she felt herself getting angry again at the tone of it, the sense of a hurt little boy looking for sympathy. And the way leaving the car seemed to buy him favor with Carter in a way that wasn't fair at all.

"And the worse part is that we can really use the car right now, since your grandfather totaled his Buick."

Betty clucked with sympathy. She had noticed that her mother frequently needed her as a sounding board and adviser, and it flattered her to play the role. "There's no reason to turn down the car, if it helps you. And it doesn't mean you're taking him back."

"No?"

"Of course not. Has he done anything to earn your trust back?"

"I guess not."

"You guess? You know he hasn't. I'm sorry to say it, because he's still my father, but he's been a dick. If Ian was acting the way he was, I'd be so out of here."

"But I can't just get out of here, like you."

"No, but you don't have to let him in. Truth is, I don't know why you haven't divorced him."

"That wouldn't bother you?" Katherine asked.

"Pffff. A lot of my friends' parents are divorced. We're all okay."

"I have to find him, first."

"He hasn't shown up here. I'm probably not as important to him as his son."

"That's not true," Katherine said.

"You don't have to defend him," Betty said.

"Where could he be, though?"

"I don't know," Betty said. "You need a car to go anywhere."

Katherine called the number of the El Rancho Motel. She talked to a pleasant-sounding voice with a South Asian accent that told her that they never gave out information on any of their guests. She then called the Military Sealift Command, in Norfolk, Virginia, to see if she could find out whether Scott had shipped out again. If he had, he would be gone for another four months at least, and that might be something of a relief. She could just put things on hold again and postpone any painful decisions, and maybe Carter would have had more of a chance to adjust to the big changes. But on the phone, she was shunted from one person to another, until finally being told that they had no way of being sure who she was, and they couldn't give out information on their employees.

Finally, she made a phone call she'd been putting off, to Scott's mother in Las Vegas. Scott's mother was named Margaret, but since moving to Vegas she'd insisted on being called Peggy, like the singer Peggy Lee. She met her second husband, a silver-haired man named Seth Paul, at a conference on motivational speaking. Katherine disliked talking to her because everything eventually was turned into the language of motivation. But she looked at the time on her Blackberry, scrolled down to Peggy's name, and thumbed the call button.

She found out instantly that Scott was not in Nevada because Peggy asked her when they were coming out to visit and whether they would be bringing Betty and Carter. She felt that Carter, especially, could benefit from a few days near Seth Paul. Katherine had to explain that Scott was not living with her and that in fact she was calling to see if Peggy knew where he was. She had told Peggy this before, but her mother-in-law never took it as anything more than a passing phase.

"Well, I can't understand why he's not living with you. I know he really wanted to be. He wrote me the sweetest letter while he was away, getting back on his feet, telling me all about what your new life together was going to be like. Imagine that! A handwritten letter. So old-fashioned."

"Just because he wanted something," Katherine said, "doesn't mean he'll get it."

"That's where you're wrong, dear. If he follows the right steps, he can achieve his dreams and get everything he's entitled to."

Katherine knew it was useless to argue with her. "Maybe that's it, then. Maybe he hasn't followed the right steps," she said. Like not losing all our money on start-ups, not disappearing for six months, not breaking into the house, not disappearing again, leaving a Fury in the driveway.

"And you can help him," Peggy said. "If you demand he follow the right steps, then you'll be demanding that he treat you like you deserve."

"Right now, I'd just like to find him."

"He's probably on some sort of quest. But he'll come back to you. I sense that his inner motivation is strong."

Katherine listened to her mother-in-law babble on for several more minutes, gathering that she was partly to blame for Scott's failings and absences, but that if she was motivated to change, a fairy-tale ending was still possible. "Just the kind of fairy tale I'm living every day with Seth Paul."

When Katherine finally got her off the phone, she walked to the self-help section of the bookstore. Peggy claimed that Seth Paul was writing a book on motivation that would be published someday, and Katherine sometimes found herself glancing at the authors whose names began with *P.*, visualizing it right there. Peggy said it would be huge, bigger than the *Chicken Soup* books or *The Purpose-Driven Life.* The weird thing was, she might be right.

The divorce shelf was amid the self-help books, as though divorce was one more phase in a continuum of books about personal growth. There were books about having or saving a healthy relationship, divorce-prevention books, and then finally the divorce how-to books, followed by books about being a single parent, like *Joint Custody with a Jerk*.

Some of the titles were about no-fault divorce. Others were witty and cute and hostile, girding the reader for battle. Protect yourself! the covers shouted. Be informed! Get everything you're entitled to! *Winning the Divorce Wars* had a cover photo with a bride and groom on top of a wedding cake. The cake was divided so that the bride got two-thirds, leaving a third for the hapless groom.

Katherine had never bought a book, had never taken the concrete steps to officially end her marriage, because she had trouble thinking of herself as the kind of person who got divorced. Her aunts and uncles had all stayed married for life, and her own father, a widower in his fifties, never remarried. Even her brother in Hollywood had finally gotten married in his forties and now had young twins.

She'd talked to her mother about it, asked her whether she should just end her marriage to Scott once and for all. Her mother, wise and silent, smiled but refused to answer. Instead, Katherine found the annoying song that had played at her wedding go through her head. "When I fall in love, it will be forever, or I'll never fall—in—love." She hated that song. And she was the one who had picked it out, for the DJ to play when she and Scott danced at their wedding reception. Now she was stuck with it. If she divorced, it would mean that the song was a lie. She knew it was stupid to care about a corny song with horns and violins that had been played some twenty years ago, but the more she told herself she didn't care about it, the more she found it in her mind. She was sick of it.

Her mother, when Katherine thought about her and talked to her, was always beautiful. Her hair was stranded with black and gray, worn straight and cut at her chin line, the gray making her face seem younger and more lively in contrast. When Katherine looked in the mirror in the morning, she already thought she looked older than her memory of her mother. That was another reason she'd been reluctant to officially end her marriage, though one she had trouble admitting to herself. Scott said he loved her, said he was crazy about her. If she gave up on him, she wasn't sure if any-one would love her again. She had trouble seeing herself as desir-able. With Scott, she had at least one person who thought she was. Without him, she was a woman with hair that was cut in too many layers and whose teeth were going to start falling out one by one.

She studied the selection of books. *Divorce for Dummies* seemed like a bad idea. She didn't like the implications. She finally picked up a book that was specifically about divorce in California. She weighed it in her hand. There were worksheets and forms in the back and a CD-ROM. The cost was $34.95, and she compared it to another book that cost $21.95 and wondered if there was $13 of dif-ference. But she decided to buy the more expensive book, decided that she was worth it. She wasn't sure what her own mother thought, but Peggy might approve her being motivated.

Back at the office, she called Carter first to make sure he had gotten Henry to and from the chemo ward successfully. Carter told her that his grandfather seemed tired, but no more than nor-mal after a treatment. She worked on her highly effective list, and when she had accomplished a number of items, she called anyone she could think of who might know something about where Scott might be. She called Reverend Nancy, even though Scott had been even less churchgoing than her. She called old neighbors from Oak Commons, but had to leave messages since nobody was home. She called the outplacement firm where he had been for a few months after being laid off, but they hadn't heard from him. A facilitator there asked if he'd found a position commensurate with his talents and experience and seemed genuinely baffled when she told him he'd been out at sea.

Midafternoon, she found time to tell Heber she'd leafed through his *7 Habits* book the night before. "I hope you don't mind," she said. "It was actually helpful."

"I noticed your Weekly Calendar this morning," he said. "I couldn't help glancing at it."

"Oh." She saw **Research Divorce** scrawled in large letters at the top of the calendar beside her computer.

"I'm sorry," Heber said.

"There's no need," Katherine said. "It's the best thing I can do now. Maybe it will be a way I can get everything I'm entitled to."

"If I can help in any way," Heber said, "let me know."

"Thanks. I think number one on my list is just finding him. It's a quest."

She'd picked up the book she'd bought once to see if it mentioned what to do if you couldn't find your spouse. It sounded like you could serve notice to an absent spouse if you put an ad in a newspaper. "A missing spouse may be served by publication." One more complication. She decided she really should just find him.

Rajni was intrigued by the book. Her parents had an arranged marriage, and divorce was rare back in Bangalore. And even in Silicon Valley, many Indian women who were here on h-4 visas felt powerless, completely dependent on their husbands and unable to conceive of divorce. She herself had an h-1b visa and a lot of autonomy. Still, she said she would probably end up marrying someone approved by her parents, though not necessarily arranged by them. There were plenty of eligible Desis in Silicon Valley. And then she would be set, or stuck, depending on how it turned out. But in the meantime, she was dating as many different guys as she could.

Near five o'clock, Katherine MapQuested the El Rancho Motel. She frowned when she saw the location. It wasn't in a good part of the valley, and she seemed to remember a meth-lab bust in a warehouse nearby. She didn't want to go there alone. But it was the only place she knew Scott had been recently, besides her driveway. When she was young, she used to pride herself on not thinking about how dangerous a location might seem, being happy to seek out blues bars in Oakland with Scott and friends. Eli's Mile High Club had always been worth the trip. Now, in her forties, with a four-door sedan instead of a beat-up Subaru, she felt intimidated. And taking Carter along to look for his father was out of the question. If she was a little scared for herself, she would never expose Carter to the same risk.

She saw Heber neatening up his desk space, gathering up a few things into a canvas messenger bag.

"Heber?"

He looked over at her, smiling and attentive.

"Are you busy after work?"

He shook his head. "Just driving home."

"There's something you could help me with," she said. "If you have some time."

"Sure," he said. "I'm always happy to help."

6

HENRY'S MEDIPORT, the shunt through which he was hooked up to dripping chemicals every three weeks, was implanted just below his collarbone. His oncologist recommended the shunt after it was clear that he would be on chemotherapy for the rest of his life. Much simpler and easier than trying for a vein in the arm or the back of the hand every time. Henry sometimes felt it under the skin, even though he'd been warned not to poke at it. The miracle of modern medicine. He was at times grateful for and at times resentful of the cold metal finger lying permanently on his chest.

When Carter brought him back that afternoon in the Fury, he settled into the easy chair in the den, put his feet up, and settled in with his weakness, nausea, fatigue. He couldn't bear to listen to the news on the radio or the television. The war didn't seem to be ending, despite what was said, but he couldn't follow it through the chemical shroud that enveloped him. He would have to be patient, wait out the side effects, to grasp those days of life that waited for him on the other side. Before the next treatment began the cycle once more.

He asked Carter to put on a stack of his records, the Duke and Ella and Woody Herman and Benny Goodman and Tommy Dorsey. His turntable, one that could still hold a half-dozen records suspended above the disk and drop them one by one into place, was so old that Betty had not believed it really could work and pronounced it *phat* when it did. Over the music, he heard Carter talk to Katherine once, tell her it was all fine and promise not to leave his grandfather alone. Then he rested, not quite able to sleep but not quite conscious, and waited to hear his daughter's voice say, "I'm home."

It would all be twilight time until he heard her voice, almost his wife's voice, in the house.

At 6:30 Carter was beside him, telling him that he couldn't reach Katherine, that she wasn't answering her cell phone. At 6:45 Carter was beside him again, telling him that he had rehearsal for *The Tempest* in a little while, but he didn't want to leave him alone. The last record had dropped and played, and the tone arm had returned to its place, and a silence ticked through the house. It took Henry some time to understand that his grandson was asking him to make a decision, to tell him what to do.

He attempted to rise, but only churned the afghan with his arms and legs like an insect on its back. He felt as though someone had replaced his brain with mush, but he knew that Carter was asking something of him, and he wanted to respond. A grandfather who couldn't help his grandson was pathetic, and he wasn't ready yet to be only that—he still wanted to be a part of the world. He pointed to the lever on the side of the chair, and Carter pulled it and returned the chair back up straight, and Henry staggered upright and threw out his arms to gain balance.

"Let's go," he said.

"Do you feel well enough, Grandpa?"

"The hell with feeling bad," he said. "Let's go."

Henry careened out of the den, pushing off walls and bookshelves that seemed to tilt into his path. Carter pointed out that he was still in pajamas and a robe, so he crashed down the hall and found an Aloha shirt and a pair of blue jeans with stretch elastic at the back of the waist. He sat on the bed to pull on the jeans, stood upright and buttoned them shut, and he grabbed a beret and perched it on his head at an angle. He thought he looked presentable enough, until he noticed that he still had on his scuff slippers. The thought of sitting down once more to put on shoes was daunting. He was afraid he wouldn't be able to get up one more time. So he decided to just go in his scuffs. Fuck it.

He pushed himself back down the hall and launched himself across the open living room to the front door, where he grabbed the door frame and held himself upright. Carter went ahead and opened the door of the Fury, and Henry lurched forward along the curved cement sidewalk that led from the front porch to the driveway and fell into the passenger's seat. He allowed Carter to buckle him in and laid his head back on the vinyl headrest. He heard Carter make one more unanswered call to Katherine before getting into the car and starting the engine.

Carter had heard that K. J. had been hit by a car and had his leg broken. He thought it served him right, and he didn't mind at all that K. J. was going to miss a few weeks of school. K. J. could miss the whole year for all he cared. But Carter had no idea that he was driving the car that had done it. He made no connection between the hit-and-run, his father's new disappearance, and the sudden materialization of a perfectly detailed Plymouth Fury in the driveway, so he didn't hesitate to drive it to school.

Henry had a handicap tag that could be hung from the rearview mirror. He hated to use it and usually left it in the letter holder where bills and junk mail ended up. He wasn't in a wheelchair, after all, and he didn't want to admit that he couldn't walk well after treatments. But Carter had taken it with them and now parked next to the Drama Building in a blue-painted spot. It was just a minute before rehearsal started.

"You go on in, Carter," Henry said. "I think I'll just put my seat back and rest here for a while."

"Are you sure?"

"Sure." He felt for the lever at the side of the car seat and reclined and closed his eyes. "Just like my easy chair at home. You go on in. You need to. I'll follow in just a little bit."

Carter tried his cell phone one more time and got no answer. Then he patted Henry's shoulder. "Thanks for coming, Grandpa," he said, and left him in the car in the growing dark.

Henry shifted to make himself more comfortable, though he knew that there was no comfort to be found. He felt empty but not hungry, and no known food would have eased him. He felt the poison in him, attacking the tumors that might shrink but would never disappear, and attacking all the tissues of his body, the healthy body that would live if it could. He settled in, again with patience. Maybe it wasn't the smartest thing to be resting here instead of at home. He probably would have been fine alone. But

Carter might not have left him, and then Carter would have missed something, and he cared more about that than his own bitter rest.

He drifted as he lay there, coming in and out of wakefulness. He didn't hear the purple Tiburon that pulled up grill to grill with the Fury. K. J. had let Mitch and Brownie borrow his car while he was laid up to see if they could locate the car that had kneecapped him. And when they spotted the Fury, they parked and got out of their car to study it.

"Might be the same one . . ."

"Looks a lot nicer . . ."

"Sure it was a Fury?"

"Wonder who owns it . . ."

"Mighta been washed . . ."

"Wasn't a kid driving it then . . ."

"Who . . ."

Henry gradually heard the voices near the car, unsure what they were saying. When he saw shadows fall into the car, he reached forward, flipped the lever, and sprang into an upright seated position, like a graveyard jack-in-the-box.

The two boys near the car jumped to see a human figure suddenly rise into view. They backed up. When the figure reached for the handle and opened the door, they turned and stumbled and piled into their car. But the time it was standing, roaring at them, they had their car in reverse and were speeding backward up the alley that led beside the cafeteria to the Drama Building.

Henry roared once more and laughed as the Tiburon reached the street and sped away. Inexplicably, he felt good. He could even stand without feeling too severely the little knives that cut into his feet. He adjusted his beret, and in his bedroom slippers, he walked into the middle of the rehearsal.

Nobody noticed him at first. The students were sprawled across folding chairs arrayed in ragged semicircles before the proscenium, and several players were onstage, reading lines. He saw Carter sitting next to a girl with black hair and two nose rings, but he walked straight to Nu. She stood at the focal point of the semicircles, a handwoven shawl across her shoulders, a loose rope of red hair down her back. She was intent upon the stage and the action, standing poised and balanced like an athlete. But when Henry came beside her, she smiled at him as though he were the person she most wanted to see at that moment. Carter had told her that his grandfather was with him, that he wasn't feeling well, but that he might come in. When Nu pressed him, he told her that his grandfather had just had a chemo treatment.

She put a hand on Henry's arm and pointed at the stage. "There," she said. "Prospero is presenting visions to his daughter and her fiancé. Visions of what their future life will be like. Wholeness and plenty, long life and healthy children."

Francisco, as Prospero, held a staff and wore a pointed wizard's hat, but otherwise was in jeans and a T-shirt. Windy and Cal, the daughter and her lover, sat at his feet, and they watched two girls standing on a platform upstage. On the wall behind them, leafy shapes and palm fronds were painted, suggesting a tropical forest receding into the distance.

"That's Juno," Nu whispered. "And Ceres, Goddess of the Harvest."

The girl playing Ceres began a speech that Henry remembered from reading the play, a speech that promised an ideal life — vineyards and orchards heavy with fruit, storehouses rich with the earth's richness, winter brief and mild and followed quickly by spring.

Henry said quietly, "That's what every father would wish for his child, whether or not he's a wizard."

"Even though it's just a vision?" Nu asked. "Even though we're all going to fall short?"

"Fathers want their children to believe in happiness. They want their children to believe in the story, even if they can't."

Nu clapped her hands, and the play onstage stopped. She could always command everyone's attention in an instant, and she effortlessly projected her voice throughout the room.

"We have a guest with us," she said. "A special guest, Carter's grandfather, Henry Watson."

Carter sat up proud, looked to make sure that Blossom Haven was paying attention.

"Mr. Watson is a Pearl Harbor veteran, I've been told. And he's the age of Prospero, and he's a father. So he's going to help us with some insights into the play by doing a little improv with us."

She held out her hand.

"Come on, Henry."

"I don't know anything about acting," Henry said.

"Just be yourself," Nu said.

She leaned closer, so that only he could hear.

"You know more about this play than any of these kids."

Henry saw Carter smiling, genuinely smiling without restraint.

"Okay," he said. He took her hand, and she took him up some stairs at the edge of the stage and out onto the boards, under the gold-lettered sign proclaiming "The Theater of California." Pieces of the unfinished set poked out from the wings. A tilting mast with antique rigging, deadeyes and lanyards and ratlines, to signify the decks of a ship in danger of sinking. A bending palm tree on a carriage, which could be rolled out to suggest the exotic island where the play takes place. All made of lath and papier-mâché, all the sham trappings of theater. Yet it was brighter onstage, and the students down in the chairs were dim and shadow faced, and Henry didn't feel as though he were stepping into fakery. The stage felt like a high place, clear and luminous.

Nu gave Henry Prospero's staff, and Francisco left the stage, but she told the students playing Ceres and Prospero's daughter, Miranda, and her lover, Ferdinand, to stay. And she said that she would play Ariel, the spirit at Prospero's command.

Nu prompted Ceres to read her speech again, and she did, again promised the blessing of abundance to the young couple.

When she finished, she looked at Nu for a sign. Ferdinand had the next line, but he looked to Nu for direction as well. Henry stood silently, leaning on the staff, gazing past everyone.

Nu began to skip and dance, lissome as a young girl, and she twirled about Henry. "Sir." She leaned toward him. "Were I human, and not composed of air, I would grow tender at this speech."

Henry smiled. He thought Nu must be at least sixty, yet her movements showed no age. "It does make me tender," he said.

"Isn't this what you would desire for your daughter?" She gestured gracefully toward Miranda with an upturned palm.

Henry nodded. "You bet. It's what every father should wish for his child."

Nu took Henry by the arm and walked him downstage and spoke with him as though the other characters couldn't hear.

"Even though it is but a vision? Even though it will melt into thin air?"

"Even so." Henry knew now that Nu wanted him to repeat what he had said for all the students. "It's better if his children believe that it's possible. Even if it's just a wish for the way we'd like things to be."

Nu went up on her dancer's toes. "I have news for you, sir. Caliban is coming to kill you."

"Caliban?" Henry asked.

"Aye, sir," she said. "Caliban, that thing of darkness you acknowledge as your own. He seeks your death."

"That's no news to me," Henry said.

Jeffrey, the weight lifter playing Caliban, hulked up to the stage. He approached Henry and leaned toward him. "All the charms of Sycorax, toads, beetles, bats, light on you. A southwest wind blow on you and blister you all over."

"It's done, Caliban," Henry said. "It's already done. I'll never be free from you."

Nu stood up, suddenly herself and no longer the spirit Ariel. "Bravo," she said.

Carter began to clap, and the rest of the students sitting in the folding chairs joined in, and the players onstage applauded Henry as well. He smiled mildly, his shoulders fell in a little, and he descended from the stage.

Henry scarcely noticed the continuation of the rehearsal. He slumped back in a folding chair next to Carter, rested his head forward on his chest, and let the lines and the scenes wash over him. He had never felt so tired. Even when Carter went up to play Trinculo, he didn't pay attention. Distantly, he heard Nu using his name, asking how Mr. Watson would understand a line—*We are* *such stuff as dreams are made on—Our revels now are ended—*or asking the cast whether Mr. Watson would think the brave new world so new, or mankind so beauteous, as Miranda exclaimed.

When they took a break, Nu invited him to join her outside for a moment. He bent forward over his knees and pushed forward and rose to his feet. Carter was at one side to steady him, but Nu took his hand and led him through the heavy metal doors to the rocky ground between the stuccoed side of the building and the chain-link fence. One streetlight filtered through the pine trees that had been planted between the parking lot and the building. Henry leaned against the building and smiled, and Nu took a cigarette from her purse.

"Thanks for that," she said. "The students really got something out of it."

Henry waved his big paw. "It was nothing."

"You're welcome to the theater anytime. Just to sit and watch." She lit her cigarette with a small butane lighter. "Smoke?" she asked.

"Naw." He half smiled. "Bad for my health."

"Here. Try this." She reached into an interior pocket of her enormous purse and drew out a single tightly rolled joint. Henry cocked his head in curiosity. She held it up to his face, and he opened his lips and took it in.

"Call it medical marijuana," she said. "White Rhino. When I light it, breathe in deeply and hold it."

Henry nodded. She thumbed her lighter and he inhaled, and the paper twinkled and the smoke was odd and sweet. He took the joint from his mouth, held his breath, and felt his lungs expand. Then he coughed out, and Nu smiled.

"That's probably good for the first time," she said.

· · · • · · ·

After the rehearsal, Carter asked if they could drop Blossom Haven off on their way home. Henry didn't understand, so Carter explained that the girl standing next to him was named Blossom Haven.

"My mother was a hippie," Blossom Haven explained.

"Yes?" Henry said. "And what is she now?"

"Now? Now she's a single mother and an LMT."

"An LMT? What's that?"

"A licensed massage therapist," Carter said.

"Sure, we can take Blossom home," Henry said. "Just drive safe. We wouldn't want to have Blossom injured."

He carefully lowered himself into the passenger's seat. Getting in and out of a car, the simplest thing that people accomplish every day without thought, was a risky task at his age, especially when he felt weakened by chemo. And he felt a certain floaty feeling that he thought might be the marijuana. He had to look for handholds to brace himself and take his weight for the moment when his knees gave out and he was going down and hoping that his bottom would land safely on the car seat. Younger people didn't know what a relief it could be to find yourself securely seated. He lifted his legs with his hands to help his feet into the car, then reclined the seat back so that he was lying out.

Carter took the driver's seat, and Blossom Haven rode directly behind him. Carter had never had a girlfriend before and wasn't sure if he had one now. He thought that Blossom Haven *liked* him, and he liked her, but he didn't know anything about what to do next. At fifteen, girls had had boyfriends, sometimes two or three, but not many boys had had girlfriends. As he drove, he felt her hand on his shoulder, and he touched it with his hand before he returned both hands to the wheel. Nine and twelve o'clock. He concentrated on the road and driving and following the directions that Blossom Haven was giving him.

She lived with her mother in an apartment complex called Cherry Creek Arms, a complex that dated from the seventies and had originally been built as "Singles Apartments." Three blocks of apartments two stories high formed a triangle around a kidney-shaped swimming pool intended as a social gathering place for swinging singles until they eventually paired off, married, and bought real estate in the adjoining subdivision. But as real estate prices increased through the eighties and nineties, with few periods of backsliding, the apartments became more like a dead end. The pool was now boarded over, and most of the studios or one-bedroom apartments were lived in by women and men in their thirties or forties, single not necessarily by choice, living without health insurance, and not expecting to eventually buy real estate in the Silicon Valley of 2003.

The unit they lived in was a one-bedroom with an efficiency kitchen, and Blossom Haven slept on a futon in the front room. Her mother had decorated the walls with chimes, and posters of yoga poses, and bearded men with the red tilak on their forehead, and handwoven hangings, and there were candles of various sizes and colors on all the low tables. She taught at the Just for Your Health College of Massage and worked at two day spas that offered massage along with facials, and she had a portable table that she took on house calls. They lived in a valley of abundance, she told Blossom Haven, and they could live like birds off the abundance as long as they were not covetous.

Blossom Haven sometimes thought her mother was full of shit. She knew who had money at school and who didn't, and she knew that she didn't. She usually hated her name. And she found her mother especially infuriating after she completed a session of yoga and came out of shavasana and just sat there, in a lotus position, with an utterly blissful expression on her face. Just sat there, on a rubber mat, on thin carpeting, with no furniture.

When she was thirteen, Blossom Haven started to stay out late with other friends from school and with older boys who had cars. She dyed her hair and found a parlor that would do piercing, even though she was underage. Her mother never criticized her except to say that she would find her own path to enlightenment. This irritated Blossom Haven more than anything.

She began to change a little when the war in Iraq started and then didn't end when it was supposed to. Her mother made her go to San Francisco for protest marches, and being among more than a hundred thousand people chanting for peace moved her. She joined her mother doing yoga again, as she had when she was eight, and tried meditating on loving kindness, though she kept the nose rings and the dyed hair.

She found herself liking Carter when she first had her hands on his face, spreading pancake and eyeliner. They hadn't been out together, or talked that much, but she could tell he liked her too. Since he had a car that night, asking for a ride home was a low-risk way to move things forward.

Henry stayed in the Fury while Carter walked with Blossom Haven to the apartment on the second floor. The steps were poured concrete, and the walkway along the line of apartments was also concrete, cracked in places. A series of identical lamps sprouted from the stucco wall down the walkway beside the metal doors of the apartments. They stopped in front of 14-B, and Blossom Haven turned.

"Your grandpa's cool," she said.

"Yeah." Carter had his hands in his pockets and his elbows stuck out at awkward angles. He felt self-conscious of his height, at least eight inches taller than her. "I think Nu is too."

"Nu is the best."

"Yeah."

"Well. Thanks for the ride."

"No problem."

She took his hand in hers and swung it back and forth. "You're shy," she said.

When Carter returned to the Fury, Henry raised his head. "You're smiling," he said.

"Yeah." He looked down, abashed.

"That's good. You should be smiling." Henry lowered his head. "Before we go, call Katherine. Let's see if we can locate her."

Carter pulled out his cell and tried calling his mother. She didn't answer. He tried calling the house as well, but just got the answering machine with Henry's voice on it.

"I don't know," Carter said.

"Let's drive home. I have a feeling she's all right, wherever she is."

Carter drove along the commercial streets toward home. He thought there was an expressway that might be faster, but he wasn't entirely confident about driving the expressway at night. He turned at the bowling alley scheduled for destruction and entered the subdivision. On Catesby Street, he passed the large house being built over the two teardowns. His grandfather's house was dark, and the driveway was empty. No Saturn. He didn't know where his mother was.

7

HEBER GRIMSHAW grew up in the town of Newcastle, in the high desert country of southern Utah, a little ways off the route tourists traveled between the great national parks, Zion and Bryce Canyon. Every July 24, they held a parade down the two-block business district to celebrate Pioneer Day, the date Brigham Young first looked down over the Salt Lake Valley from the mouth of Emigration Canyon and legendarily declared, "This is the right place," a statement later shortened in common usage to "This is the place."

The parade in Newcastle was meager every year. The few dozen children from the town and the surrounding ranches dressed up in costumes of the nineteenth-century Mormon pioneers—jeans, checked shirts and suspenders, and cowboy hats for the boys, and poke bonnets and gingham dresses with long sleeves for the girls— and either rode down the street in the backs of pickup trucks that had been hosed out the night before or, if lucky, rode on a wagon pulled by a team of horses. The only audience was their parents and grandparents and older brothers and sisters, and sometimes the children waving outnumbered those standing and taking pictures and waving back. The parade ended after a few hundred yards in front of the church at the center of town.

At the county seat or in the university town not too far away, there were more elaborate parades, sometimes with replicas of the covered wagons being pulled by oxen, sometimes with men pushing handcarts in honor of the pioneers who, without draft animals, loaded up all their belongings in rude, oversize wheelbarrows and pushed them across the Great Plains all the way to the Salt Lake Valley in 1856. But the people of Newcastle never considered doing without their own parade to attend a more elaborate one twenty miles away. It was necessary for their place, no matter how humble, to be *the* place, the Promised Land. However barren, however hard the living to be gotten from trying to ranch or farm in the high desert, every Pioneer Day it became their own lovely Deseret, the land vouchsafed to them by the Lord. And it was necessary every year for the children to act out the same roles their parents and grandparents did. Not just to help them understand the past, as something distant and closed off, but to literally claim the land again, understand it as promised to them, understand it as their own sacred ground. This is the right place. This is your family's ground, and families are forever, and now this is your place too.

When the boys were nineteen, after a year of college or a year of full-time work after high school, they were called to a mission and sent to the Missionary Training Center. In two weeks if Stateside, longer if they needed to learn a language, the boys with dusty jeans and shit on their boots were transformed into scrubbed, short-haired, dark-suited personages, wearing a nameplate that designated them Elder. For two years, they shared the Word in a place far from home, forbidden even from calling on the telephone except on rare occasions. But Newcastle knew that its missionaries would return to it, marry local girls, and within a decade be watching their own children riding in truck beds down South First Street. The bond had been forged.

Heber's voice was long and mellow, a storytelling voice that painted pictures and put those around him in the scene he described. He was telling Katherine about his hometown and where he'd come from while they were both in bed together, naked yet modest with the sheets drawn up around their chests. The mattress was thin at the El Rancho Motel, and the coverlet was stiff and shiny and creased where they had folded it back, a dark purple pattern on the top and white quilting on the bottom. They'd left a single light on in the room, a brass table lamp on the Formica-topped lowboy at the foot of the bed, and Katherine watched Heber's face as he talked about where he came from, his life before Silicon Valley. With his glasses off, it was a handsome face—not model handsome, but intelligent and animated—and as he talked, he looked out beyond the cheap prints hanging on the walls and brought distant places into the room. She felt that he was embarrassed to be near her, felt the way he jerked when she put an arm over his chest and pressed herself against him, even though they had made love twice. She knew he was a little afraid to gaze at her, unaccustomed to the intimacy of two bodies lying together, and she excused him for his inexperience. She was happy to be lying with him, listening to him talk about himself. She had been talking about herself, her family, her husband, her problems, all night long. She was glad now to let him talk, his shyness softened in talk about Utah.

· · · • · · ·

They had arrived together at the El Rancho in Katherine's Saturn a little before sunset and parked across the street alongside a chain-link fence that enclosed rental equipment for construction—Bobcats, backhoes, trailers, sitting out on cracked blacktop. The motel walls were burnt-orange stucco, showy and cheap in the late light, and the neon sign was already lit up, a yellow lariat looping around the motel's name. Below, there was a sign that read *No Vacancy* in script, but only the word *Vacancy* was lit. Katherine sat behind the steering wheel and watched. She told Heber she wanted to do surveillance for a little while, but as they watched she realized it was a silly idea.

Heber was quiet beside her, waiting for her to decide what to do. She swung the car door open. "Come on. Let's go see what we can find out."

The motel office was linoleum floored and walled with knotty pine, and on the elbow-high counter a little plaque read "Welcome." Katherine waited for a moment. Behind the counter, a computer screen was on, and she could see it displayed a webpage with writing in an alphabet she didn't recognize.

A front-door buzzer was screwed onto the counter, and she pushed it and heard it sound behind a closed door. In a moment, a Sikh man came out, wearing a turban and a large and luxuriant beard tucked away.

"Madame and Monsieur would like a room for the night?" he asked.

"No. We're looking for someone. Someone who has been stay-ing here."

"Ah, but why? When you have found each other?" He smiled and bowed at Heber. His English was strange and affected, as though he had learned it from old black-and-white movies set in New York with men in tuxedos and women in ballroom gowns and French headwaiters.

Katherine flopped her purse down on the counter. She was carrying her big purse tonight, a large red leather bag with a zip-pered center section and two outside open pockets. She carried the big purse for some weeks, gradually filling it with makeup, pens, notebooks, gum, coin purses, plastic key chains, candy, coupons, paperback books, until one day she realized that it weighed as much as a standard poodle, and she threw things out and went to a clutch. The clutch lasted a couple of weeks until it grew too small, and then she went to a midsize purse before ending up again with her big purse.

She began pawing through the purse while the Sikh man smiled politely, clasping his hands behind his back and rocking back and forth on his heels. At last, she brought forth a small leather folder with a snap clasp holding it shut. She unloosed a plastic accordion of photos and searched them for a good likeness of her husband.

"There's a trip to the Boardwalk," she muttered. "Yosemite. Disney-land, Christ, that was ten years ago. Napa . . ." She kept up a running commentary on her family photos, while the Sikh man looked on with polite interest, as though sharing memories of past vacations with utter strangers was nothing out of the ordinary. Heber looked away, embarrassed, as she continued to flip through them.

Katherine was frustrated. The problem was that Scott had so often handled the camera that there were far more photos of her and Betty and Carter than there were of Scott. The ones with Scott tended to be group photos, taken by a stranger, and his face was small and smudged and indistinct. How could she tell anyone what he really looked like, or all the bad and good things he'd been in twenty years, or why she now had to find a way to get rid of him forever?

The best photo she could find was one of her and Scott together, standing before the front door of the new house that they bought five years ago and sold last year to avoid bankruptcy. Both smiling and optimistic. *Look!* the picture said. *We've made it! We're home!* The photo made her furious. She didn't realize she'd still been carrying it around in her two-ton purse.

"Look at him." She slipped the photo out of its plastic cover and rapped Scott's face with her knuckles. "Just look at him. I can't believe it."

The Sikh bent over and inspected the photo. "He seems like a most pleasant gentleman," he said.

"Pleasant. Pleasant? You don't know what he's done to me."

Heber touched Katherine's arm and looked at the manager. "I think what she'd like to know is whether you recognize him. Whether he is someone you've seen before, whether he is staying at your motel."

"Ah. You're seeking information about him. His *whereabouts*." He used the word with great satisfaction, knowing it to be precisely the one called for.

"Yes. Exactly." Heber looked at Katherine, who was staring again at the photo. He was a little afraid of her, as though she were a bomb about to go off.

The manager leaned over and inspected the photograph carefully. He made a series of little noises to himself, *hmm*s and *ah*s and clickings of the tongue. Finally, he straightened up.

"No," he said.

"No?" Heber asked. "You've never seen him?"

"No. I cannot give you any information about any of our guests. We are a discreet establishment, you understand. *Discreet*. The privacy of our guests is *paramount*."

"So if he is staying here, you wouldn't say?" Heber asked.

"That is correct, Monsieur."

"What? What?" Katherine looked up. "You let me show you all this crap, and you won't tell me anything?"

The manager bowed with a smile of sad understanding and regret.

Heber began to sweep items from the counter back into the maw of the purse. "Come on, Katherine."

"I don't believe it." She looked at the manager like she wanted to strangle him. "Money? Do you want money?"

The manager pursed his lips. "You lower yourself, Madame, in making an offer I could never accept."

Heber took her gently by the arm and drew her backward toward the door. "Come on. We'll look someplace else."

"Where did he come from? Mars?"

They had backed out the door when Katherine realized that the one photo of her and Scott was still on the counter. She bolted forward just as they were stepping off the cement walk, and Heber's foot twisted, caught between two levels. He felt his ankle turn, and he went down on one knee.

Back in the office, Katherine snatched the photo from the counter and lifted her nose at the manager. When she turned, she saw Heber getting up and beginning to limp around, trying his weight on the ankle.

"Ha ha," she called back to the manager. "Maybe we'll just sue you, huh? Maybe we can sue you!"

She stalked out. Beyond the cyclone fences and the tall, tough-leafed shrubs that were intended as a sound break, the freeway roared and grew illuminated as night fell and the hurrying cars switched on shafts of light and the billboards that lined the winding blacktop began to glow.

Katherine rested herself against the front fender of the Saturn and let the noise and weight of the freeway press against her back. Heber limped after her. He wasn't used to seeing a woman so angry. He had never seen a woman act like Katherine. In Newcastle, even in Salt Lake City, women tended to find a way to make the best of things. When life gives you lemons, his mother used to say, make lemonade. And the girls he had dated in high school, or the few women he had gone out with in college or just after, before he left Utah, tended to be demure types who cast their eyes down and gave him to understand that his wishes were what mattered most.

Katherine's anger frightened him, but excited him too. He saw her now, half-lit by the neon from the motel sign, by the weak reflections from the flood lamps above the warehouse yards, her head slumped a bit as though tired from anger, and he wondered if all women had this anger inside them, and those he had known back home, even those who waited for their missionary boyfriends to return and got married in the temple two months later, were simply very good at hiding it.

Katherine was hiding nothing. He felt like he needed to protect her in some way, to keep her anger from causing her harm.

"How's your ankle?" she asked as he slow-walked to the car.

"It's been better."

"I'm sorry. I didn't mean for you to hurt yourself helping me."

"It's okay. I'm happy to be here for you."

"Thanks." She lifted her head. "Come on. I'll buy you dinner."

Near the freeway exit, Katherine had seen a Mexican restaurant called El Salto, which she assumed was named for the salt on the rim of the margarita glasses. If Scott had stayed at the El Rancho for a number of weeks, she was sure he would have eaten at El Salto often, maybe every night. They had always liked the Tampico Kitchen in Santa Cruz, liked getting an order of nachos con todo and a pitcher of margaritas and then some plate rich with avocado, cheese, sour cream, rice and beans, salsa. It didn't matter so much what else was on the plate. She thought about Scott's weird sense of nostalgia, obvious even in the little time she'd seen him, and she knew he would not have been able to pass up evenings at El Salto, the warmth of alcohol and reveries.

Inside, the restaurant was decorated for Christmas, with strings of colored lights around the ceiling and garlands of sparkling tinsel draped around the walls, silver, green, metallic blue. Behind the bar, big cardboard letters hung in arcs in front of the mirror, spelling *Feliz Navidad* above the golden bottles of tequila. The walls of the restaurant were splashed with different colors, golden yellow, cactus green, aquamarine, and Katherine and Heber were given a booth under a Mexican flag. An old-fashioned Wurlitzer jukebox, luminescent, played ranchero music nonstop.

Their waiter was a tall young man, slender and dressed in the uniform of the restaurant, blue jeans and a western shirt with opalescent snap buttons. He introduced himself in perfect English when they sat down. "I'm Luis Reyes, and I'll be your server tonight."

Katherine took charge, ordering a plate of nachos con todo and a pitcher of margaritas without asking Heber what he wanted. The restaurant wasn't busy, and Luis quickly brought out a tall, frothy pitcher beading with condensation and two glasses rimmed with salt. He poured two glasses expertly and set the pitcher back down. Heber picked up his glass and looked at it doubtfully, while Katherine took a quick sip and motioned Luis to wait for a moment. She hauled her big purse out onto the table and slipped the photo from a side pocket and spread it flat.

"Do you recognize this man?" She tapped Scott's face. "He was staying nearby and must have come in a few times."

"Where was he staying?" Luis picked up the photo and held it to the light.

"The El Rancho."

"That fleabag?" He smiled, delighted. "Who is he?"

"My husband."

"Oh." He looked at Heber. "So why are you looking for him?"

Katherine took a drink from her margarita. "So I can divorce him."

"Wow. Cool." Luis gazed at her with pure admiration. His parents owned the restaurant, and he had been working there most of his life, but he had just begun as a freshman at Stanford and was taking a course entitled California Noir: From Hammet to Didion and Beyond. They had been reading *Mildred Pierce*, about a woman who divorces her husband and starts a restaurant and then takes a broke aristocrat as a lover. The aristocrat ends up running away with the woman's daughter, who has become a famous opera singer, leaving the woman to get stinko drunk with her ex-husband. Luis loved the class, even though it had nothing to do with the business degree his parents wanted him to get, and he'd been thinking that nothing all that exciting ever happened at El Salto. His parents' restaurant wasn't *noir* enough. But now, a woman with a well-dressed man at least ten years younger than her was asking for his help in tracking down her husband. It *was* like something out of a James M. Cain novel! Maybe they really intended to murder her husband, or blackmail him, or maybe they were secret lovers. Maybe it was sordid. Luis loved that word. *Sordid.*

He affected a knowing look. "I'll take the photo around to the boys and get some info."

Katherine sipped her drink and smiled at Heber. "Go on, take a taste. It's good."

"Okay." Heber never drank. It was part of his Mormon upbringing that he hadn't ever wanted to upend, even though he knew that some Mormons who stopped practicing became ostentatious drinkers, especially those who remained in Utah. Jack Mormons, who used drink like a badge to prove they had left the church. He sipped cautiously, afraid he would be drunk with one taste. The salt on the rim grained pleasantly across his tongue, and then the taste was fruity with lime.

"Nice," he said.

"Good." Katherine grasped the pitcher and refilled her own glass.

Luis brought out the plate of nachos con todo, carrying it with a towel and warning them that the plate was hot. He told Katherine in a half whisper that he was making inquiries and he'd have some straight dope for her pronto. They ordered combination plates and pulled at the nachos while they waited, taking gobs of cheese, salsa, refried beans with every chip. Heber took one mouthful of sliced jalapeño peppers and gasped it out onto his plate, half chewed. Katherine laughed as he gulped down water, and she offered that a frozen margarita is especially good at putting out jalapeño fires.

As they ate and drank, her more than him, she began to talk about Scott, her husband, her soon to be ex-husband. The things about him that had first attracted her to him: his endless sense of being special, of being certain that he—and therefore she—was destined for something glamorous. That California dream, of being in the right place where something wonderful was about to happen. And it was always just out of reach, so close, yet always just beyond the fingertips, in the magazines and in the movies and in those vacations where he posed her like a movie star in front of a vineyard filled with the brilliant yellow of mustard in early spring, as if they owned it. That was it, *as if* they owned it, instead of being just two more workers in Silicon Valley, in midsize companies that were not going to go public in a splash of instant millions and champagne. And she saw how he grew more desperate as he passed forty, he grew more desperate and he grew more needy, and he looked increasingly to the past even as their son, Carter, was having problems. It was a kind of nostalgia he had, she thought, but not a nostalgia for anything they ever really possessed. A nostalgia for the life he had dreamed they *might* have someday, rather. He'd lost their money, and that was partly her fault. She'd been willing to let him deal with things like that and had signed papers she didn't understand. And he'd lost their house, and that was partly her fault as well, since she'd let herself be convinced that they could afford that beautiful house with the cathedral ceilings and the gourmet kitchen with the trophy stove. And he'd lost his job, and that really wasn't his fault, since a lot of people in a lot of companies lost their jobs that year in Silicon Valley. But choosing to run away, go on board a ship in the Arabian Sea, a job he hadn't done since he was in his early twenties? That was crazy. He wasn't twenty-two anymore—he was almost fifty. And it wasn't World War II, and he should just understand it. He was caught, he was trying to relive a past, and it wasn't even his own past. There was something messed up about that.

"He's gone crazy. And he wants me to enable him. But I'm through being an enabler. I've been enabling him for twenty years. I've enabled enough."

Their food came, again with a warning that it was hot, and Katherine immediately shoved a forkful of beans and rice in her mouth. She drank more of her margarita.

"You know what really sucks? That I don't even know what I wanted before I met him." She was speaking with her mouth full, but she didn't realize it. "I don't remember! I don't remember!"

Listening to Katherine, Heber felt he wanted to protect her, soothe her, heal her, but he didn't have a clue how to do it. He had never heard anyone talk the way she did. He guessed she was sharing her feelings. That was supposed to be healing. So he listened and nodded and agreed with her when it seemed like that's what she needed. He had a desire to lay hands on her and give her a blessing. But he wasn't in Utah, would never again be in Utah in that sense, within the comforting strictures and precepts of the church, even though he had never truly stopped believing. He could only improvise his comfort and healing out of his own capacities and limited experience.

"What should we do, Katherine?" he asked. "I don't think Scott is coming here tonight."

Luis Reyes brought their bill over in a padded wallet, and he kneeled down close to Katherine's side of the booth. "I've got the lowdown," he said. "Interested?"

"Sure," she said, leaning toward him a little sloppily. "What's the scoop?"

"The party in question was a regular for a month solid. Three or four nights a week. Number 6, Burrito Jalisco and a bottle of Corona with a slice of lime. Fair tipper."

"See?" Katherine said to Heber. "I told you."

"But where is he now?" Heber asked.

"The only bar nearby is Darlene's," Luis said. "One of the boys heard him say once he was heading there for a nightcap."

"Good work." Katherine slipped her Visa card inside the wallet. "You'll find the tip to your liking. Share it with the boys."

Luis doffed an imaginary hat to her and took the check. Katherine stood up, feeling warm but not wobbly on her feet. She realized that she had been accusing Scott of living in the past, convicting him in absentia of hollow nostalgia. Yet she herself was reliving the past, out for Mexican comfort food and drinking enough to know it and talking about herself and feeling the person across the table was interested in her. She could feel new and enchanting, new to Heber at least. And now they were going to a bar together. Reliving the past wasn't so bad. Maybe she liked it.

"You coming?" she asked.

Heber felt the need to protect her grow.

. . . .

Darlene's was a small blues bar with low ceilings and painted green walls decorated with neon beer signs and tattered posters of old blues acts and cardboard record covers. The bar itself was rich green marble, while the barstools were cheap steel with vinyl seat covers patched with cloth tape. The floor was carpeted, and even years after smoking was outlawed in public places in California, it seemed to exhale an odor of warm tobacco and nicotine. Darlene's still smelled like a bar and seemed comfortable with that. On Thursdays, a single blues singer accompanying himself on the guitar took the stage, covering songs that most of the patrons would know by heart—"I'd Rather Drink Muddy Water, Sleep Out in a Hollow Log"—and when he went on break, the bartender played CDs over the sound system or occasionally vinyl from the owner's collection.

The first thing Heber noticed when he and Katherine walked in was that they were the only white people there. In Newcastle, he had grown up surrounded by white people, and in Salt Lake City, he found himself staring when he saw a black person. Then he would feel embarrassed for staring and would train his eyes on the sidewalk beyond the person so that he wouldn't have to make eye contact. He hated that he couldn't act naturally around other human beings. When he moved to California, it took months for him to accustom himself to the regular presence of people from all races and many countries, to see and greet them all equally. He thought he finally managed it. But he couldn't remember being in a situation where *he* was the minority, where he had to worry about others seeing him equally.

Several people turned to look at them as they paused on the bar's threshold, then went back to their conversations. The regulars were used to white blues fans dropping in.

Heber touched Katherine's arm. He felt his smile was unnaturally wide. "I don't see Scott here," he said.

"Well, we're going to have at least one drink," Katherine said. "A vodka tonic. It will cool your mouth down after the Mexican food."

They sat down at a table adjoining the dance floor, a small square of parquet cut into the carpeting. Nobody was dancing. The singer on stage shot a grin and a wink Katherine's way. Katherine smiled back at him. A waitress came over wearing black slacks and a red blouse loose over her hips, and Katherine ordered two vodka tonics, on the rocks, with lime.

"Top shelf?" the waitress asked.

"Sure. Top shelf. We deserve it."

Heber's ankle still hurt. He thought he might have sprained it. RICE: rest, ice, compression, elevation. That's what he needed. But he didn't want to leave Katherine's side. He had let her drink more of the margaritas because he was unused to drink and because he had fantasies of protecting her. That's how he thought he could serve her best, by being ready to protect her. It was a gallant, chivalric notion, though in Darlene's it seemed utterly stupid. What was he doing to protect her here besides sitting with a big stupid smile on his face to show that he was a nice man and thought well of each and every person he saw? But he was glad to let her down three-fourths of the pitcher anyway. It didn't make her drunk and sloppy—it made her ardent, vehement, and reckless in a way that he found fascinating. Now that they were seated, he was looking forward to having another drink, to see what she would be like afterward. He began to wonder why her husband had been stupid enough to run off and expect her to be waiting.

He leaned forward across the small round table. Katherine leaned in to listen.

"I don't know why your husband would be stupid enough to run off and expect you to be waiting," he said.

Katherine smiled. "That's a sweet thing to say."

The waitress brought their drinks on a round plastic tray, brown with a layer of cork in it. She looked at Heber, waiting. Heber looked back at her and smiled broadly. She put a hand on her hip and turned down a corner of her mouth.

"Oh," he said. "Sorry." He fumbled out his wallet and paid for the drinks and added a big tip.

"There you go," he said.

The singer called the waitress over, and she nodded at Heber and left the table. Katherine lifted her drink toward Heber, and after a moment he lifted his as well, and they touched glasses. She sipped her drink. Heber seemed so young to her, so inexperienced, but in such a sweet way.

On the small platform that served as a bandstand, the singer leaned into his mike. "We're going to have Ruby here sing one that the great Koko Taylor sang last time she was in town."

He began to lay down a twelve-bar blues rhythm, and the waitress, who had put down her tray and picked up a microphone, swayed with the music. She let the rhythm repeat itself and then began a song about a woman who didn't care much if other women were sneaking around her husband, since he was just a husband. But she wouldn't put up with anyone sneaking around her *man*.

Halfway through the song, Shirelle Jones walked over to Katherine and Heber's table. Shirelle was a mean, complaining woman who was always convinced that others had it better than her. Other people had better jobs, better lovers, better cars. Other people were having a better time than her. They always had something to laugh about and someone to laugh with. And she knew, for someone to be having such a good time, they must be doing something wrong. She had decided that if a person was acting right, they would be just as miserable as she was.

She frequently sat down at a table of white people, skinny and wearing a dress that tightened over her flat chest, and talked a drink out of them. She was sure they were doing better than she was, and if they were, the least they could do is buy her a Long Island iced tea. Darlene and Ruby and the other cocktail waitresses knew Shirelle, knew how she acted, knew what she drank. They let her act out because it didn't seem to bother the customers. Some of them even liked it, judging by the tips and the liquor downed.

Shirelle sat down at the table without asking and looked at Katherine and Heber. "Hey," she said.

"Hey yourself," Katherine said.

Heber said nothing at all, just smiled at Shirelle. He didn't think about asking her what the hell she was doing at their table. It wouldn't be polite, and she might think he didn't want her at his table because she was black.

"What are you drinking?" Shirelle asked.

"Vodka tonics."

"Hmmmpf." Shirelle snorted as though she knew they would be drinking something like that. "Hey. You two are sneaking, aren't you?"

"What?" Katherine asked.

"You two are sneaking." Shirelle said it as a statement, not a question this time.

"No, we're not sneaking."

"He's not your husband, is he?"

"No."

"I knew that. I knew that from across the room."

"That doesn't mean we're sneaking."

"Hmmmpf." She looked at their vodka tonics. Katherine's was below half, but Heber's had just been sipped on. She began to tell them the story of the last time she'd been sneaking, when she was stepping out with a married man, a man who had little ones at home. "Little ones at home! And did I care? No!" She knew it was going to end bad, and it *did* end bad, and she was the one who was treated mean.

The waitress Ruby was singing another song. Shirelle glared at her, but Ruby ignored her. Shirelle thought that when Ruby was up there singing, it was just her trying to be someone she wasn't. Ruby was never going to be Koko Taylor. Now Shirelle, she *knew* she wasn't going to be Koko Taylor, and didn't pretend otherwise.

She turned back to Katherine. "But when you're sneaking, it's the sweetest thing there is. That's what you got to know. You two need another drink."

Heber covered his glass with his hand. "I'm fine," he said.

Shirelle shook her head in disgust. "You two need another drink, and I need one too. Why don't you order us one?"

"Okay." Katherine waved toward the bar. She was enjoying listening to Ruby sing, listening to the blues in a kind of bar she hadn't been to in twenty years, enjoying the way the drink made her feel, and enjoying sitting across the table from Heber. She was even enjoying listening to Shirelle rant about how life always treated her like shit.

Darlene brought over a tray with two vodka tonics and a Long Island iced tea in a tall glass that looked exactly like a normal glass of iced tea, with a wedge of lemon. Katherine gave her thirty and told her to keep the change. Darlene said thanks. She walked back to the bar, shaking her head.

"Now, you see, he don't want to drink, and he got to drink." She pointed at Heber, sitting back from his two vodka tonics.

"Why does he have to drink?" Katherine asked.

"Because you want him to get up and take you by the hand and take you out to that dance floor, even though nobody else dancing, and put his arms around you and dance you around. And he ain't doing it unless he's drinking."

She looked at Katherine and smiled meanly.

Partly to prove Shirelle wrong, Katherine stood up and took Heber by the hand and led him to the dance floor. He surprised her by holding her with confidence, a hand on her hip, leading gracefully.

"Where did you learn to dance?" she asked over the music.

"Ballroom is big in Utah. In a lot of wards, they have a ballroom night once a week. Fox-trot. Rumba. Waltz. I also learned square dancing in Newcastle."

"Wow." Katherine looked at Heber's face as they glided around, in a dance not right for the music being played. He looked happy now, confident, in a way that he hadn't since they left the office. He looked happy to have her in his arms. Her specifically, not just anyone, but her. She felt special, even though as she thought that she knew it sounded like a cliché. *He makes me feel special.* It sounded like an item from a list in *Seventeen* magazine, "Ten Ways to Know If He's the One."

But she did—she felt special.

He looked happy. She thought that if this were a movie, she'd know just what would happen next. She'd take his face in her hands and kiss him, right there on the dance floor, and even though they had stopped twirling, the room would still seem to be twirling about them.

If this were a movie. But what did it matter? She didn't care that it wasn't a movie. And she didn't care that she would be acting as if she were in a movie. The hell with *as if.* What she most wanted to do was take his face in her hands and kiss him.

Then the song ended. Heber took his hands off her and applauded Ruby and the guitarist. Katherine was dazed suddenly. Her mind wasn't working well at thinking. Heber turned to go back to their table, and Katherine's mouth suddenly seemed unable to express simple thoughts.

She grabbed his hand. "N-n-n-no," she stammered. "S-s-stay."

The blues singer began another song, and Katherine waited for his left hand on her hip, and then she felt as though it belonged exactly there. And they danced, and when she felt ready she took her hand from his and stroked his cheek and rose up to him and kissed him on the lips, once quickly, and then a second time as she felt him understand and put his arms around her. She closed her eyes and felt the room twirling.

"Hmmmpf. I knew that was coming," Shirelle said to herself. "And she said they wasn't sneaking? Hmmmpf." She sipped her drink. She'd been right. And she'd gotten her Long Island iced tea. It had been a good night.

Katherine drove them back to the El Rancho Motel. Home seemed impossible, with her fifteen-year-old and her father in bedrooms on either side of her own, and Heber lived more than an hour away. And the El Rancho was close, and it seemed important not to delay, important to hurry. Any delay might upset everything, so that what she wanted to happen wouldn't.

The *No* in front of the *Vacancy* was still unlit when they pulled into the lot beside the office. As they stepped out of the car, the neon lariat that bordered the sign flashed on and off, washing their faces with a cheap yellow light before leaving them darkened again. The Sikh manager was delighted to see them, smiled as though he had expected them all along. Katherine asked for a room as Heber hovered near the door. The manager complimented them on their good sense in patronizing his motel and stated in a pleased way that they had taken the last vacant room. He handed Katherine a key on a long diamond-shaped piece of plastic that had the motel's address on it and requested anyone who found it to drop it in a mailbox.

"This is for staying, yes?" the manager asked. "Not for spying. No one else will be coming in tonight."

"Not for spying," Katherine said.

Katherine was delighted with the kitschy sleaziness of the motel. She pointed out the way the *No* light flickered when it came on in front of *Vacancy*, the concrete steps crumbling a little at the corners on the way up to the second floor. She had not seen a motel key like this one for decades. It reminded her of family driving vacations in the early seventies, when the goal was to get to the motel in time to use the swimming pool. She began to think she had married too early. She should have had more flings like this one. Her daughter was having a time, living in Aptos. So Betty was peeling shrimp? So what? Betty was having a time. Katherine thought she deserved one too.

Heber nodded at the tawdry aspects of the motel as Katherine pointed them out to him. He didn't understand why he was supposed to find them amusing, but he didn't want to admit it. He wanted to play along, act cool, act like he knew what he was doing. But he was terrified. He didn't know how to admit to Katherine that he was a virgin.

In southern Utah, in his community, premarital sex was rare and shameful. Young people worried about hitting the big Two-O while still single, and they seized on each other to escape into the haven of marriage, within which decisions about sex could be safely made. Even those who were engaged held off, since the big event of their lives, a temple wedding, required that they be pure. If a wedding wasn't held in the temple, it could be taken as a tacit admission that the couple had fallen short of virtue.

The time Heber spent on his mission, which should have solidified his testimony, had caused him to question the church, in part because of sex. One of his mission companions in Northwest Ohio, Elder Branson from Fayetteville, Arkansas, had confessed to him that he was afraid of being a homosexual. Heber tried to convince him that it was just a stage, that they were all having trouble, that he thought that everyone, including himself, had called the mission president at one time or another to confess to masturbating.

And the mission president, with a bored voice, had told him that he could still be a good missionary. But Elder Branson told Heber that it was different for him. He had to fight every day to act as he knew he ought to. He knew that if he controlled his behavior, it wouldn't matter what his thoughts were. But it shouldn't be so hard to be good, should it? Shouldn't being good seem natural and normal, as God intended?

They had prayed together, and for the three months they went door-to-door as a pair, Elder Branson spoke with a fervor and passion about the church that Heber had not seen in anyone else. And then they were rotated to other companions. The missionaries were not supposed to become more attached to each other than to the scriptures. After their missions were completed, Heber received a letter from Elder Branson telling him that he had gotten engaged to be married just three weeks after returning home. The church had sponsored a social where young people could meet others of the faith, and he had found her there. Elder Branson expressed wonder and awe that he had found someone who would have him as her husband. The church was true. His testimony was strong. In the letter, he said that he was writing Heber first among all his mission companions, because he felt closest to him. And Heber remembered the confession Elder Branson had made and heard an undercurrent of wishful desperation in his expressions of wonder at his bride-to-be.

After his mission, Heber finished a degree in information technology and then moved to Silicon Valley, another valley about which it could be said "This is the place," though without any notion of divine revelation. Heber switched jobs several times in his first few years, floating on the manic energy of the Internet arising from nothing, from the crackle in the air, from Netscape, Hotbot, Yahoo, Google. From the notion that everything you knew before was ancient history. When the crash came, he was young enough to find a place in the shrunken job landscape, not one of those middle managers who had let their programming skills erode and now found themselves on the outside.

Heber lived chastely in California, uncertain what the shape of his life should be. He had isolated himself from the structures of

Mormonism, but he found he had not left them behind. He had refused the model, but this refusal felt like a failure on his part, and he didn't know how to replace it.

Katherine was opening the door of their motel room. The El Rancho. He would always remember this. He hadn't expected his first sexual experience to be with his coworker Katherine. But now it seemed right, inevitable. He was comforted by the fact that she was more than ten years older than him. She was leading him down a pathway she already knew—he wasn't tricking her or seducing her or taking advantage of her. She was older, but she was passionate, and he found himself surprised and grateful that she was passionate for him. Ardent Katherine, vehement and passionate Katherine, with just a touch of the comforting mother attending her.

Yet he was still terrified. He wasn't ignorant of the physical act of sex. Even in Utah, there were soft-core films that were shown at bachelor parties, pornography with the most explicit parts edited out to keep them legal within the state. "Training films," they were jokingly called. Available also to be piped discreetly into bridal suites, even in conservative Provo hotels. Yet now the knowledge he had seemed abstract, seemed to have nothing to do with the scary and shivering anticipation he felt.

He couldn't bring himself to admit to her his utter lack of experience. He was a man, after all, and felt that pressure to project competence. He let her go first into the room and locked the door behind them. He looked at the dresser, the television, the ventilation unit under the window next to the door. He looked at the prints on the wall of Mission Carmel, Mission Santa Barbara, the whitewashed adobe walls and red tile roofs and bells hanging within arched bell towers. The bed itself had a stiff green coverlet and a square Formica headboard. None of it seemed to displease Katherine, so he didn't allow any reaction to show.

He had decided to let her guide him, without letting on that he was being guided. "Let her set the pace"—that was a phrase that he'd heard somewhere, maybe at a bachelor party, maybe at one of those ward house gatherings where the young men clustered together before breaking apart to mingle. He would let her set the pace.

"I'll let you set the pace," he said. She smiled, and he felt he had said the right thing, felt smooth and debonair. *Debonair,* a word that, when he was nine, he and his friends would pronounce "De Boner" and laugh hysterically, even though they didn't know why.

She set a fast pace, eager and anxious. Fortunately for Heber's self-confidence, since he knew nothing about attending to his partner's wants and needs. It was all over quickly, before he really knew what was happening, and he was lying on his back with Katherine lying on top of him, soft and warm and molded to his body. He was embarrassed by her telling him that she had to pee. No woman had ever used those words in his presence before. But when she returned, without him willing it, he felt himself become ready again, and he saw pleasure in Katherine's eyes. And she guided him more slowly, a second time, to the same place again.

Afterward, he lay back and covered his face with both hands. He felt shame, he couldn't help himself from feeling shame, and looking at Katherine would have made it worse. He knew it wasn't fair to her to feel that way, and it might make her feel awful to know that he wouldn't look at her and why, but it felt easier for him to close his eyes, to cover his face, to look at nothing for the time, not even the dim outlines visible in the half light reflecting from the bathroom.

Katherine cuddled up next to him. At first, when they undressed, she found herself wishing she could lose ten pounds before she was completely naked, but then she had forgotten about her age or how she looked, and she felt wonderful. She pressed her cheek up against his chest. It wasn't a bad chest, a little bony toward the clavicles, but broad enough, hairy and masculine. She rested there for a minute and then noticed Heber covering his face.

"Hey," she said. "Peek-a-boo." She tried to peel his palm from his cheek.

"I'm sorry," he said.

"What? You have *nothing* to apologize for."

"No. I . . ."

"What." Katherine raised her head, present and attentive now. "What's the matter?"

"I've never done this before."

"Been in a sleazy motel room with an *older woman*?"

"No," Heber said. "This."

"This?"

"Yes. This."

"This," Katherine said it as a statement.

"This."

"Wow." Katherine didn't think she'd ever been with a virgin before. The boy she'd lost her own virginity to in high school had some experience. Not enough, that was certain, but some. Enough experience to please himself, but not her.

She had thought of this as a fling, but now she saw that to Heber, it was all very serious, an event of substance and gravity. She felt bad, as though she had taken something from him.

"Hey," she said. "Are you crying?"

"No," he said. "It's just not what I'd imagined it would be."

"But it's okay, isn't it? Whatever we do isn't what we imagined we'd do. We're all failures in some way. Here." She settled down alongside him. "Why don't you tell me what you imagined? Tell me about yourself. You don't have to look at me. But I'll be right here. You've been listening to me talk about myself all night long. Your turn."

She tugged gently at his hands again, and he slid them off his face and smiled at her sadly. Then he looked up at the ceiling, white plaster mixed with asbestos.

"Something sacred, I guess."

"Sacred?"

"That's how I was taught. I haven't thought that way for a long time, but it sticks with you."

"Tell me about it," Katherine said. "I want to know about you."

So he began talking, about Newcastle, about being one of the kids in the Pioneer Day Parade, the parade that lets every person say "This is the place" for themselves. Then being one of the returned missionaries watching the next generation and feeling the expectations that he would take part in the same story as his ancestors. Even though, at that point, his testimony, what other religions might call his faith, was already weakening. And he'd begun to think that the point of mission service was not only to win converts to the church, but also to win the young missionaries themselves and bind them to the church once and for all.

He told her about Elder Branson and the night they prayed together. A few years later, while still in Utah, he received a letter from Elder Branson. He had split up with his wife and was being excommunicated. He knew now he was gay, and he hoped the church would have a place for him someday. He apologized to Heber if he'd ever tempted him in any way, as that had never been his intention. The last time Heber wrote to him, in 2002 at Christmas, Elder Branson was living in New Orleans, happier, but missing his two daughters terribly.

In his long storytelling voice, he told her about his time in Salt Lake and his move west. His mother called him a hippie. That's the only category she had for someone who moved to California and drifted away from the church—as though working in a tech firm was like wearing love beads and tie-dyed T-shirts.

"When I was a boy," he said, "my mother told me there was an angel standing outside our door, to protect us at night. Now, there is no angel outside my door. Sometimes, I miss that angel."

He told her he didn't know how he would find love, once he left the church's social customs of courtship. He didn't know how to look. He didn't know what it would look like. And maybe he hoped love would find him. There would be a sign, a vision, a revelation.

"And instead there was just me," Katherine said. "Forty-seven, and ten pounds overweight, and over the hill."

"No." He put his arm around her. "You're beautiful. You're just who you should be. Maybe it says something about me, that I *couldn't* imagine this."

"Hey," Katherine said. "Maybe Shirelle was an angel."

"Maybe so," Heber said. "Funny angel."

"Fond of Long Island iced tea."

"Yeah." He looked at Katherine. "Maybe this is the place."

"It's not so bad." Katherine put a hand over his brow and stroked an eyebrow with one thumb, slowly and thoughtfully.

8

EVERY MORNING, at his mother's house in Henderson, Nevada, Scott took a cup of coffee and sat in one of the squat brown leather armchairs in the living room and waited for his mother and her husband to leave. He tried to be as inconspicuous as possible, sipping his coffee quietly, making himself small beside the large potted ferns that sat on the floor amid the furniture. He hated to be noticed. His mother would ask him brightly what he planned to do with the day. She asked in a way that sounded innocent and interested but was always critical. Seth Paul, her husband, didn't bother to ask him anything. He just smirked as he walked by, obviously judging Scott a waste of time as he went about preparing for his important day. Scott had never liked Seth Paul very much, even at the wedding between him and his mother, when he knew he was supposed to put aside personal feelings and wish everyone well. But now that he was staying in Seth Paul's house and was dependent on his generosity, Scott hated his guts.

The house was a five-thousand-square-foot southwestern-style ranch, located fifteen miles south of the Las Vegas Strip in a gated community of other similarly spacious homes. It had broad, open floors of terra-cotta-colored tile and open archways painted Navajo white leading between the front foyer and the dining room and the living room. The kitchen adjoined the living room, separated only by a counter with stools, and copper-bottomed pots and pans hung from a rack above the island range. French doors opened from the living room onto a patio enclosed by two arms of the house. Bright flowering vines climbed the squared columns that held up wide, overhanging eaves, and a fluted fountain imported from Spain splashed in the center.

Seth Paul bought the house with the proceeds from his seminars on motivational speaking, which he gave on a regular basis at the

MGM Grand Resort Casino. Relocating his business to Las Vegas had proven a brilliant decision. He had tapped into the convention circuit, booking himself several times a week for presentations to trade groups and associations of sales reps. This led to connections for presentations elsewhere in the country, at the headquarters of corporations. He had self-published a book about motivation that he had originally sold only at his seminars—back-of-the-room merchandising—but now it had been picked up by Regan Books and would soon be given distribution, publicity, end-cap space at Books-A-Million and Barnes & Noble. And he still had groups who came in to Las Vegas for his three-day "Motivational Boot Camp."

Scott watched him move through the house, surrounded by a little cloud of smugness and self-satisfaction, and he despised him. He knew that some part of his intense dislike for his stepfather came from envy, which only made him despise him more. And seeing his mother spend most of her time playing along with the game, catering to his wishes, praising his speech and his decrees, making him feel like he was the center of the universe, made Scott want to vomit.

They didn't leave the house until after ten every day, when they drove matching BMW 5-series sedans to the offices Seth Paul maintained in a glass tower just off the Strip. They could leave their air-conditioned garage, drive in their air-conditioned cars, arrive at the climate-controlled parking garage, and ascend via the elevator without ever exposing themselves to the weather. Neither the black-capped inversions that made the air thick and foul smelling, nor the dry desert winds that could desiccate plants in a half hour, nor the still, breathless days of 110 in the shade, nor the rare monsoon rain that could suddenly overwhelm the storm-drain system and float off cars beneath the overpasses affected them on their journeys. They never drove in the same car, even when they knew they would return at the same time, and, more frustrating to Scott, they never thought to leave a car for him to use during the day. Even the gardeners from Michoacán had a pickup truck. Scott had been staying with his mother for three weeks, and he was going crazy.

He'd panicked after he drove over that kid's legs in San José. He knew he'd panicked. In the rearview mirror, he saw the boy moving, and he knew he was alive, but what he did afterward made sense only for a man who felt powerless. He drove the Fury to a car wash that looked like a Mississippi River sternwheeler, from the days of Mark Twain, and he paid $175 for the Works, custom detailing after the wash. Then he checked out of the El Rancho and drove to the bank and withdrew five thousand dollars. At the Greyhound Bus depot, he found a late bus to Las Vegas. He didn't want to fly to Las Vegas and have a name and a credit-card number following him there, and he didn't want to drive and have his car recognized and stopped. And he didn't want to leave the car parked at the depot. He reasoned it would be only a matter of days before the car was declared abandoned and then traced both to the hit-and-run and to him, and someone would recognize a photo of him and place him on the Las Vegas bus. Craftily, he decided that the only place he could leave the car where it wouldn't end up being processed by the police was on Catesby Street. And if leaving the car made him a hero to his son, even better. At the time, he hadn't thought that leaving a car involved in a crime and encouraging his son to drive it might be a bad idea and certainly wouldn't be a winner with Katherine.

He'd had a taxi meet him at the house on Catesby Street and then left the Fury there and went to the depot to wait for the bus, dressed in Ben Davis jeans and a hickory-striped shirt, his seagoing clothes. He had his belongings in a seabag at his feet, cash folded into the special wallet that hung around his neck and inside his shirt. When he looked around at those traveling with him, he realized that he looked like he fit in. Everyone was traveling with the last scraps they could gather, traveling on cash only, ties broken with all institutions of finance. Men who looked lean and beaten, who looked like they had not worked for a salary for some time. Women who kept children gathered close to them, watching over their young heads for the danger that threatened them. All heading for the most western of cities, the most American of cities, Las Vegas, where open spaces replaced personal history, where the freedom to reinvent yourself from nothing seemed still bright.

His mother immediately invited him to stay with them as long as he needed to, and Seth Paul agreed with a careless ease that Scott soon identified as condescension. Seth Paul certainly didn't have to worry about his wife's emotions being divided. He had an abundance of her care and attention. And if Scott had been a weak rival for her love before, he was completely insignificant now that he had sought refuge under Seth Paul's roof.

When they finally left in their BMWs, after ten, Scott felt a bit freer to move around the house. He emerged from his corner seat and scrambled some eggs with cheese and ate them with salsa fresca, fresh-sliced avocado with lime juice squeezed over the top, a slice of papaya, and more coffee. Then he set himself at a glass-topped table with a view of the patio and opened up his laptop. He hadn't been the only one on the bus to Las Vegas to be traveling with a computer. Even the desperate and down-and-out in Silicon Valley seemed to have scraped together the hundred dollars it took to buy a used Dell, and he saw one of the single mothers, possibly fleeing from a husband who habitually did her violence, open up a laptop and encourage her son to pass the time by playing Doom. The boy typed in "iddqd," the cheat code that made him invincible, and slaughtered the monsters who came before him.

The first thing Scott did every morning was check his in-box for an email from Carter. There was never anything from his son, though a few messages sneaked past his filters, messages promising penile enhancement (Add inches! Drive her wild!) or cheap Viagra or tips on penny stocks. He tried to delete them without looking at them.

Then he wrote an email to Carter. He emailed Betty as well, from time to time. But he thought he had a better chance of breaking through to his son. In his emails, he asked him how he was enjoying the car, how he was enjoying school, how he was. He asked how Katherine was. He told him he was working a few things out, but that he would be back soon. He asked Carter not to tell his mother just yet that they were in contact. He wasn't quite where he wanted to be, and he was afraid that if she knew where he was, she would make a rash decision that they would all regret.

Scott thought about telling Carter that the car had been in an accident and that perhaps he should be careful about driving it to school. He thought about it every morning. But he always found some reason to put off doing so. He told himself he would wait until Carter wrote him back, at least once, and that allowed him to avoid the painful admission that he'd done something stupid and criminal.

After writing Carter, he opened up a file labeled "Greatscott.doc." "Great Scott" was the working title for the novel he had decided to write, an homage, he told himself, to *The Great Gatsby*. He was keeping it a secret from everyone until it was finished, and though he had no reason to think anyone would try to pirate his manuscript from his hard drive, he still felt a little thrill when he called up "Greatscott.doc," knowing that nobody else would know what it meant. He didn't know what the novel was about yet, but he was sure it would have a hero who was forty-eight and went back to sea.

He'd sit with his open laptop, and sip coffee, and contemplate the patio, and when he was just about to begin typing, the cleaning lady showed up. Her mother called her Señorita Lopez and always said she was pure gold, but Scott found her insufferable. Señorita Lopez had quickly sussed out the relative stature Scott had in the house and decided that she belonged there every bit as much as he did, if not more. After all, she was paid to be there as someone with an important function, while he was there on sufferance and had no function at all, so far as she could see. So she felt free to order him out of her way, to run the vacuum cleaner whether it bothered him or not, and to sigh theatrically whenever he left behind a juice glass or coffee cup. If he went outside, to one of the café tables, the din of lawn mowers, edgers, electric clippers seemed to assault him, whether it was from his mother's yard or one of the many similar yards within the gated community. Also, there were misters arranged along the overhanging eaves that went off at odd times, suddenly spritzing the dry desert air with water. He never got used to them, and between the discordant noise of yard work and the sudden light showers, he never got much writing done.

After closing "Greatscott.doc" in the early afternoon, he went to the bedroom he was using and counted his money. Five thousand dollars sometimes seemed like a lot of money when he was laying it out in stacks of hundred dollar bills, but he knew that it really wasn't. Five thousand was about what he had in his Etrade brokerage account after it had spiraled downward from six figures and he cashed it out to pay the mortgage and hide the truth from Katherine for one more month. Still, counting it helped him feel he was still a man with options. It felt good to have options. It helped him feel not so dependent on his mother and her asshole husband. One option he'd have to think about soon was shipping out again. The war was still going on, carrier battle groups were still in the Arabian Sea, and he could still find a berth aboard an oiler. His official vacation time was up, and he'd gotten another month of unpaid vacation, but soon MSC was either going to have him shipped out or terminate his employment. And he didn't want to be terminated. He wanted to be the one exercising the options.

On the Monday of his fourth week there, Scott heard Seth Paul saying goodbye to his mother, *See you at the offices,* and moving to the air-conditioned garage. It wasn't much different from other mornings. Sometimes, they even left at the same moment and had to operate the automatic garage door only once. He waited for his mother to follow, so that he could open up his laptop, see that Carter hadn't emailed him, and get on with his day.

But he didn't hear his mother leave. And the atmosphere in the house didn't change. He didn't feel the liberating emptiness he looked forward to every morning, when he could walk around with a sense that his time was his and there was no one to judge him. He sat in his place in the armchair, under the fern, and he could sense his mother waiting for him to emerge. He thought about trying to wait her out. Surely, she would have to go to the office at some point. But he wasn't sure what she did at the office that was so vital, besides reading and praising Seth Paul's latest screeds, making sure his hair was in place, and generally reflecting his own brilliance back to him. Seth Paul could probably forgo that for one day if she needed to have a little heart-to-heart with her son.

He stood, picked up his coffee cup so that Señorita Lopez wouldn't bitch at him when she came in, and walked to the kitchen. His mother wasn't there, so he knew that she was waiting for him in the room they called the library. He decided it was stupid to try to avoid talking with his mother. He had an idea what she would say, and delaying it wouldn't change anything. He felt a choice looming up before him, a choice with consequences.

The library had a large adobe-colored beehive fireplace in one corner, and a wall of white bookshelves filled with hardcover books chosen by the interior designer, who also chose the Navajo rugs hanging from the walls, the overstuffed leather chairs with ottomans facing the fireplace, and the tasteful paintings by two local artists whom the designer deemed "Potentially Collectible." Scott had looked over the books and found them shelved haphazardly, hardcover novels mixed in with history, travel books next to *A Brief History of Time.* A matching set of books on artists—*Goya! Matisse!*—stood together with matching leather covers. Scott had never seen his mother or Seth Paul read any of them. His mother generally read lifestyle and health magazines, with cover stories about sex and aging and diet or books that began with the phrase *What Your Doctor May Not Tell You About* . . . Seth Paul read and reread what he called the classics of his field: Napoleon Hill's *Think and Grow Rich,* Dale Carnegie's *How to Win Friends and Influence People,* and others. He also read what he called "the competition"—Rick Warren's *The Purpose-Driven Life,* and *The Secret.* There were always new ones to keep up with. He didn't have a specifically religious element to his seminars, preferring a more generically spiritual tone, but he wanted to keep up with what was hot.

As Scott suspected, his mother was sitting in one of the leather chairs. Even though it was eighty degrees and the air conditioner was running, she had the gas logs lit in the fireplace. It was November, and she liked the cozy feel of the crackling ember effect. She saw Scott and smiled and stretched.

"It's so beautiful here," she said.

Scott sat down in the chair opposite his mother. He did not put up his feet. She made him nervous. He hadn't seen her for more than a year before he showed up on a Greyhound bus, and in that time she seemed to have grown younger. She actually looked younger than he did. He thought she must have had plastic surgery, because the skin of her face looked strangely tight and she always seemed to be forcing a smile, as though two invisible hooks were tugging at the corners of her mouth. But she would admit only to Botox and instead credited the bioidentical hormone-replacement therapy she was on, as well as various juice fasts that left her bowels clean as a newborn's. She was prone to launching into long monologues about the benefits of wheatgrass, or pomegranate juice, or the bowel-cleansing powers of eating only quinoa and corn for two days, and sometimes she called on Scott to witness her rubbing an ointment made of natural estrogen onto her thigh or asked him to feel the glands under her chin.

Hearing his mother talk about her hormones or her bowels made Scott feel ill. Seth Paul seemed to have mastered the art of smiling absently as she talked about those things, which made her focus even more intently on Scott. And when Seth Paul wasn't around, she confided to Scott that it was him and his genius, above all, that were responsible for how she felt. Scott thought that she was referring to her sex life, and so he never asked for details.

"So beautiful," she repeated.

Scott looked out the window toward the central patio. A mister shot the air full of water droplets.

"Dear," she continued, "both Seth Paul and I are concerned about you."

"I'm all right," Scott said.

"There. You see how defensive you're being? How high your barriers are?"

Scott knew he was already screwed. If he denied being defensive, he would only prove her point. If he admitted it, he would also prove her point.

"We know you're trying to work through a hard time, and you want to find a way to heal your marriage with Kathy, and we want to help you."

"You are helping me," Scott said.

He thought he was agreeing with her. He was wrong.

"No we're not," she said. "I'm afraid we're enabling you."

When she spoke, she also nodded, as though she were miming the agreement Scott was supposed to find with her. The two corners of her mouth pointed up, like little arrows, giving her an incongruous smile even when she was expressing gentle disapproval.

"Before I went through Seth Paul's workshop, I was so much like you," she said.

"You were still married to Dad," Scott said.

"Yes, but that wasn't a true marriage. And I was settling for it."

Scott wondered how his father would feel about being told that his marriage of thirty years wasn't true. He hadn't been to see his father since he'd arrived in Las Vegas, though he knew he was working as a doorman at the New York-New York Casino.

"Now, the question for you is how to find a true marriage again with Katherine. She shouldn't have to settle for less. And neither should you."

Scott knew where this was headed. He suddenly wished he were counting his money, making neat stacks of hundred-dollar bills.

His mother told him about a Motivational Boot Camp, starting tomorrow. A three-day intensive. Both she and Seth Paul thought that it would be the most important first step he could take.

She nodded as she spoke. And how could anyone disagree with someone who was in her sixties and had such flawless skin?

"Okay," he said. "I'll go."

"And sweetie. I haven't even talked to Seth Paul about this. But he's thinking about franchising out his seminar. He's so needed, everywhere, and there's only one of him. Wouldn't it be wonderful if . . . ?"

She smiled and left the rest unsaid. It was clear to Scott that the more he was like Seth Paul, the more she would think of him as a success. He could even go on the road, an avatar of Seth Paul, and help spread his word. His mother was sure that it would make Katherine love him as he deserved.

"I don't know," Scott said. "I don't know when I could be ready for something like that."

"That's just the kind of self-limiting thinking that the seminar will help you overcome." She patted him on the knee.

. . . • . . .

The casino floor, even at nine thirty in the morning, seemed suspended in an odd kind of light, both flashy and dark at the same time. Around the banks of slot machines, electronic bursts of orange, red, flamingo pink exploded from screens, along with the arpeggio of electronic tones that mimed the sound of coins spilling forth. A cooler luminosity enveloped the table games, the arcs of blackjack tables and the long green fields of the craps tables where a low, steady patter was punctuated by occasional yells. But the islands of brightness all hovered in a warm half-light, completely uncoupled from the surrounding world, the same subtle indirect illumination of walls and ceilings at all hours. The people at their tables and their machines had the comfortable feeling that the vast space helped them, protected them, uplifted them in their individual pursuits.

Scott walked through the gaming floor to get to the conference center at the MGM Grand, wearing khakis and a blousy, long-sleeved Oxford. If there was a way to get to the conference center without passing gambling opportunities, he hadn't found it. As he walked on the carpet printed with the heads of lions, he was aware of the travel wallet he had hanging from a nylon cord inside his shirt. His five thousand dollars in cash. He'd decided he didn't trust Señorita Lopez not to clip it if she found it, peel off a hundred-dollar bill or two. And it gave him a sense of autonomy. Even if he was following his mother's directives, taking the seminar as the price of staying in the house, the cash gave him the conviction that he could walk out at any time. He also carried a nylon computer carrying case with his laptop, containing Greatscott.doc.

At a folding table outside the Vista Ballroom, Scott picked up a registration folder from a young woman who had everything laid out in neat alphabetical rows. Inside the folder was a blank pad of paper, a blue pen with the words *Motivational Boot Camp* printed in gold, an agenda, and a registration badge with his name in red.

Scott was glad that his mother had gone back to her maiden name, so that nobody would ask him if they were related. Inside the ballroom, tables were arranged with folding chairs in shallow arcs around a raised stage with a podium. He saw his mother talking to some hotel employees, gesturing at the buffet in the back of the room that held urns of coffee, pitchers of orange juice, baskets of tiny muffins, croissants, and danishes. When she finished with them, she turned and hurried out a side door. She hadn't noticed Scott filing in among the other conferees.

Scott spread open his folder and drew circles on his pad of paper while the seats around him slowly filled. He kept his laptop at his feet, but he saw a number of people open computers on the tables, ready to type notes directly into a document. He also saw a number carrying Seth Paul's book *Your Best Self: A Motivation-Based Program* and leafing through it. Some of the books had the worn look of having been read many times.

The lights dimmed slightly, warmer lights bathed the podium, and Seth Paul strode out, saluting the audience with a half wave. He was dressed in black linen slacks, a dove-gray silk shirt open at the throat, and his silver hair swept back from his perfectly tanned face. He smiled at the warm applause, his teeth very white against his tan, and waited at the podium for it to taper off. Some people turned his book over and compared the large back-cover author's photo with the man standing before them.

When he began to speak, the people around Scott grew intent, focused. Scott noted this with surprise. He disliked Seth Paul so much that he had assumed that anyone who went to his seminars must have been duped in some way, and they would all end up feeling about him the same way Scott did. But they were listening carefully, taking notes, and Scott noticed that the woman next to him had a name tag from a motivation seminar that she had taken last year. She had gotten something out of the seminar, enough that she would come back again.

He began to listen, and unthinkingly he began to take notes. The goal was to *rechange* yourself. We've all changed from people who do believe in our dreams to people who don't. We need to leave our induced state of believing that there was only one way to live, the way we had ended up, the rut we were living in. And to rechange, return to our natural state of limitless possibilities.

At the end of the boot camp, you would be able to write down a description of your best self. And you would be able to articulate a true dream you want to achieve, the maximal expression of your best self. Finally, you would identify the obstacles between you and your dream and grow motivation to overcome them. Grow motivation. Organically. Like a tree, growing within you. The tree of life, which is already there.

Scott watched Seth Paul move easily from behind the podium with a remote mike clipped to his shirt, making eye contact, engaging the audience, finding humor, asking people's names and a snippet of their story, and weaving them into his presentation. And Scott began to wonder himself who his best self was and how his true dream exemplified his best self, and he found himself forgetting that he despised the man speaking in front of him.

When Seth Paul completed his remarks by telling everyone that he expected them all to find something life changing by the end of three days, the attendees applauded, and he applauded them back, saluting them for coming to be motivated and for committing to carry their motivation out into the world. Scott applauded with everyone else, and he looked at the agenda in his folder of material. There were breakout groups before and after lunch and some "dreamstorming" tasks to be completed in the evening before the next day's sessions. He saw that his mother was facilitating one of the groups, but fortunately it wasn't his. He looked at her standing below the podium, answering questions, directing people to the correct conference room, looking poised and competent. And she looked happy. He had misjudged her role in Seth Paul's enterprise. If he was the creative, she was the production. And it contented her, and even allowed her to baffle time and grow younger. It suddenly didn't seem so bad to Scott.

He met his breakout group in Room 203. The facilitator was a woman named Barbara who looked around thirty-five, but Scott wondered whether she wasn't really forty-eight, his age, and had grown younger looking like his mother. She said she had taken Seth Paul's seminar in San José five years earlier and had moved to Las Vegas soon afterward. She now worked in guest services at the Mirage when she wasn't helping with the seminars, and she introduced herself by talking about how much motivation helped her give world-class service to her guests. She had found her best self by helping others.

The members of Scott's group were all leading lives very much like the one he had led before he lost so much money in the stock market, before he lost his job and his house. They had jobs with health insurance and 401(k) plans—they had families. They had managed to buy real estate in the Bay Area or Los Angeles or San Diego or Phoenix, managed to climb onto that ladder of price escalation they thought would never end. They were white mostly, two women of Chinese parentage and one woman originally from Nicaragua who worked in banking. More women than men. They lived in the center of the land of affluence. They were successes in the normal, ordinary sense of the word. But they didn't feel like successes. They were seeking a door to open for them, into a bright space they could not define.

One by one they introduced themselves, said where they were from, told how they made a living. They struggled to articulate what they wanted to get from the seminar, but Barbara was gentle and encouraging, assuring them they would know more by Saturday evening.

Scott had an urge to lie as the round of introductions approached him. He wanted to erase the past four years and return to that slumberous American peace he'd found so unsatisfying. There would be no bursting of the tech bubble, no split-up with Katherine. There would be no 9/11. No war in Iraq, no need for able seamen with experience on fleet oilers. He would fit in with them and their unhappy aspirations. He had the odd feeling that if he had taken this seminar instead of investing in Internet start-ups, his life would have been different.

The woman next to him worked in sales for a transportation firm, selling space in containers that began in China and were shipped across the ocean and then moved by railroad and truck to

Chicago. She talked about feeling that she was just selling empty space, that there was something unreal about it, and the sales targets kept rising and the incentives kept rising too, but she realized that exceeding targets and making incentives weren't making her happy. She wasn't sure if she wanted the seminar to help motivate her to continue in sales or to help motivate her to find a new passion and purpose.

Everyone nodded and then turned to look at Scott. He hesitated.

"Scott Cochran?" Barbara said warmly.

"I want to write a book," he blurted.

To his surprise, nobody laughed—nobody looked skeptical. The smiles were warm and comprehending, and several people tapped themselves over the heart and mouthed, "Me too." They all wanted to write books, it seemed. Scott, unwittingly, had voiced the group's common unspoken desire. To write a book, to explain themselves, authenticate them, justify themselves once and for all. And then, most important, to have their book published, with cover art, and an author's photo to validate their endeavors, so that forever afterward they would be able to refer back to that artifact, brilliantly and indisputably existing—My Book.

Encouraged, emboldened, Scott began to describe what the book was about, losing everything, fighting back, learning lessons. He told about his life, just as everyone else around the table had done, but he told it as though it were already in a book, already a story. He couldn't tell them how the story ended. Maybe that, he said, was what he wanted the seminar to accomplish. To tell him how to write the happy ending he deserved.

When he finished speaking, rushing his words, he saw the others look at him admiringly. Barbara nodded at him and began to speak before the next person could introduce herself.

"Scott's presentation is exemplary in several ways," she began, "and we can all learn from it. First . . ."

For the rest of the day, through the buffet lunch and all the afternoon sessions, Scott felt as though a bright aura had settled about him. He had stumbled into a social circle that would accept his most vain and self-justifying statements about himself and congratulate him for them, encourage him to put them into action. During the breaks, he exchanged email addresses with several men and women who wanted to form an online writing group and keep in touch after the seminar was over.

One woman named Helen touched him while they spoke. She wore narrow black glasses and had bleached blonde hair, and she asked him what he was doing that night. He had made it clear in what he said that his main goal, above all else, was to regain Katherine's love and be again the man he had been before in the past. But such frank statements only seemed to make him more desirable to her. He tried to put her off with a promise to stay in touch, but she didn't want to have a spiritual or artistic connection in the future. She wanted a physical connection in the here and now. She wanted fornication. And she finally convinced him to meet her later in the Paris Casino.

He saw his mother in the hallway after the last session, and he told her he didn't want to ride to Henderson with her. He had his laptop, and he wanted to get right to work on the "dreamstorming" tasks he'd been given—to write down, in a single sentence, his purpose in life. His mother smiled and told him to come home anytime. He had the security code, and he could let himself in.

"It's working, isn't it?" she said. "You're rechanging."

"I think so," Scott said.

Barbara walked by then, and she paused. "Peggy, your son is wonderful."

His mother nodded at Barbara, and Scott felt a blush of pleasure similar to a third grader whose teacher had praised him to his parents.

He walked back through the casino floor, through that buoyant, half-lit space, and through the two sets of doors to emerge into the sunlight of early November. The lights hadn't yet come on, but shadows from the hotels on the west side of the Strip angled over the slow-moving cars. The sidewalks were crowded, and it was still warm enough for tourists to be walking in shorts and polo shirts and running shoes. Some walked with their video cameras held before them, guiding their steps by the small rectangular image in the flipped-out screen. Others paused and stretched out their cell phones to arm's length and took a photograph of themselves with the casinos as a backdrop. Above them, giant video screens showed people like themselves, at a show, at dinner, at the tables, having fun. A booming but indistinct noise hovered over the street, the distant and continuous construction. On the corners, young Hispanic men handed out pornographic photos of women accompanied by phone numbers. They offered them to all men with a distinctive snap of paper, regardless of whether the man was accompanied by a woman. Alongside them, missionaries in white shirts and black slacks handed out Bible tracts.

The Eiffel Tower, half the size of the original and much brighter, loomed above the Strip, and Scott walked into the noisy, air-conditioned casino space. The pits of table games were stylized with bronze art deco sculptures similar to the ones found at the entrance to Paris Metro stations, labeled Sainte Honorée, Etoile, Tivoli, Concorde, and the banks of slot machines were called "French Kiss Slots" and "Parlez Vous Poker." The dollar- and five-dollar machines were set apart in a separate section labeled "Champagne Slots."

Scott had several hours before his date with Helen—he guessed it was a date—and he walked through the casino to the restaurant and shopping area called Le Boulevard. It was designed to resemble a winding cobblestone street in a French provincial town. The roof overhead was painted in sky blue and clouds, and there were artificial trees and greenish bronze streetlights. Shops of various kinds sold *Les articles* and *Le journal,* and above the ground-floor shops were features of a nonexistent second story, tiny mansard roofs and red shutters around fake windows and shallow wrought-iron balconies.

He found a French-style café called JJ's Boulangerie, ordered a caffè latte—the names of coffee drinks were in Italian—and sat down at a small table. He breathed in deeply and decided the air smelled French. There was an aroma of baguettes freshly baked, the good smell of strong coffee and steamed milk hissing from the ornate bronze and copper espresso maker, an indefinable and perhaps imaginary scent of lavender from a French country garden. He found it easy to ignore the bare-kneed tourists going by, the young girls in shorts and tank tops, the old men with pale and hairless shanks, the couples with their cameras, the same crowd he'd walked with along the Strip. He opened his laptop, opened a document, and entitled it Parisdreamstorm.doc.

It was hard to imagine a better place to write than this. He felt at one with the milieu, as though he fit right in with the scene, an American writer in a European café, alone with his work while the world busied itself about him. He hovered his hands over the keyboard and then wished someone would take a picture of him with his fingers poised, just about to lay down the first word of the day.

He paused and thought about checking email. He hadn't yet checked that day, and he hadn't written Carter. He didn't know whether his son would have finally answered him, but he had an urge to write him, now that he felt that something was changing, now that he felt he was taking action to fulfill his dreams. He ached for his son's approval, the same ache he felt for his wife's acceptance and love. And he thought that if he could express in an email the sense of passion and purpose, the sense of his best self, that he had received, he was sure Carter would write him back.

He checked the upper bar for a WiFi signal, but he couldn't find one. He promised himself he would find Internet access and email Carter as soon as he had finished writing in the café. And he thought how much more authentic his email would be if he had just spent two hours on his novel.

Scott opened Greatscott.doc and looked at the first page, those aspiring first two words: Chapter One. Then he returned to Parisdreamstorm and hovered his fingers over the keyboard again.

He began to wonder if he should buy a beret. They probably sold them someplace in the casino. It would probably be easier to write if he was wearing a beret. Hemingway wore a beret. Who else wore a beret? Besides Frenchmen. Salvador Dalí? Picasso? Mitch Albom? He thought about leaving the café to find a beret. And he thought about the croissants in the pastry display at the counter. A beret and a croissant. Or a beret and a muffin. Banana walnut.

One hint Barbara had given everyone was to write about yourself in the third person if you're stuck. Even if you couldn't imagine yourself doing such marvelous things, you might be able to free yourself if you imagined you were writing about someone else. Scott closed his eyes and began to type.

Scott Cochran has given voice to his generation.

He looked at those words, in Times New Roman. On a computer screen made up of flickering pixels, yet suddenly seeming solid and authentic, as though already printed, as though already true.

He wrote another sentence. *On "The Today Show," first-time author Scott Cochran discussed his book with Katie Couric.*

Suddenly, writing was easy. He wrote about how the book would be received, what it would mean to people's lives. He wrote blurbs the book would have on the back cover from famous authors—he wrote snippets from the reviews the book would get. He wrote about himself, reading from the book, signing the book, being interviewed about the book.

> "Mr. Cochran's book explores the dilemma and promise of the sons and daughters of the Greatest Generation."
> —The *New York Times*

> "Mr. Cochran's book, finally, proposes a fulfilled lifestyle."
> —usa *Today*

> "A heartfelt cross between novel and memoir."
> —Mitch Albom

> "Good work. Good man."
> —Ernest Hemingway

> "In this deep and honest work, Scott Cochran describes the way to finding one's best self."
> —Seth Paul

He wrote about the book he wanted to write, knew he could write. And he wrote about the praise he would receive, the success he would enjoy. He wrote in the present time about himself in the future, wrote as though he had achieved his dreams, as though the dreamstorm had revealed his purpose in life and he had already overcome the barriers between him and the brightness that awaited him. And underlying it all, unspoken, was the reception he would receive from Katherine and Carter and even Betty.

He signaled the barista for another caffè latte, and she brought it even though they didn't normally have table service. He offered her a twenty-dollar bill, and she took it and told herself that she would give him change when he asked for it, though she suspected he wouldn't. She got monster tips several times a day, from the generous types nicknamed "George," and she knew it paid to cater to the eccentric in Las Vegas.

The desire Scott expressed through writing about himself was the same desire that everyone in his breakout group felt. Beneath the various languages of self-fulfillment, the goal to which they all pointed was love. The people in his group wanted to open doors for themselves, find their authentic voices, develop confident personae, even learn to make boatloads of money. But always, at the end of their labors, was the desire for love.

Scott turned off his computer, stood up, transfigured by his vision of himself. He staggered down the French village street, past the shop windows with colorful awnings and the fake workshop of Alexandre Gustave Eiffel. The same streams of tourists were walking, dressed in shorts and sandals and T-shirts, holding up digital cameras or small video recorders or cell phones, talking, happily oblivious to Scott's feelings. He thought his face must be shining, like a prophet come down from the mountain, but nobody seemed to notice.

The casino area opened about him, spacious and filled with chimes and rattles and the noise of human play. Everything about him seemed suddenly animate and meaningful. All the scraps of light and color, the twisting smoke of a cigarette, the pleas and shouts of the craps players, the glint of sequins on a woman's dress, the pattern in the carpet, the smell of bodies, all seemed to speak to him in a language he understood and had no need to translate. He walked as though a god went before him, feeling utterly safe and secure.

He entered the Champagne Slots area, the dollar- and five-dollar machines tall and bright, beacons in the hovering half-light. He stopped at one, oddly humanoid in shape, broad shouldered with a smaller head capping it off, and he felt the machine communicate to him. He took his wallet from within his shirt and drew out five hundred-dollar bills and fed them into the slot and watched the credits for play mount up. He selected maximum play, five dollars a spin, and hit the big button and watched the animated reels flash and pop.

He hit his first jackpot in ten minutes. The lights on top of the machine flashed, and bells rang, and he saw three double bars of gold across the center line of the machine. Two hundred to one. A thousand dollars. He pushed the large Credit button and saw the electronic numbers spin up. He pushed maximum play again, watched the animated reels, rich in cherries, and stars, and stack of gold bars.

He hit another jackpot, and then another. An attendant came by, dressed in smart black slacks and a white blouse and had him fill out a W-2G form for a payout of fifteen hundred dollars. He had her write down the information for him while he continued to play, showing her the able-bodied seaman's card that carried his Social Security number. He didn't want to stop. The numbers on his credits for play continued to spiral up, and other slots players, attracted by the sound and light, began to fill in the machines near him. A cocktail waitress, dressed like a French gamine, brought him a gin and tonic, and he tipped her ten dollars. He didn't know what time it was. He communed with the machine in front of him, listening for its message, and its message was always the same: Place Maximum Bet. He hit the Play button with a satisfying smack, and the reels spun and told him he was immortal.

Finally, a hollow plastic splashing sound broke his concentration. Beside him, an old man in a shiny shirt with a string tie had unzipped his fly and was urinating into a large plastic change bucket. It was a long, slow pee, the work of an older man with an enlarged prostate. Scott stopped playing while the sound continued, looking away from the change bucket with the script Paris logo. The old man continued to push the Play button, spinning the reels three times before he finished. On the third spin, he hit three cherries for a twenty-to-one payout. As the machine began to tone and chime, he noticed Scott had spotted him, and he winked from his seamed and gnomish face. Scott pressed the Cash Out button on the machine and hoped the attendant would come before he wet his own pants.

The men's room off the casino floor was splendid with black marble counters and black-and-white tile floors. He was disappointed there was no ice in the urinals. He had always wanted to be able to say he was pissing on ice, and he felt like he was. His five thousand was more than doubled, to ten thousand. He walked back onto the casino floor and felt buoyed up by the cash in his wallet.

He cast his eye about with a certain air of mastery, as though choosing where he would next win, since he was indisputably a winner. He still didn't know what time it was. When he was twenty-one and driving from the Bay Area to Reno to gamble legally for the first time, he had played blackjack and craps. He now gravitated toward the craps tables, toward the music of the patter and call, the dealers and the shooters calling for bets, calling for numbers, *Coming Out, Hard Way, Yo, Big Six, Big Eight*. He found a place at the rail, pulled out his wallet, and waited until the shooter made his point. Then he laid down two stacks of hundred-dollar bills to buy chips, the black ones worth a hundred dollars apiece. One of the dealers called out "Change, two thousand," and stuffed the bills with a plastic blade through a slot in the green felt table.

Immediately, he began to win. He placed two chips on the pass line, and the shooter rolled a seven. He dragged the winnings and waited for the next roll. The shooter rolled a six, and he backed up his pass bet to take the odds and placed two more chips on the come line. The shooter rolled a four, and he took the odds and the shooter rolled a four again. Then the shooter rolled a six, and all of his bets were winners.

The first shooter made three points before crapping out, and Scott saw the lines of chips in the wells before him grow longer. He felt like a magician. The chips he threw onto the table returned to him doubled and tripled. The table grew loud and frantic as shooters made two or three points before losing the dice, long rolls that allowed players to press their bets. The noise of winning, the happy, frantic noise of humans who feel themselves touched by fortune, attracted more people to the table, until there was hardly space to stand. Everyone was pouring money onto the table, Hard Ways, Proposition Bets, Field Bets. The dealers called the roll, and chips were pushed back to the players, and everyone felt they would never lose again. People crowded around the table, watching over the players' shoulders, wishing they could get into the game that was hot, the table that was hot, promising themselves that they would be in the right place next time, and they would know to commit themselves totally—they would know it was their time to win.

Scott felt someone lean in against his ass, felt a woman draping herself over his back, and he turned and saw Helen propping her chin over his left shoulder. She still wore her narrow black glasses, and her bleached blonde hair, flattish on top, shimmered weirdly in the casino light, as though it were going to lift up off of her head. She had changed into a looser blouse and casual jeans, and she'd had one martini while waiting for Scott at the Zinc bar.

"Hey," said Scott. "Am I late? I lost track of time."

"It's all right," Helen said. "I just looked for the hot table. I knew I'd find you here."

Helen had been attracted to Scott even before he announced that he wanted to write a book and had become the ideal and exemplum for the breakout group. His thick hair, just curling over his ears, still black even though he was surely the same age as her. His taut neck and defined jawline indicating a slim body, still boyish in the hips. And then the timbre of his voice when he spoke, a man's voice, yet still youthful and searching. She chose him before he'd finished speaking.

Helen attended workshops on life coaching, self-actualization, dream envisioning, inner motivation every six months or so. She continually sought a key to understanding herself and her career in real estate, and each workshop made her feel good about herself for a few months. Then a buzzing dissatisfaction settled deep into her chest again, and she found herself online, looking for some weekend retreat that made the right-sounding promises. She never lost faith that the key could be found, even though each workshop's pathway proved lacking. There was always another workshop to try, and she was a believer in believing.

And there was always a guy waiting for her at every workshop. A cute guy who understood her needs, since he was seeking the same help she was. And a cute guy who wouldn't follow her home and make demands on her while she tried out her new way to her own centered self. The times she had met someone who was also from San Diego, it had ended badly and sent her in search of another workshop even more quickly. Scott was from San José. He was seeking. He was cute. He was perfect.

"I knew I'd find you at the lucky table," she told Scott. "I knew you'd be luck."

"New shooter," the dealer cried. "Coming out!"

"Play eleven for me," Helen said.

Scott gave her a grin and threw a twenty-five-dollar chip on the table. "Give me a yo," he called.

"Yo, yo," the stick man called. "Bet."

The shooter was a young black woman in a metallic silver dress. She had her boyfriend blow on the dice, then sent them crazily down the felt, over the stacks of chips on the pass line, and against the low multifaceted surface surrounding the table.

"Yo," a dealer sang. "Yo-leven. Winner, winner."

The dice showed a six and a five, sitting beautiful against the green, and the dealer placed fifteen twenty-five-dollar chips next to Scott's one placed on the eleven. He remembered something his father said. Elevens often repeat. His father, who was working as a doorman. Drawn to Las Vegas in the wake of the woman he loved and would continue to love for the rest of his life. His father, whom he hadn't even called since he'd arrived.

Elevens often repeat.

"Let it ride on the yo," he called.

"Let it ride, let it ride," the music began. "Ride on the yo."

"Yes," he heard Helen say in his ear. "Yes yes yes."

The pit boss came and stood behind the dealers to watch. At a sign from the man sitting box, a dealer dumped four dice on the table to mix with the two that had just been thrown, and he pushed and pulled them several times with the stick, so that it was impossible to distinguish them from each other. Then he pushed them down the table to the young woman in the silver dress. She picked two and winked at Scott.

"Yo, baby," she said as she cast the dice.

The table exploded in shouts and cries of anguish, envy, admiration. The blessed six and five, again on the felt, and the players on the rail and the spectators behind them yelled and cried and swore they had thought of making the same play themselves, they had dreamed it, and even though they had faltered at the brink this time, they had seen it, by God, they had seen it happen for someone, and that meant it could happen for them as well. And next time, when the magic moment arrived, they would recognize it and seize it and not prove diffident and meek. The dealer quickly calculated the payoff, four hundred times fifteen, and pushed six thousand dollars' worth of chips out to Scott, and everyone watched him to see what he would do. Even as their own pass-line bets were paid as winners, he seemed the only winner at the table, and everyone's luck was only a reflection of his luck.

"Drag it," Scott said, and the stick pushed the chips toward him, and he took all his chips off the table and wondered how he would carry them all to the cashier's window.

"Can we color that up for you, sir?" the dealer said.

"Sure." Scott placed all his chips down and watched the dealer quickly and expertly exchange all the small-denomination chips for stacks of blacks. Scott gave a hundred-dollar toke to each of the three men working the table and saw Helen gaze at him admiringly. Before he turned away, a suited casino rep was at his side, asking him if he had lodging for the night, if he would like to stay as a guest of Paris. And if he'd like to dine as their guest, reservations could be made immediately.

The players and the spectators watched Scott go, and the mood at the table collapsed. Everyone was certain now that it was he who had been the key to the winning streak and that he had taken the luck with him. They cut their bets back to the minimum, waiting to see if they were right, and the woman in the silver dress threw a three, and they lost, then a two, and they lost again, and one by one they began to gather up their chips and winnings and regrets.

For Scott, the rest of the evening moved swiftly, taking its course with an empty-headed inevitability. He went to dinner with Helen, at Mon Ami Gabi, the waiters wearing white aprons and black bow ties, and they split a bottle of Bordeaux and had a flute of Veuve Clicquot with enormous desserts. They had a nightcap at the Eiffel Tower Bar, halfway up the replica of the tower, where they had a view of New York, Venice, Rome, and Scott was stupefied to find himself treated like a winner, called a winner, a winner at last. Then they went to the room that was waiting for them, that was always waiting for winners. Helen pressed Scott against the wall in the hallway several times to kiss him before they got to the door, so that when he finally slipped the card in and turned the handle, they seemed to fall in on top of each other. Scott was carrying, still carrying, his small laptop case, and it was a relief to finally have a place to set it down and not worry about it. He had his hands inside Helen's blouse, and he discovered he still knew how to loose a bra with a quick snap of his thumb and fore-finger. She reached into her purse around his back and fumbled for a condom as she pushed him back toward the bed. They fell together, still mostly clothed, and only then did Scott remember that it was the first day since he'd left San José that he hadn't emailed Carter.

9

KATHERINE WONDERED ABOUT LOVE—the outrageous promise of it all. She'd come home early in the morning after the crazy night with Heber, pulling into the subdivision at four a.m. under the quiet dark of stars, finding the Fury safely in the driveway and knowing her son and her father were safe. She hoped to get three hours of sleep. Heber decided to just stay at the motel and wear the same clothes to work the next day, since it wasn't such an issue for a man. Katherine wasn't going to show up wearing the same outfit two days in a row, not with Rajni the gab queen sharing her bay of desks.

She thought she could steal in and wake up at her normal time and not admit how late she had been, but she found her father sitting up, listening to Rosemary Clooney sing with Duke Ellington and rubbing a cup of coffee between his hands. She was astonished to find him up, and not prostrate from chemo, but strangely enlivened. And though finding him up and waiting for her was ludicrously similar to something that could have happened when she was fifteen, he didn't ask her about where she had been. She poured herself a cup of coffee as well, and they sat across the table and talked about her mother. Katherine listened, mostly. Her father talked about how much he missed her still and how much he'd loved her. She was a woman who went for the story, he said, who believed that their life together was going to follow a story line with a happy ending. And he also talked about how being alone was no way to get through your sixties and seventies. Loving someone else wouldn't have meant that he'd loved Mary Katherine less.

He also told her that he thought Carter was getting a girlfriend. He didn't think Carter would tell her himself, so he was letting her know. A girl with a funny name, and a nose ring, but he supposed it didn't matter so much. Katherine felt herself become jealous for a moment, possessive of her only son, even though she had just spent the night with a man sixteen years younger than herself. But she felt something loosen in her chest, open, as her father talked about how Carter was joining the club, joining those who had loved.

Five hours later, at the office, Katherine and Heber were polite with each other, but distant. She didn't ask him if he wanted anything when she went to the copy room where coffee was on. She didn't include him in poking fun at odd emails or absurd requests from clients planning on attending the users' conference. They hadn't talked about how they should act in the office, but Katherine knew it was best to keep it quiet for now, and she would have found it impossible to act exactly as she had before. Heber hadn't known what to expect, but he acted similarly distant, and when he spoke her name he pronounced it with careful formality, so that no hint of passion or affection showed through. Kath-uh-rin. Three syllables, modulated like a tape teaching English as a second language.

Katherine and Rajni went out for lunch together, to a place with a stand-up order counter called Café Benedetto. Katherine found herself ravenous. She'd only had time in the morning for a bagel with cream cheese and strawberry jam, and midmorning she had a doughnut, which seemed to make her hungrier. She had intended to get the low-cal chicken Caesar salad, dressing on the side, but she ended up ordering the meatball sandwich with fries and a diet Coke. Rajni got the chicken Caesar and a bottle of Calistoga. She had worn a sari, as she sometimes did, iridescent blue with blackish highlights, and she looked slender and elegant when she sat down. Katherine looked at her enviously across the table and suddenly felt dumpy and defeated. She tore a bite out of her meatball sandwich and wiped her chin.

"So did you and Heber have some kind of fight?" Rajni asked.

"No," Katherine said. "Why?" She stuffed three fries into her mouth. She was eating so poorly that she could serve as the Don't Girl in a feature in *More* magazine—"Diet Do's and Don't's."

"You've just been a bit peculiar with each other today."

"Hmm." Katherine paused. "He is a bit of a peculiar man, don't you think?"

"Oh, he is," Rajni agreed confidently and leaned forward. "I think it's that Mormon thing."

"Oh, you think that's it?"

"They must keep the boys very separate from the girls. Just like some traditional Indian men. They know nothing about women. Imagine a wedding night with one of them." She shivered in disgust.

"Oh."

"And then he's so geeky, don't you think? Those glasses he wears are like goggles. Nobody has worn glasses like that since the seventies."

Katherine listened as Rajni continued to list Heber's shortcomings. She had been feeling like she didn't deserve Heber, like she was too old for him, like her female fat zones were too round, like everything on her body would start to sag in a year and he would find her unattractive. Now, listening to Rajni, glamorous and elegant, find fault with Heber, she began to wonder if *he* deserved *her*. Or maybe they were both just losers.

Back in the office, she discreetly observed some of what Rajni had noted. The glasses for his nearsightedness that made his eyes appear tiny, his geeky way of chewing the caps on pens. But, in a manner that surprised her, everything she observed became endearing. She saw that he had shaved, but badly, and guessed that he had begged a disposable razor from the motel's front desk and had tried to use soap lather for shaving cream. The prominent mole below his left ear had been cut and looked angry. She had discovered that mole while nibbling on his ear, and she felt sorry for it and protective of it. And she wondered about love and whether part of the outrageous promise of it was to find that flaws made it grow. Was she like a teenager, willing herself to be blind to flaws and limitations? Or was she acting maturely to embrace imperfections? She wasn't sure.

Heber lived in a subdivision in Tracy, an hour by freeway from San José. He'd bought a modest ranch house there, on the edge of the Great Central Valley, because it was the only place he could afford. And he wanted to be building up equity, real estate equity in California. Now it made life difficult. There was no chance he and Katherine could make the long drive to his house to be together and still allow Katherine time to return home and tend to her father and son.

They didn't meet that afternoon after work, and Katherine didn't dare send him even an email love note. She'd heard too many stories about emails at work becoming public. At home, she found that her father felt well enough to go with Carter to his rehearsals. He wanted to go. They could make it a driving lesson there and back, and Henry said he enjoyed watching the rehearsals, and Carter's drama teacher welcomed him. That freed up Katherine's time. She used her son's computer to send Heber an instant message and suggested they see each other after work tomorrow. He replied almost immediately. She loved thinking of him sitting at his computer, waiting for her—she loved that she had fulfilled his wishes and expectations.

They met at the El Rancho the next day, and the day after that. Katherine rushed home and put dinner on the table and then drove out to the motel to find him standing on the second-floor walkway outside an open door, waiting for her. What surprised her was the swift ferocity of his love, the way it seemed to have suddenly elevated itself into a vast monument. He was especially moved by her physical responses to him. Each quiet cry that she gave out as though from a distance, her eyes half-closed and her head turned to the right, the skin prickling at the base of her spine, seemed to leave him in a state of gratitude and wonder at becoming a lover, her lover. She tried to tell him that it was his inexperience that made him feel that way. She tried to tell him that she was not unique, that any secrets she had were secrets common to all women, she tried to tell him that he thought she was unique only because he was so young—she wanted to ease what she thought sure would be the gradual fading of his enchantment. But he would not listen. He loved her, he said. And each small nuance of sex she showed him, each motion he could put into practice that brought her more pleasure, made him love her more.

Katherine hadn't thought she would ever be anyone's first love. The thought was ludicrous, incongruous, for a forty-seven-year-old. The stories she sometimes read in newspapers, about schoolteachers falling in love with fifteen-year-old boys, made her think the women who did things like that were strange and extravagant creatures, who must have failed at some point in their lives. Now not only did she have a lover who was much younger, but he was furiously and naively in love with her, despite his thirty-one years.

She had no one to talk to about him. She hadn't had time to make any new friends in her father's neighborhood, and she hadn't lived long enough in Oak Commons to grow close to anyone. Talking with friends at work was impossible, of course. One week went by, and then another. Two weeks of love. She hardly thought about Scott, about the fact that her mad search for him had brought her together with Heber. She spoke with her mother, while driving to and from work, teased out the plusses and minuses of what was happening, talked about the possible consequences of having Heber in her life, the future. He was in love with her and wouldn't want to share in just a corner of her life. He had already posted his résumé on Monster.com, so that he could change employers and avoid the awkwardness of an office romance.

Katherine asked her mother whether her father had been her first love, whether that had made it special and precious, or whether she too had considered all the dunning practicalities of life. *You'll do better than me,* her mother had said. She asked her now if being able to fall in love again meant she was doing better.

Her mother, as always, had no answer. So Katherine waited for an evening when she and Heber were taking a night off and Henry and Carter were at drama rehearsal, and she called her daughter in Aptos.

Katherine heard a bored note enter Betty's voice as soon as she identified who had called her. She wondered if it was a special voice daughters cultivated to indicate that they were beyond the concerns their mothers had for them, but would humor them by pretending to take them seriously. Katherine hit the normal topics, updating Betty on her grandfather's health, on Carter's doings. She asked about work at the restaurant and asked her again about her plans to take classes at the community college beginning next semester. Betty replied with shortish answers intended to satisfy her mother—she loved living in her boyfriend's house, though she was thinking of moving on from her job if they didn't start training her on the wok soon. Yes, she had signed up for two classes at the community college. There was no need to rush.

Katherine wanted to talk about love, but she didn't know how to bring it up. Her own emotions were utterly beyond the scope of their normal conversations. She had always played the mother's role of placing her daughter's welfare and happiness at the center and intent of their talks, and she was unused to placing herself at the center. So she asked about Betty's boyfriend.

Betty's voice immediately grew guarded. "What about him?"

"Well." Katherine thought about the questions she had about Heber. Was he just naive? Was it only about sex? Was there a difference if he loved her or if he just thought he loved her? Would he change with experience?

"Do you think he's committed to you?" she asked.

"For now," Betty said. "We're not talking about getting married or anything."

"But do you think he could grow tired of you? Or too used to you?"

"It's not something I think about."

"But maybe you should," Katherine said. "Were you his first? That would make a difference."

"Mother . . ."

"He might decide he needs to experience more. And then where would that leave you?"

"Mom, you're asking me about my boyfriend's sex life. Yuck."

"Oh." Katherine looked down at the paper she'd been doodling on. She'd drawn a number of arrows with feathers and long shafts and arrowheads, and they all suddenly looked like penises to her. "I'm sorry."

"What are you being so *weird* for?"

"Oh. No reason."

Betty's voice hushed with a sudden suspicion. "Are you going out with someone yourself?"

"Kind of."

"You *are.*" Betty's voice pitched high and delighted. She began pumping her mother for details and was a little disappointed to find that it was someone at work who was more or less at the same level as Katherine, not some kind of Internet mogul. She asked what kind of dates they had gone on and was disdainful when she heard that at times they didn't really go out at all. She advised her mother to think about what she was getting out of the relationship, how it benefited her.

"I *know* what I'm getting out of my relationship," she said. "And if I weren't getting enough, I wouldn't stay in it."

When they finished talking, Katherine wondered how she had raised someone who'd become so unsentimental so young. Betty *knew* what she was getting. Katherine envisioned her toting things up—the house by the ocean, no rent, a job she could take or leave, a lifestyle. Talking with Betty had only helped Katherine see things by contrast. Whatever sort of goodness she was gaining from Heber, it was a kind her daughter, at the age of eighteen, knew nothing of.

· · · **·** · · ·

Carter received emails from his father every day, and every day he read them and deleted them without replying. They showed up in his in-box from an AOL account, with determinedly optimistic subject lines: "The Right Stuff," "Going Strong," "The Time Is Now." And they contained a mixture of reports from his father's life and advice and guidance for Carter. His father told him that he spent every day engaged in an "ambitious project"—those were his words—the exact nature of which was difficult to describe, but which would finally bring them all together again. Each day, he talked about the progress on his project. Then he advised Carter to start weight training and perhaps join a dojo so that he could learn tae kwon do, and he sometimes attached articles he found online about strength diets and supplements. Once, Carter opened an attachment and found a crude cartoon strip of a young man changing from a ninety-seven-pound weakling to the Hero of the Beach.

Carter felt that his father wanted him to share these emails with his mother. He thought that his mother was the real addressee. His mother would probably just delete emails from his father without reading them at all, but she would pay attention to them if Carter brought them to her. He never did. His mother was pulling away from him during those weeks, distracted, often gone, often disappearing right after dinner, giggling at odd moments when she was at the table with them. Carter resented this, used to being the focus of her attention. But he also enjoyed the independence that was unthinkingly being granted to him since the Fury showed up in the driveway.

In the early evenings, just after his mother rushed off, he drove his grandfather to the rehearsal. Nu always greeted his grandfather with ceremony, seated him close to the stage next to where she sat, and made sure he was comfortable. When she was watching the actors run lines, she strode about, considering the blocking from various angles, sometimes calling a direction out of the darkness. But she frequently returned to Henry's side, sometimes talking to him low and quiet, even while the action continued, sometimes asking him a question aloud, so that the actors in the scene and those not then onstage could hear what he had to say.

Carter discovered that Nu's embrace of his grandfather meant that he was accepted and welcomed by everyone. He was known now as the guy with the cool grandpa who came to rehearsals and was liked by Nu. Anytime he came to the picnic tables outside the theater, where Jeffrey and Cal held court, he was immediately part of the group. He was forgetting the awkward adjustment to Montalvo High, how out of place he'd felt with his antiwar T-shirt. He hadn't worn the T-shirt since early October, and hadn't felt the need to. It was easier for him at fifteen years of age to simply be with those who were against the war and have that understood, instead of wearing a shirt and being tossed into a Dumpster. He hadn't had any more run-ins with K. J. and his buddies, since K. J. had been out of school with a broken leg.

He saw Blossom Haven several times during the school days and again at rehearsals. She usually sought him out, running to him at lunch period and hugging him from the side. Face-to-face hugs were a little too explicitly sexual for the school grounds, but she always wanted to touch him. Carter had a small part and was onstage only infrequently during rehearsals, so it was easy to sit with her and hold hands or disappear for a time behind the theater building to talk. They talked about their families more than anything else, weaving together a common knowing of the past, and could have forgotten time in their talk if not for the clocklike appearance of Nu to smoke a cigarette that told them a section of rehearsal had ended. Sometimes, his grandfather came out to keep Nu company. After the rehearsal, he drove Blossom Haven home, with his grandfather stretched out in the seat beside him.

He began driving the Fury to school in the mornings as well as using it to drive to rehearsals with his grandfather. He knew he didn't officially have his license and wasn't supposed to drive without his grandfather in the car. But it made sense to him in several ways. First, he knew the way perfectly, and it was safer during the day than at night. Second, he was saving time by driving instead of walking. Third, his mother was so distracted and was paying so little attention to him that he felt entitled. He decided that because she was rushing in and out of the house and he was hardly seeing her, it was like she was giving him permission to do what he wanted, as long as she didn't specifically tell him not to.

The first time he did it, he had slept in after a late night and would have missed class if he walked. His mother was gone, and his grandfather was sleeping, and he took the Fury without asking anyone. When he came back after school, his grandfather didn't mention it, so it seemed to Carter that he thought it was all right. Carter didn't test this thought by actually asking. He just took the Fury again the next morning.

That second day, he drove Blossom Haven to her home after school. She said that she hated being away from him, and sometimes, when he dropped her off in the evening, she held his hand at her door and didn't want to let go. He had to gradually slide his hand from her grasp, promising he'd talk to her the next morning, and then walk back to his grandfather snoozing in the Fury. He had never had someone else (a girl!) declare him to be so important to her life, and it generated odd and conflicting feelings within him. He felt protective of Blossom Haven, as she had given him the power to protect her. Yet he also felt superior to her, as she had given him the power to make her happy or unhappy. He hadn't asked for these powers, and to have them rendered to him so completely both pleased and confused him. He hadn't asked to be her boyfriend, but now he was, recognized by the theater kids as part of a couple, and he carried his new status uneasily.

She was happy when he told her he could drive her home after school. He had to park two blocks from the school, on a side street, and they walked together to the car, holding hands, each with a messenger bag slung from the opposite shoulder. She leaned against him as they walked, her head barely coming to his shoulder, and he didn't feel awkward or odd, didn't hunch over to take up less space as had been his habit. When they reached the car, they flung their bags into the backseat, and then she leaned back against the passenger-side door.

"Kiss my eyes," she said. "I want to be the kind of person who is kissed on the eyes."

She closed her eyes, looked as if she were deep in a peaceful sleep. Carter ran a hand across her straight hair, dyed black, and along her round cheek. He was in love, as far as he knew, and that gesture seemed like something someone in love would do. Then he leaned down and gently touched his lips to each of her smooth eyelids.

She smiled and opened her dark eyes.

In the Fury, she told him to drive her home slowly, not on busy streets. When they were moving, she leaned across the broad bench seat and put her head in his lap. She kissed him through the cloth of his pants, pulled down his zipper, and then released that part of him that she thought most important to making him love her.

"Guys like this," she said.

Carter drove, keeping his eyes ahead, and glancing down in wonder at what was happening to him. He swore to himself that he was in love, that he would always love her, that life was miraculous. He felt an unconquerable happiness then, to know that she loved him, and to know that the happiness of their love would never end. Then he realized he was driving into a cul-de-sac. He slowed down and cranked the big boat of a car to the right, then hard to the left, so that he would not have to stop. The right front fender nearly took out a mailbox, and a woman working in her garden looked up at him disapprovingly.

He came back to the corner, which had a stop sign, and tapped the brakes quickly. Anytime the car stopped, he felt as though it became transparent, and everyone would see what was happening. He drove around the subdivision, trying to keep in motion by avoiding major roads. A man walking a dog, a woman pushing a stroller, terrified him. They waved at him, and he waved back with a smile that he was sure looked guilty. He went 'round and 'round blocks of ranch houses with small green lawns and shade trees on the front strip, trying to keep his love secret and separate from the graphed landscape. Then at last, he leaned back his head, and the Fury sighed to a halt.

By the time they reached the apartment complex where she lived with her mother, Blossom Haven was sitting beside Carter, leaning her head on his shoulder. She didn't mind that the shoulder was thin and that the bones were barely sheathed in skin. It was her shoulder to lean against, and she claimed it, and no one else could have it. After he parked, she held his hand.

"Will you drive to school tomorrow?" she asked.

"Yes," he said. "Yes, I will."

· · · • · · ·

A week later, Mitch spotted the Fury as it was pulling out from the curb. He recognized it immediately as the car he had seen at the theater. A Plymouth Fury, a big-ass American car with a peeling vinyl top that looked as though a cat had clawed it and rusted metal underneath. A squared off body, wide enough to hold a V8. Old California license plates, yellow lettering on blue. The body painted the color of lime Kool-Aid. And he was sure it was the same car that hit K. J.

K. J. had suffered compound fractures in his leg from the hit-and-run, and he now had thirteen titanium screws in his tibia and fibula. After several painful operations and physical therapy, he was walking on crutches and almost ready to go back to school. When Mitch told him that he'd spotted the car, the first thing he asked was whether he'd recognized the driver or not.

"Somebody from high school, I'm pretty sure. He had curly hair, and a girl with him. But I only saw it from the back."

"And you didn't get the license plate."

"No."

"Shit." K. J. thought for a second. "If it's a guy from school, I bet he drives and parks in the same block most every day. See if you can spot it and make whose it is. I'll be back in a couple of days, and we'll figure out how to take care of him."

"'Kay."

After Mitch left, K. J. took up his crutches and poled his way around the living room. He was ready to go back to school, past ready. He wanted to be back with his friends, back to being the smart kid in the group, the leader. He wanted to be back at his job, working as a busboy in a local steak house, getting a cut of the tips and sometimes a joint or two. He was sick of being the crip and sick of being stuck home. He hated his parents' house. As he swung around on his crutches, he scowled at the frilly country-kitchen curtains his mother had put up and enjoyed, the decorative plates with yellow ducklings wearing blue ribbons, the handmade birdhouse painted orange that she decided would look cute, the two-dimensional wooden angels dressed in gingham skirts with aprons. He especially despised the little framed sayings she hung up in the kitchen and the front hallway—"Rule #1: Mom is always right. Rule #2: If Mom is not right, see Rule #1." "The Lord is my Shepherd, I shall not want." Some of them hand lettered, some done in needlepoint and bought at craft fairs. All of them claiming without fear of contradiction that this was a happy family in a happy home.

K. J.'s parents had bought this house—ranch style, three bedrooms, one bath, built on a slab—in 1987, when his brother was three and he was a newborn. It was a Braden-built house in a sixties suburb called "Revere Montclair," poorly planned and poorly constructed. But it was California real estate, and they'd felt like successes when they closed on it, and K. J.'s father felt secure enough in his civilian job at Moffett Field Naval Air Station that his mother quit her job to be a full-time mother.

Six years later, Moffett Field was closed, and K. J.'s father couldn't find maintenance work that paid decently and had benefits, and his mother went to work as a secretary for the school district so that they could keep up with the mortgage. K. J. always had to wait, after first grade, for his unemployed father to pick him up. When his father finally found work, it was helping to lay carpets, truck and toolbox work, irregular hours. He later trained as a cable installer and worked hooking up houses for cable TV and then satellite TV and the Internet. But he didn't work for one of the big companies that might have given him some security. Installation work was contracted out, to small companies that bid low against each other and kept a cap on wages.

K. J. watched his father's attitude toward the world, sometimes anger, sometimes a certain bitter pride that he was making it despite the fact that the kind of job he'd thought he would have had vanished. He heard his father complain about how much a broken leg cost, how the insurance co-pays added up, how the system was rigged to soak normal people. And he had seen his brother, on graduating in the year 2000, look around and decide that the army was better than any other option he had.

The broken leg forced K. J. to sit still, and he didn't like it. He couldn't make money at the restaurant. He couldn't drive the car and talk to girls, or hang with his friends. And he wondered what would happen if the screws in his legs kept him out of the army. He refused to live like his father and feel screwed every day. And his friends felt the same about their old men. They all planned to go in a group and enlist together. K. J. didn't know what he'd do if he couldn't join up.

When Mitch brought over the forbidden Grand Theft Auto to play while his parents were out, he began to dwell on that piece-of-shit car that ran him over and wish that the game was real and that he could hold an AK-47 or a Micro Uzi to the head of the driver, and tell him to get out, and watch him exit the car with his hands over his head and fear in his eyes. K. J., holding the gun on him, could feel himself in control, could feel himself become exactly the person he wanted to be.

He'd been getting homework assignments over the computer, and his parents preferred that he spend time online instead of just playing games while he was recuperating. They thought as long as he was on the computer and it wasn't pornography, he was learning something. So he began to search the Net for means of revenge. It gave him a goal while he was online. Pipe bombs. Timing devices. The oxidizer and the combustible. The mechanics of explosions. None of it seemed difficult.

· · · • · · ·

Carter drove to school every day he thought he could get away with it. His grandfather didn't seem to mind or perhaps didn't notice. He'd had one more chemo session and was recovering and was usually still resting when Carter left for school. And his mother didn't know, since she left for work early and came back late and seemed distracted when she was home. And it made Blossom Haven very happy every time he said he could drive her home from school. They held hands during lunch, and she put her head in his lap on the way home, and then they sat with each other in the evening at rehearsals. His grandfather, when he wasn't with Nu, looked upon them benevolently, like an old god who knew everything and was beyond approving or disapproving.

One time, Blossom Haven invited him into the apartment where she lived with her mother. The apartment had no front hallway, and Carter noticed, as he walked in, that the living room had no sofa. There was a collapsible metal massage table near the counter that separated the kitchen area from the rest of the living room and a small Buddhist altar made up of brightly colored scarves draped over three tiers of cardboard boxes against one of the windowless walls. Purple and blue meditation pillows sat on the floor near the altar, and yoga mats were rolled up neatly in the corner. A low shelf held foam blocks and straps and eyebags for yoga practice, along with a small stereo to provide ambient music. There were posters on the wall of Indian men in white robes and a very large poster from a Buffalo Springfield concert at the Fillmore in the late sixties. Blossom Haven's mother had never been at the Fillmore because she was only six when it closed, but she still felt nostalgia for times past.

"Where do you sit?" Carter asked.

"On the floor," she said. She pulled up two of the squat meditation pillows near the altar and told Carter to sit on one while she lit two sticks of incense. Carter sat with his long legs crossed at the ankles and his bony knees sticking way out on either side. Blossom Haven instructed him to keep his back straight, like a tree growing toward heaven, and place his hands palm up over his knees. She sat down comfortably on a pillow beside his.

"Now, concentrate on thinking about nothing." Blossom Haven was trying to recall some of the things her mother said to begin meditation practice, but she knew she was leaving things out. "Your mind is like a monkey, always ready to scramble away. When it does that, notice it, and bring your monkey mind back to center."

"Okay." Carter sat quietly and glanced sideways at Blossom Haven. She had her eyes closed, and the thumb of each hand formed a circle with her index finger. Carter touched thumb and forefinger in the same way. He found himself thinking about sex. He'd been masturbating more frequently since Blossom Haven had introduced him to oral sex. He wondered if this was normal, or if he was a pervert. He thought sex should take the place of masturbation, but it seemed to make it worse. The more sex he had, the more he wanted it. Was that normal? The morning shower was the best time, since he knew nobody would disturb him. The rest of the day was a problem. He hated sharing a bathroom with his mother. He'd had his own bathroom at their old house in Oak Commons, but he hadn't needed it as much then as he did now. Having his own bathroom again would be great. Or being married.

"Monkey Mind," Blossom Haven said.

"Oh." Carter realized his pants were bulging out. He looked over at Blossom Haven. Her eyes were closed, and she breathed in and out with a deep sound from the back of her throat.

Carter closed his eyes and tried to breathe rhythmically, like her. He decided to center his meditation on the last email his father had sent. The subject line simply read "Hi from Las Vegas."

Hi from Las Vegas. Hi from Las Vegas.

Hi from Las Vegas.

Hi.

Minutes passed. From the center of the deleted message, an image of his father appeared. There were no words. Just his father, alone at a kitchen table. As Carter meditated, he realized that he recognized the kitchen table. It was a table with a fake wood grain, and they had that kitchen table not at the Oak Commons house but at the little house they had owned when Carter was born.

His father was waiting for something. That's what Carter felt as he concentrated on the image. He wondered whether he was remembering a specific time he had seen his father at that table, and what he was waiting for, or whether this was simply a general feeling that had floated up from thinking about what his father wanted from him.

"Now," Blossom Haven said, "think about someone you have trouble with. Bring them into the room and say, 'May you be well, may you be happy.'"

Carter brought himself back to concentrating on the image. Father waiting. For him? For his mother? For someone, something, to tell him he was well, his path was a right one? It would have been easier to have a father who simply knew he was well. But how many of those were there, really? Perhaps they were all filled with doubts, all waiting for self-assurance. And with his father, more than most, those needs were open and exposed.

Father waiting. May you be well, may you be happy.

He'd talked with Blossom Haven about *her* father. She didn't know him well. He was an optician from Redding who had met her mother in Santa Cruz when they were both in their teens, and they broke up when she wasn't willing to move with him back north. He had never understood that, for her, teaching yoga, giving massages, leading meditation groups, and joining in a drum circle weren't things that she looked on as youthful activities she would leave behind when she decided to act like an adult. They were the things of her life. Her father tried to sway Blossom Haven away from her mother by sending her Christmas and birthday gifts that might change her interests, like a microscope, a telescope, a book about being a successful teen. And when she wasn't interested, he didn't think to blame himself for not trying to understand her—he simply gave her the feeling that she didn't meet his standards.

Blossom Haven told Carter that his father was showing more interest in him than her father had ever shown in her. She would have been happy to have one message from him in six months. Carter's father was trying, at least.

Father waiting.

Carter heard a small chime and opened his eyes. Blossom Haven had tapped a small tubular bell lying horizontal in a polished wooden case to signal the end of meditation.

"How was it?" she asked.

"Great, I think."

"You're the only guy who has ever wanted to meditate with me," she said.

Carter thought about the daily email message from his father. Every time he marked a message for the trash and then told his email to dump the trash, he saw a dialogue box pop up and ask, "Are you sure you want to expunge the selected messages?" *Expunge*. It seemed so much more definitive than *delete*. He'd looked it up in the dictionary, and it meant to obliterate completely, annihilate. In other words, are you sure you want to annihilate the selected message? And the word came from Latin, *ex = out* and *pungere = to prick*. Carter had smiled, thinking about obliterating the old prick. And when the dialogue box came up, he always clicked on "Yes."

That evening after rehearsal, when he booted up his computer, he thought about reading the message. He didn't tell himself he would answer it, didn't promise to himself he would show it to his mother. But perhaps he wouldn't expunge it. Maybe that's what his meditation was telling him to do.

He logged on to his email server and was astounded to find no message from his father. Nothing at all. His father had not missed a single day for weeks, ever since he left the car in the driveway. Carter had come to depend on receiving that gesture from his father in his in-box. It was like a daily affirmation of his father's need for him and his own power to choose whether to respond to that need or not. It was all right for him to choose to delete the messages and keep his father waiting. But he hadn't foreseen that his father might have some choice in it as well. Carter felt betrayed.

He checked his email account again in the morning before he drove to school. Nothing. At lunch, he and Blossom Haven sat cross-legged facing each other for fifteen minutes on a bench outside the Drama Building, and he meditated on where his father might be. He began to wonder whether his father was in trouble, in danger, lost in the desert in Nevada. As he meditated, he saw a cartoonish image of his father, crawling on his hands and knees through a two-dimensional yellow sand landscape, a three-day growth of beard on his chin, his face haggard, his clothes tattered, a buzzard sitting on the branch of a nearby Joshua tree with black-eyed anticipation. That would explain the missing email.

Carter talked with Blossom Haven that afternoon as they walked toward the Fury, trying to think through what might be happening with his father and how he should feel about it. He didn't notice until they were on the same block as the car that two boys wearing hoodies and blue jeans were lounging against it.

Mitch pushed his hood back, and their eyes met. Carter thought briefly about walking by them, pretending he had no connection to the car, but he saw from Mitch's look of recognition that it was already too late. He had seen the way Carter reacted to them leaning arrogantly against the fenders.

"It's you?" Mitch exclaimed. "This is too fucking good."

"Yeah," Brownie added.

Carter stopped cautiously a short distance from the Fury. Blossom Haven stayed half a step behind him. "What's up?" he asked.

"This your car?" Mitch asked.

"What if it is?"

"We're looking for the guy who was driving this car. Last month. The day K. J. got his leg broken."

"What?"

"You know who it is, don't you? We know it wasn't you."

Carter remembered the note from his father. The way the car gleamed on the driveway. Newly washed. Polished. Detailed. Clean of evidence.

"If I know," Carter said, "I'm not telling you."

"No?"

"Why don't you call the police if you think this is the car?"

"We don't need the cops," Mitch said. "What do you think, Brownie? You think he knows?"

"Yeah," Brownie said.

"Or maybe his *girlfriend* knows," Mitch said. He used the word *girlfriend* as though he didn't think too much of it. "What do you say, Blossom? You still like riding in cars with boys?"

"No," she said in a small voice.

"Hey!" A man's voice hailed them from the end of the block.

Mr. Johnson was walking toward them with his always-energetic stride. Mr. Johnson worked at the high school, but the students didn't know exactly what his position was. He didn't seem to have an office, or if he did, nobody had ever seen him in it. He spent the school days walking around, keeping arguments from starting, keeping fights from breaking out, keeping couples from being too hands-on during school hours. He was always walking, with a fine round paunch swelling out a short-sleeved white shirt and a muddy-colored tie, showing up just before trouble broke out. He wore his black hair slicked back, accentuating his widow's peak, and he had sharp black eyes and a sharp nose and a penetrating voice. When he saw a boy and girl embracing, he relished the chance to call out in a loudly embarrassing way "Gettin' pretty friendly!"

Mr. Johnson lived in the neighborhood and walked to and from the school nearly every day in the mild California autumn, and he'd never hesitated to carry his school-authority voice into the streets around the school. Mitch and Brownie stood upright as he approached, put their hands in their pockets, looked at the ground.

"You can't hang out here, guys," Mr. Johnson said. "The neighbors will call the police on you for loitering. Whose car?"

"Mine," Carter said.

"You all leaving together?" He looked at Mitch and Brownie and kept them pinned with his eyes until Mitch scuffed the cement with his shoe.

"Naw," he said.

"All right, then. You," he said to Carter and Blossom Haven, "head out. And you two better walk on home."

Carter opened the door for Blossom Haven and then got into the driver's seat. He was glad Mr. Johnson hadn't thought about his age and asked to see his driver's license. In the rearview mirror, he saw Mitch and Brownie slouch back in the direction of the high school and Mr. Johnson begin again with his quick stride.

He drove Blossom Haven to her mother's apartment, but they didn't talk much. Carter felt humiliated that he needed Mr. Johnson's help to get into the car, and Blossom Haven had seen his powerlessness. And he was beginning to feel uncomfortable thinking about guys Blossom Haven had been with before him. He hadn't thought about it before, but after Mitch asked her if she still liked riding in cars, he remembered her saying that he was the first guy who would meditate with her, and he remembered her saying *Guys like this*. What guys? How did she know?

They said they'd see each other at rehearsal, but Carter was holding himself stiffly and Blossom Haven understood that a distance had grown between them and she didn't try to hug him.

Carter drove through the quiet blocks of low ranch houses, past the one with the fake window shutters, past the one with the cement oriental lantern near a dry stone riverbed and a Japanese maple, past the small front lawns shaped with curvilinear cement edging and bordered by fall flowers and junipers. He wanted to speed, but the roads were a little too narrow and had gentle swerves at random intervals. He parked the car in the driveway of his grandfather's house and leaped from the car and went directly to his computer, without even announcing he was home.

There was still no email from his father, so he hit "Compose" and began to write.

Hi, Dad:

Some boys today claimed that the Fury hit one of their friends and broke his leg. They say they recognized it. They're like a gang, and they asked me who was driving the car, but I didn't say anything. What happened? Can you come back?

I miss you.

Carter

10

HENRY WAS DUE for a CT scan, and Carter stayed home from school to drive him. Henry teased his grandson about whether he could take a day away from his girlfriend, and Carter had turned quiet, but Henry took the long view of such things and thought that ups and downs between teenagers were nothing extraordinary.

For Henry, a scan was at best a way to reset the clock. If he had a scan, and it showed the lesions on his liver were the same size, then he could believe that the chemo protocol he was on was good for another few months. He knew what palliative care meant, and he knew that treating cancer as a chronic disease was just a way of talking. It could be revealed as a flimsy stage set of a life anytime cancer cells stopped responding to treatment. He had already had two crises. The first when they thought they had completely killed the tumors through surgery and chemotherapy, used the magic word *remission*, stopped treatment altogether. In six weeks, the lesions were back, and he was put on a regular once-every-three-weeks regimen. The second when the cocktail of poisons stopped working and a scan showed two lesions on his liver growing larger, and he had to switch to a new protocol, with a new set of pains to adjust to.

But he had adjusted. Once, when he was with Nu behind the theater, he'd asked her why she liked being around an old wreck like him. Nu had looked up at him, raised an eyebrow.

"You've obviously never been a sixty-year-old unattached woman," she said drily.

"So I'm the best of a poor lot." They laughed, and Henry said, "Well, I'll take that. Can't expect much more at my age."

He looked at her, the bright eyes in her lined face. "You know, the kind of surgery I've had done."

"I know." She put a hand on his shoulder. "You're still interested in life. You think there are still things to find out about. That's why I like being around you."

She'd told him something about himself there, and he knew it. Even with regular fathoms of pain, he still found the world an interesting place, and he was in no hurry to leave. He liked having his grandson around to surprise him with a girlfriend, he liked seeing his daughter fall in love in her forties, he liked looking forward to seeing Nu and laughed at the idea of smoking his first marijuana when he was eighty-one. He might find out, from today's scan, that his clock was winding down, and there was no guarantee that a new protocol would work. But he might not. He didn't want to let Caliban take away the savor of each day. There were so many reasons to live.

He and Carter stopped by the break room to say hello to the oncology nurses before he checked in. Henry loved the nurses, especially Diane, who had been on the unit for many years. She was originally from New Orleans and still had some of that gentle lengthening of vowels in her speech, and she liked being bossy with her patients. "Now one day after treatment," she would say, "*one day* can be a jammie day. You can stay in your jammies all day long and feel sorry for yourself. But after that, you get your ass out of bed!" Henry liked being bossed by her, in that accent, and liked talking back. "What if the spirit is willing, but the ass is weak?" he asked. And they could laugh, even when she was getting ready to hook him up to an intravenous drip through the Mediport implanted in his chest.

When she knew that his condition was chronic and that he would be coming in on an ongoing basis, she gentled with him. "These others, I want them to see me as someone to get beyond. But you've got to like coming in to see me, so I'll be nice to you."

Henry and Carter found her sitting on a plastic chair at a small table in the break room, a narrow space with a refrigerator and microwave and two coffeemakers that were largely unused since a Starbucks had opened nearby. When she saw Henry, her plucked eyebrows, dyed red to match her hair, arced up.

"You're not here to see me today," she said. "You just turn around and march your ass on out of here."

Henry smiled. "CT scan," he said.

"Oh." She knew better than to say that she was sure everything would be fine or even that she hoped everything would be fine. She didn't know how anything would be, and she didn't want to be part of anyone's disappointed hopes. And she knew that Henry didn't expect her to say something bright and optimistic. Those kinds of words didn't mean much.

"And I thought I'd see who you liked at Golden Gate Fields today." Henry knew she liked the races, and they always talked handicapping together.

"Any horse being ridden by Russell Baze," she said. "How are you, Carter?"

"Fine," Carter said.

"He has himself a girlfriend," Henry said.

"Well, that doesn't surprise me a bit, handsome as he is," she said. She liked making people blush.

Henry gave her a little wave. "See you soon."

"You bet, honey," she said.

Carter walked with his grandfather to the counter and watched while he gave his information to a woman behind the desk, who printed out a small paper band and wrapped it around his wrist. Then his grandfather was escorted through some double swinging doors, wide enough for a gurney to fit through, and Carter walked to the waiting area he had grown used to in the time he'd been coming to the oncology unit. The waiting room, a beige-carpeted space open to the corridor, was hushed and calm. The area had a number of cloth-covered sofas and love seats arranged around coffee tables and end tables spread with magazines. There were lamps on the end tables, but most of the light came from the banks of fluorescent bulbs overhead. Carter had developed a little ritual while waiting for his grandfather here. He walked a slow circle around the carpets, looking at the large framed posters on the wall that showed scenes of beauty, like a soaring eagle or a lighthouse shining through a dark storm, with captions underneath counseling

Vigilance, or Courage, or Fortitude. Then he chose a certain love seat with its back to the wall. He could keep watch over the quiet hospital traffic from here, and nothing could sneak up on him. He'd sat in this same spot every time, and so far his grandfather had been fine.

Carter rarely spoke to anyone in the waiting area. Even though it was arranged to resemble a living room, each person seemed to hover within a self-contained sphere of anxious hopefulness, so Carter retreated within his own sphere, hiding behind a book. He had learned to watch but not be noticed watching when truly sick people were helped by or wheeled by, people whose faces were haunted and gaunt and hollow. When he saw a boy or girl walk by wearing a paper cap, he had learned to whisper *leukemia* to himself and avoid meeting their eyes. He kept lookout silently and subtly, and if he went unnoticed, it made him feel safe, as though he had kept something at bay.

A television was suspended from the ceiling in one corner of the area, but it was muted, showing the face of Donald Rumsfeld with block letters appearing above his right ear. Carter watched his lips move, then settled in to his spot with the book he was reading for English class, *Lord of the Flies*. When his mother saw the book, she exclaimed that she had read the same book in high school. She couldn't remember much, but she thought that a character named Piggy wore glasses, and that symbolized wisdom. When the glasses were broken, things went downhill. And she asked him if they were going to read *A Separate Peace* as well. Carter said he didn't think so, and she said good, she'd hated that book.

Carter began to read about the boys marooned on an island. It sounded cool, like that other book he liked about a boy who went to live in the woods and built himself a home inside a tree. He wondered if the class was going to talk about it today. He would miss it. That would make two days in a row of class he missed, once because he had faked feeling sick and once because of his grandfather. He couldn't keep skipping school, just to avoid K. J.'s crew. But he didn't know if it was better to drive in the car they said hit him or to walk and try to escape notice that way. He remembered being thrown into a Dumpster twice while walking home, so that wasn't safe. Maybe being marooned with boys wouldn't be so great.

He wondered about driving and Blossom Haven as well. If he walked, they wouldn't be able to drive around together. But he'd begun to wonder just what she'd done with other boys before she got together with him. Why couldn't he be the first boy she'd been with, just like she was the first girl he'd been with? Was someone's love less love if it had been given before?

He looked down at his book again. There was Piggy. Wisdom in a pair of glasses, knowing how to master fire. He grew into the book, reading and only occasionally glancing up at the quiet passage of hospital traffic along the polished tile corridor. Time passed, and there was his grandfather, smiling before him, and Carter marked his place in the book. They were leaving the hospital, safe once more.

· · · • · · ·

Scott awoke in a tangle of six-hundred-thread-count sheets and was immediately aware of his penis. It felt as though an army of tiny men had spent the night jumping up and down on it. It felt as though someone had attached a block and tackle to it and stretched it out like an elastic band and then let it snap back and flap against his balls. It felt as though a clown had attached it to a helium tank and blown it up like a balloon and then tied knots in it so that it resembled a dachshund, before letting the air escape and seeing it deflate in a limp *pfffft*. He was usually completely unaware of his penis first thing in the morning except for the need to pee. At some point, waking up with an erection had been replaced by waking up with a bladder in undeniable stress. Perhaps that was a measure of age. He swung his legs over the edge of the bed and cradled himself. In the dim light, it looked utterly normal and harmless. Yet every molecule of it seemed sentient and suffering and determined to ache its way into his consciousness.

He stood up, disoriented. The room was filled with a half-light through the heavy drapes, and a dull thud and hum came from somewhere outside. He had no idea what time it was. He turned around once, the carpet plush under his bare feet. There were the cardinal points of nearly every hotel room he'd ever stayed in to anchor him. An armoire with a television enclosed in the upper half. A chest of drawers. A table with two padded chairs near the window. A king-size bed with tiny lamps on matching night tables. It was growing familiar to him.

He saw in the bed the rounded rump of Helen, covered in a white sheet, as she slept on her side with her back toward him. An odd sound exited her, something like a wet washcloth dropped on the floor.

His pants were hitched carelessly over one of the padded chairs, and as he looked at them, an image formed in his head. An image of a large number of black chips at the cashier's window. Placed in identical stacks, counted and recounted. Then hundred-dollar bills being counted out for him, piles of them. And his travel wallet growing bloated and gross with them and some of them going in the front pocket of that pair of pants.

He lunged toward the chair and fell on his knees beside it. Helen gave out a snarfing sound. He groped at his pants, rumpling them between his hands until he felt the comforting bulge of his wallet, the solid wad of cash in the pocket. It was there, all there, and he rocked back onto his bare buttocks. Then, quietly, he got dressed.

Counted up on the table, the money amounted to more than twenty thousand dollars. More money than he'd had when he was paid off from his ship. He sat with his back to the curtained window, his pants now on, looking past the money to Helen still sleeping. He found himself speculating how long he could live in this hotel room, just live there. Something about the room, in its anonymity, in its interchangeability, in its complete lack of distinctiveness, made it seem cut off from the past and the future. It had always existed as it did now, always would exist as it did at this present moment. How long could he stay, separated from past difficulties, severed from consequences? The room could contain such a life. How long, just living there, before something caught up with him?

He stood up and went to the window. It was eleven. The light and heat tensed behind the curtain. He drew back the edge and saw the boom of a construction crane, rising thirty stories from street level. Below, the noise of construction rumbled, carpenters building forms, welders placing rebar, cement trucks coming and going over the pounded earth. The sun was out, and the heat, even in November, seemed to fade and curl the mountained horizon, giving the land a weathered and yellowed look.

He gathered up the cash and shoved some into the wallet he wore around his neck, the rest into his pockets and folding wallet. Then he leaned over the bed.

"Helen," he said quietly.

"Mmmm." Sleepily, she reached out and cupped a hand around his right buttock. He started back, but she held him with a positive force, so that he had to continue with his thighs pressed against the bed.

"I'll go down to the café and get us coffee and croissants," he said. "And then we can go out for breakfast."

"Mmm-hmm." She tightened her hold on him and pulled. Her fingers were burrowing to a region where no one's fingers but his own and his proctologist's had been for many years.

"So should I go?" he asked, leaning forward to lessen the pressure.

"Mmmm. Ysss."

"Yes?"

"Mmm-hmm."

"Okay." He reached back and loosened her death grip and then patted her hand. On his way to the door, he saw the black padded case that held his laptop. It seemed to beckon him, not with the file of his novel, Greatscott.doc, which he realized had only two words in it: Chapter One. Rather, it beckoned him with the promise of connection, beyond this hotel room, beyond the broad desert valley that held Las Vegas. He slipped it off the dresser and stole into the hallway, closing the door behind him with a firm pneumatic seal.

The casino floor was quieter. Dealers stood attentively behind several blackjack tables, waiting for players, and only a single craps table was in action. Electric chimes burbled up from the banks of slot machines, but only a few tourists who would be catching a morning flight were playing. Scott walked back along Le Boulevard, along the fake cobblestones and artificial trees, and found JJ's Boulangerie, where he'd been so creative the day before. It wasn't crowded, and when he asked for two croissants and two lattes to go, the barista told him to have a seat and she would bring the lattes out to him.

As he waited, he decided it wouldn't hurt to check email quick. Helen was still half asleep. He flipped open the laptop, and this time saw that he had a WiFi connection. While he was waiting for his login screen, he began munching on one of the croissants.

His in-box showed a message entitled "Your Best Self." It was from the workshop, cheerily encouraging everyone to reflect on the progress they had made that day, so they could build on it further. The next message had a subject line that read "Hi from Bette Cochran," and even though his daughter's name was misspelled, he thought it might be from her, so he opened it. A woman's face appeared on the screen above the question "Would you like to see me? Click here for hot photos."

The barista brought his two lattes, glanced at the screen, then glanced away. Scott quickly pressed "Delete," which brought up a screen offering to increase his penis size, a prospect that made him involuntarily clamp his thighs together in a protective gesture.

He dipped his half-eaten croissant into the latte and bit down. It was delicious, butter, milk fats, and caffeine. He realized he was famished and gobbled the rest down.

Back in his in-box, he set about deleting spam without reading the messages. His filter was not working or needed updating, he decided.

When he scrubbed one screen of new messages, a second screen appeared, and he saw the message from Carter. The subject line said "Help."

He felt himself suddenly breathing hard, and he grabbed the second croissant. He hadn't received an email from his son since he had come to Las Vegas, but this one showed that he wasn't forgotten, that he was needed. *Help*. He opened the message and saw what Carter had written, and he felt himself unthinking and guilty, stupid to have left that car with his family, naive to think nothing would come of it, whether or not it could be identified to the police. At the same time, he felt grateful to be called back into the drama of his family's life by his son, grateful that the strange hiatus in Las Vegas was all coming to an end. He would rather be connected through error and crime than isolated and without consequence, and he wondered for a moment if he had left that car expecting at some point the very message he saw before him.

He ate the rest of Helen's croissant and made for the door of the casino. A taxi took him to a strip of used-car lots west of the Strip, places where cars were parked at the front of the lot with their hoods up and poster boards propped over their engines spelling out B-I-G S-A-L-E. He had the taxi cruise slowly until he saw it, a '97 Mustang, yellow with a black ragtop, gleaming on a grassy mound at the corner of the lot. Within an hour, paying out half his cash, he was on Interstate 15, driving southwest, aiming around the southern edge of Death Valley toward Barstow, Tehachapi, Bakersfield, and then over to Interstate 5 and up the long Central Valley of California until he could jump over to San José. To home.

· · · • · · ·

Carter noticed his grandfather walking a little more quickly than normal on their way out of the hospital. He didn't have to slow his pace to walk beside his grandfather, as he normally did. They walked down the quiet corridors, past the pharmacy, past the line of wheelchairs waiting in the open and airy atrium, through two sets of sliding doors, and out onto the covered circular drive at the hospital entrance. Then his grandfather stopped and leaned over and braced his hands on his knees. He was breathing heavily.

"Carter, can you bring the car around for your grandfather?" he asked.

"Sure." Carter hesitated. "Did you need to make an appointment to find out about your results?"

"There's time enough for that," Henry said.

"But you've always done it right away."

"You know what your grandmother would have said. 'Good news will wait, and bad news will refuse to go away.'" He patted Carter on the shoulder. "I'm sorry you never knew your grandmother, Carter. She would have liked you."

They drove in quiet toward the house. Henry watched the strip malls and the big-box stores set back behind acres of asphalt pass by the windows. Carter's show opened in a week, on a Thursday. He'd scheduled a chemo treatment for the Friday following. The bowling alley and the café were going out of business that weekend. He had a bad feeling about the CT scan he'd just had, and he wondered if he felt as good now as he ever would.

"Why don't you drop me at the Garden Spot?" he said. "One of my buddies will bring me home."

"You're sure?" Carter asked.

"You'll be safe enough driving six blocks," Henry said. "And I'll be home in time to go to rehearsal with you."

"Okay."

The parking lot of the bowling alley was nearly deserted, except for a little clot of cars around the entrance that led directly into the restaurant. The last league play had ended a few days earlier, and there was seldom much traffic in early afternoon. Carter pulled near the curb and watched his grandfather get out. He waited until he saw him walk up three steps, pull open the glass door, and step inside.

When Carter turned down Catesby Street, a chunk of yellow disturbed his vision. It broke up the normal line of lawns, green hedges, leafy trees, the parklike setback behind which sat the ranch houses of the subdivision, the array of small landscapes he had grown used to. The yellow was in his driveway. A yellow Mustang. And he knew who was leaning his butt against the front fender.

Carter saw his father grin as he pulled the Fury alongside the curb. He was wearing khakis and a loose shirt open at the throat, like he'd just come from a resort, and Carter found the grin irksome. It looked like he felt he should be congratulated just for showing up.

"Bet you didn't think I'd get here so fast," Scott called.

"No, I didn't." Carter walked up the drive, and his father went in for the hug, masculine, all chest and shoulders.

"Nice car," Carter said.

"Yeah." Scott gave another version of that self-satisfied smile. "I see you've been getting some use out of the Fury."

"I've got to be the one taking Grandpa to the hospital now," Carter said. "He crashed his car."

"Was he hurt?"

"No, but the car was totaled."

"Well, then, it's even better that I left you the Fury."

He smiled again his irritating smile. Carter thought of all the things that had happened in the weeks since he'd seen his father. The pieces of his life were sliding like the floor of a fun house. His mother's growing absences. The place he thought he was finding at the theater, helped by his grandfather. His worries about his grandfather's health. Blossom Haven, the sudden commitment they had to each other, that he now didn't trust. And the threat from the boys who identified the car.

His father, standing now in front of him, seemed an unlikely choice to bring it all into order. He wondered now why he'd emailed him, when so much of it seemed to be his fault.

"The Fury is great," Carter said. "Except you ran somebody over with it."

"No, I didn't."

"You didn't?"

"If somebody got hit, it was some other car. There must be lots of old Furies around."

Scott had been practicing that line on the drive from Las Vegas. Lots of Furies around.

"Tons of 'em," he continued. "Furies abound." Even with practice, it sounded like a lie.

"They're probably going to try to beat me up the next time I go to school." Carter spoke in a tone that asked, *What are you going to do about it?*

"They can't prove anything."

"That doesn't matter to them."

"Okay. Well, let's try to be smart here."

"Smart?" Carter asked skeptically.

"Yes. Smart. Motivating success." He said that they had to think through the obstacles that were standing in the way of their desired outcome. Once they had identified the obstacles, they could motivate themselves to overcome them.

"So," Scott said, "what's the first obstacle?"

Carter thought his father had gone a little crazy, wherever he'd been. But he had an idea. He thought about what Betty would do. She would turn this into a situation that could get her what she wanted. And what Carter wanted right now was the Mustang. It was almost new. It had a multidisk CD player. It wasn't a beater car. It was probably faster than the Tiburon. It was cool.

"The first obstacle is that they see me driving the car that broke K. J.'s leg," Carter said.

"The car they *think* broke his leg," Scott corrected.

"Okay," Carter said, neither agreeing nor disagreeing.

"So. You could not drive to school."

Carter gave him a look that told him that he'd made a suggestion that was stupid and without any merit whatsoever.

"I was just thinking out loud," Scott said. "Dreamstorming."

"At night? I have to drive to rehearsal. And I take Grandpa with me." He explained that he was in *The Tempest,* and his grandfather had become friends with his drama teacher. Not taking a car wasn't an option.

"It opens next week," he said.

"Mom can't take you?"

"Mom's busy."

"Is she working late?"

"I guess. She doesn't say." Carter didn't want to let his father in on much. That's how he thought Betty would operate. Once you let information out, you no longer have control over it.

"She's working too hard," Scott said. "Does she know about these three boys? What they said about the car?"

"No."

"Good. She's got enough on her plate to worry about." Scott felt relieved. He was sure that she would immediately have believed that he had committed a hit-and-run. And she would blame him for leaving the car for Carter to drive, even though it had obviously come in handy. She was inclined to think the worst of him right now and would take the word of some hoodlums over his. Even if they were telling the truth, that didn't make it right.

"I've got an idea, Dad," Carter said.

"Yeah?"

"You could leave me the Mustang. You take the Fury."

"Oh. Huh."

"I know Mom would appreciate it. Even without knowing about the boys. The Mustang's a lot newer, and I bet it's more dependable."

"It's newer all right." Scott looked at the yellow Mustang, bright and shiny, and then over at the Fury, old hubcaps nicked up, the dull aqua green and the ripped vinyl roof. He had enjoyed driving the Mustang back from Las Vegas, enjoyed thinking of himself as a winner, someone who just won a new car at the craps tables and was now coming back to help his son out of a jam. He'd wondered, as he passed cars up on Interstate 5, if they saw him and wondered what his errand was, wondered about the glamour and drama of his life. He enjoyed thinking of himself through Carter's eyes, thinking how he appeared, leaning against the fender of a shiny new car, suave, calm.

"It would take care of the first obstacle," Carter said. "K. J. himself hasn't seen the Fury. He just came back to school yesterday."

"So . . ."

"So then they *really* wouldn't be able to prove anything," Carter said. "They won't do anything without K. J. telling them to. And if he isn't sure, I'm safe."

"I want you to be safe, of course."

"I know you do, Dad."

Carter's smile looked guileless and genuine. Scott began to feel trapped. He tried to think about some other way to overcome the first obstacle. Take Carter with him back to Vegas. Win enough to buy a second car. Return driving a pair of Mercedes.

It didn't seem too likely.

"Okay," Scott said. "Okay. But you have to promise me something."

Carter nodded.

"Promise you won't tell your mother anything about these boys and what they're saying."

"Okay."

"And promise you'll tell her that I wanted you to be safe. I'll see her soon. We have to talk because I might be going back to Iraq."

"I'll tell her."

They exchanged keys, and Scott walked down the driveway to the Fury, the car he'd bought eight weeks earlier when he first got back to the States. Carter watched him go, the shirt seeming a little less elegant, clinging a bit to the curves of flesh on either side of his spine, the khakis bunched up around the belt loops in the back. The back of a man nearing fifty.

"Hey, Dad."

Scott turned.

"Mom bought a book on divorce. I saw her reading it." After the car, Carter wanted to give his father something in return. "I thought you should know."

"Thanks," Scott said. "I need to work on that."

Carter watched his father drive down the street, turn the corner, head out of the subdivision on Country Lane Road. Then he walked all around the Mustang. He ran his hands down the fenders. He tried the key in the door, making it lock and unlock several times. He sat in the driver's seat and put his key in the ignition.

He wished he could see himself. He wished a movie camera was rolling that would show him in the driver's seat, turning the key, hearing the engine roar to life. He wished everyone else could see him.

That last part was easy. He looked at his watch and saw that school let out in fifteen minutes. He put the car in reverse, backed out onto the street, and drove to school.

The Drama Building was set back from the street and parking lot, so he couldn't drive by the benches where he'd expect Cal and the others to be. He cruised by the side of the school where they might be walking out, but he didn't see them.

He hadn't talked with Blossom Haven for two days, since he dropped her off after their run-in with Mitch and Brownie. He'd missed one night of rehearsal, two days of school. He hadn't emailed her or ɪᴍ'd her or called her. He'd been embarrassed and uncertain and hurt, not thinking that she might feel the same. And if his solution for his feelings was to avoid her, he didn't realize that she needed the opposite, to see him, to be assured by his presence. But now, as he drove around the school, he realized that the person he most wanted to see was her and no other.

He parked the Mustang on the same block where he had usually parked the Fury, and he ran to the school grounds to find her, before she started walking home.

· · · ● · · ·

As Carter was looking for Blossom Haven, K. J. was looking for him. He had been back in school for two days, and when class ended he gathered his crew into the Tiburon and cruised the streets surrounding the school grounds, looking for either the Fury that had hit him or for Carter, who could lead him to it. He believed Mitch, but he wanted to see the car with his own eyes before deciding what to do.

K. J. was getting most of his ideas about honor, respect, and revenge from his brother. Before checking for homework, he always looked first for an email from Iraq, from Baqubah. His brother had told him things that he didn't share with their parents. It was a goat fuck. Some soldiers in his battalion had been ᴋɪᴀ, and every night they were busting down doors, kicking ass and taking names, but they were never sure if the *hajis* they got were the right ones. They wanted an identifiable enemy—they wanted to close with the enemy and destroy him. They were infantry, and that's what they were trained to do, close and destroy, not this bullshit.

The first day back, he didn't see Carter or the Fury. He drove with the others up and down the street where they'd spotted the Fury before, but didn't find anything like it, and he drove along the route where they had jumped Carter and thrown him in the Dumpster. Brownie and Mitch were happy to be riding around again, and they tried to make jokes and keep everything light, but K. J. thought he needed an identifiable target to strike back at, just like his brother, and he was in a foul mood when they found nothing.

The next day, on their second loop around, Brownie spotted Carter and Blossom Haven together, crossing the street away from school.

"There they are," he said.

K. J. pulled the car to the curb. He saw them turn down the same side street where Mitch had seen them before.

"Let's give them a couple minutes," he said. "Bet we catch them right by that piece-of-shit car."

They waited, tense and silent. Then K. J. pulled forward and turned right. There were many cars parked along the street and cars parked in the driveways between the squares of green lawn, and at first he didn't see them. He thought he'd lost them in the landscape of cars, none of which resembled a 1977 Fury. But a block up, he saw two people standing, pausing beside a car, and one of them bend down to put a key in a door.

"That's them."

He stepped on the gas. He had a new walking cast on his left leg, and he thought himself lucky that he'd never needed to learn to drive a stick shift. He saw the two people turn at the sound of his engine, and he roared beside them and stepped on the brakes.

"What the fuck?" K. J. turned to look at Mitch. Carter and Blossom Haven were standing beside a newish Ford Mustang, bright yellow, and they were staring at K. J.

Mitch gave a bewildered shrug. "That's not the car they were in before."

K. J. swung out of the driver's side, leaving his door open. His car boxed in the Mustang, and he walked around the front of it, his leather jacket bulking over his shoulders. He still walked awkwardly, unevenly.

"Hey," he said, "where's your other car?"

"I don't have another car." Carter stood close by Blossom Haven, leaning toward the passenger side of the door. He thought about pushing her inside and telling her to lock the door.

"You know what I mean. That beater car you were driving two days ago."

"That old Fury?"

"That's it. The one that broke my leg."

"How do you know it was that one? There must be lots of old Furies around." Carter heard his father's lame line come out of his mouth. And, with a kind of wonder, he saw K. J. looked confused.

"Lots of old Furies?"

"Sure," Carter said with increasing confidence. "Tons of 'em. Furies abound."

"When I see it," K. J. said, "I'll know."

"But you haven't seen it yet."

"So where is it?"

"I don't know," Carter said. "It's my father's car. He doesn't live with us anymore."

"Where does he live?"

"I don't know. He might be going back to Iraq." Carter didn't know what to believe of what his father told him, but he saw how effective it was at baffling K. J., and he was momentarily pleased with his father.

K. J. looked past Carter and Blossom Haven to where Mitch and Brownie stood. Mitch shrugged again. K. J.'s face pinched in ugly frustration. He pointed his eyes at Blossom Haven.

"Hey, flower girl," he smiled contemptuously. "You know where the car is? Bet you got a good look at it."

Blossom Haven shrank a little beside Carter. She'd been afraid this would come out. It was when she was thirteen that she found out older guys were interested in her. Because of the way she dressed, or because of the way she talked. And, growing up without a father, she was delighted that they paid attention to her, asked her to ride with them in their cars, got her high. Oral sex didn't seem like much to give in return. It gave her personality a boost, and it made her popular with a certain group of boys.

When she began to go to peace marches with her mother, and to spend time around the theater, the boys who had liked her personality began to ridicule her, and they found other thirteen- and fourteen-year-olds with good personalities. But she knew they hadn't forgotten her, and at school there was a group, including K. J., who gave her leering, knowing looks.

She looked up to Carter. Long-limbed, goofy Carter, who had come looking for her. He put his arm around her shoulder protectively, and she leaned against him.

Behind the Tiburon, a giant suv with tires the size of small elephants and dark tinted windows pulled up. The driver gave a quick honk of his horn.

Mitch closed the Tiburon's doors, but the suv still couldn't get by. It inched forward and stopped as its bumper, which was close to the level of the Tiburon's roof, was about to run a crease through the smaller car.

The driver honked again.

"Okay, okay." K. J. jerked back to the driver's side of his car, and he and his crew got in. Then he glared through an open window.

"I'm going to find that other car," he said. "Then I'll be your daddy."

He started the car and screeched away, followed by the lumbering suv.

Carter and Blossom Haven got into the Mustang. He'd wanted to impress her with the car. Now he just wanted to take her safely home.

He took her hand, to be sure of her, and stepped on the gas.

11

THE EDUCATION Heber had received in Cedar City High School had not given him a sound understanding of female anatomy. The school, though public, was almost entirely Mormon, and discussion of sex usually centered around the notion that chastity was the best form of birth control, because it was both foolproof and part of God's plan. At times, the gym teacher would read from a study that proved that condoms were ineffective against venereal disease. In halting speech, with his eyes on the paper, he informed them that the disease-carrying germs were smaller than sperm and could slip through the molecular barrier provided by latex. The analogy he used was that it was like trying to catch minnows in a basketball net. "The safest sex," he ended, "is no sex." And he pursed his lips, looked out at the fourteen- and fifteen-year-old boys, and nodded approvingly at his own words. Once, he showed a series of old slides showing penises ravaged by syphilis, and for weeks afterward the most popular locker room insult was to call someone else a syphilitic dick. Heber later figured that the presentation was meant to discourage boys from driving to Las Vegas once they were old enough and losing their virginity with a prostitute in one of the economy motels off the Strip.

Eventually, Heber gained an accurate account of what intercourse was, how children were conceived, how born. But he had still understood little until he knew Katherine. The pleasure she took with him made him think she was unique, one among women, even when she tried to convince him otherwise, and he felt he loved her completely. Yet whenever he thought himself becoming competent in his understanding of her, the messy complexities of the human body intruded. She began to talk frankly with him about her pains and cramps, the feelings of ovulation, the increasingly irregular and heavy flow of blood, the monthly rise and fall of different hormones, perimenopause. If for a time he had thought of her as possessing a constant desire for sex, as he himself did, he was beginning to modify that notion, trying to grasp the concepts of cycles and moods.

Currently, standing in the doorway of Room 12 of the El Rancho Motel, he was hearing about yeast infections for the first time and understanding that they weren't going to make love that evening. She was describing an itching, almost burning feeling, and something else. "It's kind of like cottage cheese," she said.

"Oh." He had trouble picturing this.

"One-day creams never work for me," she said. "I'll try a three-day cream. That's not too long to wait, is it?"

"No, of course not." He let himself fall back on the squishy bed, fully clothed, his arms stretched out to both sides. Katherine crawled beside him and rested her head on his chest, and they lay together, looking at the cheap furnishings on the wall. The walls of this room had prints of bullfights in flimsy brass-colored metal frames. Other rooms had images of the California missions, or the Napa Valley vineyards, or the redwood trees. Heber had held the notion that they would come back and always have the same room. He was already eager for a semblance of home with Katherine, even someplace as obviously temporary and conditional as a roadside motel. But the El Rancho didn't allow anyone to reserve individual rooms, and so they were always placed where the chance of room occupancy allowed them.

"Someday," he said, "I'd like to spend the whole night with you. Wake up together."

"That would be nice," Katherine said. She moved her cheek against his chest, feeling the silk of his tie against her skin. She was glad once again she hadn't spoiled anything. She didn't like talking about her body with him, because he was so much younger than his thirty-one years. She wished she could be as free and spontaneous as her twenty-year-old self had been, when the body's capacities had not yet begun to deviate from the mind's desire, and she'd had no notion that they ever would. But she wasn't, and so far it hadn't driven him away.

"It's not because I don't want you, you know," she said. "It has nothing to do with you."

"I know."

He had been asking to meet her family. She temporized, changed the subject, in part because she wasn't sure how to think of him. Boyfriend, lover, sexual pupil, fling, possible long-term partner? She wasn't divorced yet, either, though that seemed just another way to evade the question, since her father had grown only more open and accepting with time, and Carter was old enough not to be bruised. And Betty . . . well, Betty was Betty. To make up for the lack of sex, she invited him to the opening night of Carter's play. He could come as a friend from work, and then they could all go back to the house for ice cream. And they would see how things go.

"How does that sound?" she asked. "This Thursday."

· · · • · · ·

Two doors down, in Room 14, Scott lay on a motel bed in a posture similar to Heber's, though without Katherine's cheek against his chest. In his sickly imaginings, he saw all the different ways his wife was having sex with another man. Into his mind came step-ladders, chandeliers, trapeze swings, white silk handcuffs. It was nothing like the knowing married sex he'd had with her, a familiar path to a shared destination. It was happy and savage and cease-less. If he'd been in the next room, he would have held a water glass up to the wall, like he'd seen in old movies. The water glasses at the El Rancho were flimsy plastic, in a plastic wrapper to signify cleanliness, but he thought they would work just as well. This was the torment he sought out every night.

Scott had begun trying to shadow Katherine after he exchanged cars with Carter. He didn't know what else to do. He had accomplished nothing in the nearly two months since he'd been back. He was again driving a 1977 Fury and living in a freeway motel, and he had about the same amount of money he'd had when he first got paid off his ship. He hadn't made anything better with his wife. He hadn't made anything better with his son, though he seemed to have unwittingly given him a car. He hadn't written a book. He hadn't found a new job. He didn't have any clothes, because he'd left them all in Nevada. His leave from Military Sealift Command was almost up, and he had to make some kind of decision.

Scott knew nothing about trying to follow another car without being spotted. In the movies, the streets were dark, spotted with the hanging globes of streetlamps that illuminated only themselves, and the cars were all black and high-fendered, blending with the night. But in Silicon Valley office developments, the parking lots were broad and flat, with trees too young to offer any shade still supported by cross braces in cement planters at the end of each row of yellow lines. There was no place to lie in wait.

He found her Saturn in the lot outside BPI, and he decided to park three rows over, next to a Hummer, so she wouldn't walk past him on the way out. He wasn't sure he actually wanted to talk to her, because of what Carter had said about the divorce books. But he wanted to find out what Carter meant by saying she was always late, never at home.

After five, people began to trickle out. There wasn't a sudden rush. In Silicon Valley companies, people frequently worked into the evening. There was always some deadline, always some sense that a competitor would come out with a project first if you didn't push yourself. And sometimes there was a competition to be the last one to leave, even after productive work had stopped, to prove who was the most committed.

He spotted her around five thirty, walking out with two others, a woman and a man. He could tell it was her from a great distance by a gesture he knew, a way she had of holding up her arm and flipping her hand from the wrist in a dismissive way, to indicate that anything being discussed really wasn't worth the bother. He loved that gesture. When she made it, she was in a good mood. When he was with her and she made that gesture, it meant that the things out there weren't so very important, wouldn't come between them.

He missed that gesture.

He was about to turn the key when he heard a rap at the window. He looked up and saw a fifty-year-old man wearing camo pants and a T-shirt and a ball cap with the Hummer logo stitched on. The owner of the Hummer, grinning at him.

Scott rolled down the window.

"Hey!" the Hummer man said. "Cool ride!"

"Thanks." Scott looked up, to see if the Saturn was moving yet.

"Got to have, what, the four-barrel 400 V8? That's one hell of an engine."

"Yep."

"So what are you going to do? Strip it down and pimp it up? I know a guy."

"Sorry. Gotta run."

Scott turned the key and the engine roared.

"Whoo-wee!" The Hummer man stepped back and listened admiringly. Scott saw the man's mouth moving as he backed out, but he couldn't make out what he was saying.

Scott lost Katherine's car before he left the parking lot. He was caught in a crawl of traffic nosing toward the one exit with a traffic light, and the Saturn slipped through on a yellow light while he was still twenty cars behind. He thought he saw her take a direction away from the house on Catesby, but he couldn't be sure. When he oozed out with the next light change, he took the nearest freeway entrance and gave his four-barrel 400 V8 engine the gas. He knew it was stupid to cruise the freeways, thinking he might encounter her car. It was still rush hour. The cars were moving, but the traffic was chunky, and he felt a great anonymity now on the road, not like the glamour he'd imagined driving back from Las Vegas. He felt like only one among a multitude.

After an hour, he pulled off at the exit for the El Rancho Motel. He had taken a room there for a week, not knowing where else to go. And in the parking lot, completely unexpectedly, he saw the white Saturn. He knew the license plate. It was hers.

He parked the Fury on the street behind the motel, and from his room on the second floor, he kept watch through vinyl blinds. Evening darkened over the small asphalt parking area, stitched with shiny black lines of patching. The motel's neon sign clicked on while he watched, and beyond the cyclone fence and shrubbery, the freeway boomed and glowed, an indistinct light brimming above the traffic lines.

The Saturn waited, alone and untouched.

At eight thirty, he saw her. She had been in one of the rooms on the ground floor, and she had been with a man. He saw her squeeze the man's hand before they parted, he toward a maroon Camry. Scott smiled with half his face. Katherine had never liked public displays of affection, PDAs she called them. At least she hadn't changed that for this other guy, whoever he was. Nights after that, he waited at the motel for her to arrive. Sometimes she did, arriving a little before or after the Camry. Sometimes she did not.

He began to follow her home on the nights he spotted her at the El Rancho. He knew the route she would take from the motel to her father's house, and he could quickly get the Fury moving after she had pulled out. He told himself he was escorting her, seeing her safely home. And when, after allowing a few minutes to pass, he drove by the house and saw the Saturn snug in the driveway, he breathed happily and thought her secure for the night.

Sometimes, lying on the bed in his room, thinking about Katherine with another man, he wanted to break in, rise above them and hurl down words proving his own rightness. But whenever he imagined the scene, he found the words turning on himself. He had fallen so far short.

· · · • · · ·

On that Monday before the first performance of *The Tempest,* a storm swept in from the Pacific and lowered the sky over the Santa Clara Valley. The rains, absent every summer from California, fell darkly over the valley and darkened the streets and parking lots and rooftops. The water that fell on the shaped and paved landscapes of the cities was shunted into gutters and drains and culverted streams, sent profligate into the bay.

The yellow Mustang was parked in the handicap spot near the theater that evening, as it was during every rehearsal, and K. J. sat alone in his Tiburon one block away, waiting. He still had not seen the car that had broken his leg, and the Mustang was the only connection he had to it. He felt ugly and little from the injury, and he wanted to find that car, to restore himself.

He had worked up a basic pipe bomb, easy to make. He drilled a small hole in the center of a threaded length of pipe, mauled a candle down to the wick to use as a fuse. Then he mixed potassium chlorate, used in chemistry class to produce oxygen, with sugar. He placed it in the pipe with some stones and nails, left some space free to allow it to pressurize, and then capped the other end. He found a plan for a delayed igniter on the Internet, using brake fluid and swimming pool purifier, which he had a kid whose house had a swimming pool get for him. He didn't care if the bomb hurt anyone, as long as it scared them, as long as it showed that if anyone fucked with him, they'd get fucked with themselves.

K. J. hadn't actually tried out his bomb. But the Internet told him it would work, and he had complete faith in it.

A little after eight, he began to see people trailing out from the theater. Then the Mustang nosed slowly between them, and K. J. turned the key and began to follow. He thought the dark purple of his car would make it less distinguishable in the low weather.

The Mustang first drove along the four-lane streets to Blossom Haven's apartment. K. J. expected that. He knew where she lived. He didn't know where Carter lived, since there was no house or phone number in his or his mother's name, but he was going to find out. He drove past as the Mustang was maneuvering slowly into the lot that adjoined the apartment. The asphalt was liquid with rain, and as he slowed for a U-turn he could hear the water picked by his tires and swished against the underside of his car.

The Mustang was ahead of him as he came back the other direction, and he followed it as it turned right onto Country Lane Road and into the subdivision. Now it was easy. The streets were mostly at right angles, with an occasional curve or cul-de-sac. He saw it turn on Catesby and settle into a driveway.

He drove around the block once, to get a slightly longer look at the house and double-check the address after Carter had gone inside, and he found himself following a white Saturn. The Saturn pulled into the driveway next to the Mustang, and K. J. once again continued on past, intending to make one more round after the house was quiet and everyone was inside.

He turned onto Catesby one last time and found himself looking at the wide, unmistakable rear end of a Plymouth Fury. There were the sharp body lines, the dinged and rusty fenders, the silvery rear bumper. There was the vinyl roof, clearly ripped and peeling back. It was the car that had hit him, he had no doubt.

He saw the car slow past the house where Carter had parked. By the two streetlights on the block, he saw the man driving the car wave at the house, even though there was no one to wave back at him. Then the car sped up.

K. J. lost the Fury on 101, heading north. He wasn't sure if the Fury knew it was being followed or not. On the glary wet surface of the freeway, the traffic clotted and unclotted, and big trucks threw spinning shields of water beside them, and he peered through the wipers slapping at the liquid film, and in one moment the Fury disappeared. But he knew he'd made the car, and he knew he had his house.

· · · • · · ·

On Thursday, the day the play opened, the Garden Spot Café at the Blue Skies Bowl served food for the last time. Asbestos removal would begin within days, and then the large and saurian machines would move in on tank treads, equipped with pistons and jaw-like shovels and electromagnets suspended from heavy chain. They would chunk away at the building, crumbling it into pieces of concrete and twisted metal that would be pushed into mounds by bulldozers, sorted out and punched into smaller pieces, and finally dumped into long rust-striped containers to be trucked away. The mounds would grow until the last corner of the building was demolished, then gradually shrink until a lone bulldozer smoothed out the soil, and grass seed and fertilizer were spread as a temporary ground cover. Construction on the luxury condominiums would begin in 2004. At the edge of the bowling alley parking lot, a sign was already advertising—*A Home in the Heart of Silicon Valley*—and offering attractive terms and conditions.

Henry and the men he had lunch with on that last day had seen similar signs a half century earlier, at the edge of newly cleared orchards—GIS, *No Money Down!*—but they paid no attention to the sign foretelling what would replace the Blue Sky Bowl. It was not directed at them. They ate the pastrami sandwiches on rye, the corned beef sandwiches, the roast beef with horseradish au jus they liked. Some, whose dentures weren't up to deli meats, had rich tomato soup and crackers and cheese. And they talked over where they could meet now and then for lunch and coffee. Across the street, at the Western Horizons Shopping Town, there were only the chains—Starbucks, Olive Garden, Red Lobster. George Lee, who had been running the Garden Spot for twenty years, was retiring, or they all would have gone to wherever he was working. After he had served them all, he came from behind the counter and joined them, and they stayed through all the afternoon, telling stories, making long the time before the doors finally closed.

At five o'clock, Henry stood up and shook hands with everyone and said, "An attractive young woman is picking me up today."

They laughed. They shared the tales of their aging bodies among themselves, they knew who had a pacemaker and who was incontinent, and they knew about Henry's radical prostate surgery. Two of them had had the same. But he told them to come and see for themselves.

He walked out the door, stepped gingerly, felt the numbness on the soles of his feet cut like tiny knifepoints. As he walked down the concrete steps to the asphalt, Nu pulled up in her 1969 Ford Fairlane, red with a white top. She had washed it on the way to pick Henry up, and the chrome gleamed and the white stripe down the side shone. She got out of the car and stood up, her own red hair pulled back in a soft rope, wearing silver and turquoise around her neck and a loose white blouse.

The men had expected to see Henry's daughter, or perhaps granddaughter. They didn't expect to see Nu, sixty years old, but lithe and limber, face lined and eyes bright. They watched, from the door of the exhausted coffeeshop. Nu stood near Henry as he lowered himself carefully into the white bench seat, then walked to the driver's side, got behind the wheel, tossed her hair back. She smiled and waved, and Henry waved as well, and the men watched as the Fairlane sailed off for the opening night of *The Tempest*.

· · · · • · · ·

In the house on Catesby Street, Katherine spread a new yellow tablecloth on the dining room table and set out spoons and paper napkins and cake forks and small plates and bowls. She put candles in the candlestick holders and a seasonal centerpiece of russet and gold leaves and golden apples and brown acorns. She had ice cream in the freezer and a cake from Safeway in the refrigerator decorated with a square-rigged ship and the words *O Brave New World*.

Betty had allowed herself to be persuaded to come over Highway 17 from Santa Cruz for the play, feigning reluctance even after her mother told her that she wanted her to meet Heber. She helped smooth the tablecloth and opened the packages of oak-leaf-printed napkins with an amused smirk on her face.

"This is so corny," she said. "Is *this* what your new boyfriend likes?"

"This is for your brother. Heber likes Mexican food. And blues bars."

"Hmmm." Betty was skeptical. That sounded too cool for someone dating her mother. "What kind of a name *is* Heber, anyway?"

"It's . . . his name." Heber had told Katherine that his name was not uncommon in Utah and that there was actually an old trading center called Heber City east of the Wasatch Front. But Katherine didn't think that would impress her daughter.

"Heber *Grim*shaw." Betty shook her head as though baffled, and she went to the mirror in the front closet to inspect her new tattoo for the fourth time. She was wearing a low-cut pair of tight jeans and a stretchy top that rode up her midriff and left a couple of inches of bare skin. "I can wear Abercrombie and Fitch like you're supposed to," she'd told her mother. "No muffin top on me." And, since the last time she'd seen Katherine, she had gotten a tattoo across the back of her hips, a black-and-red filigree that peeked partway over the waist of her jeans. She inspected it now, turning her head over her left shoulder and looking at her backside in the mirror and pouting. She hadn't announced to her mother that she'd gotten a tattoo. She'd simply made it a point to conspicuously consider it in front of her mother and see if she got any comments.

Katherine said nothing about it. She hadn't been asked what she thought, and so it was safer to say nothing. She couldn't compliment it. She couldn't help but see it as a sexual come-on, and she'd found out online that a tattoo there was called a "tramp stamp." Complimenting her on it would be like complimenting her on having sex. *Yuck,* as Betty herself might say. Yet she couldn't criticize it. She had given up on criticizing her daughter's clothing even before she moved out, and criticizing her tattoo now would be like criticizing her for having sex.

And Katherine wanted and needed her daughter's approval. She'd first told Heber he could meet her family as a way to make him feel better, but now she wanted to bring him in and wanted the fractured circle of her family to form again. She wouldn't pitch a fit over Betty's tattoo, just as she didn't over Carter meeting with Scott and now driving a Mustang. She needed both of them to understand and approve of her. So she'd welcome Betty, and her tattoo, and she'd welcome Carter's nose-ringed fifteen-year-old. Her father wanted to bring the drama teacher, with whom he'd become friends, so she welcomed her too. She would welcome Scott as well, to come and settle things and not disappear. When Carter had told her about meeting him and exchanging cars, she found she was not so angry anymore—since Heber, perhaps—and she would welcome him in as a friend.

"It's too bad Ian couldn't come," she called over to her daughter.

Betty raised her eyes from her butt.

"I was *not* going to bring my *boy*friend to see my little brother in a high school play."

"He would have been perfectly welcome," Katherine said.

"God," Betty said, in perfect amazement at the simple-minded witlessness of mothers.

The doorbell rang. Betty opened it immediately, before her mother could get there. Without saying hello, she surveyed the man standing there. He didn't look like any prize, in her opinion. Kind of thin-faced with busy eyebrows and skinny through the chest. Not buff, not someone who worked out. Wearing an Eddie Bauer jacket and driving that Toyota Camry parked on the street, the most boring car ever. The only thing that made him at all interesting was that he was at least ten years younger than her mother.

"Hello?" Heber said through the screen door. "Am I in the right place?"

"Heber, come in. This is my daughter, Betty." Katherine swooped in behind Betty and opened the door and drew Heber inside. "Betty, say hello."

"Hi," Betty said in her already bored voice.

"Hello, Betty. I've been looking forward to meeting you."

"Come in, come in," Katherine said in an artificially high voice. "We have some time before we have to leave."

"So this is the house you grew up in." Heber walked into the small living room.

"It's not much," Katherine said.

"No, it's fine." He went to the dining room table, set and decorated. "Hey, nice napkins," he said. "You went all out."

Betty gave her mother a smirk.

· · · • · · ·

In the music room adjoining the theater, a bank of makeup mirrors was set up on long folding tables, and the young actors were applying pancake with round sponges, penciling in their eyebrows, aging themselves with crow's feet and lined foreheads. The boy playing Stephano, the drunk, was giving himself a bulbous and reddened nose, while Francisco as Prospero was whitening his hair with spray color. Behind temporary dividers, students were putting on doublets and cloaks and long embroidered gowns, and crowns and necklaces and rings.

Henry sat apart, where Nu asked him to wait, out of the way. He watched Blossom Haven applying greenish and black makeup to the face of the monstrous Caliban, matching the frog-colored bodysuit he wore, and giving him gills on both sides of his neck. Caliban, whom Henry had seen and addressed as his cancer on that first evening in the theater. He watched his grandson emerge from behind the divider, dressed in motley and wearing a fool's cap, belled and tricolor.

When Nu entered the room, thirty minutes before curtain time, the shouts and songs and invented Shakespearean insults quieted. She went to the music room's grand piano and played a G major chord and held down the damper pedal, and as the sound wavered and held, all the actors gathered around her.

She played a simple ascending and descending series of notes, and everyone warmed up their voices by singing along, deep, from the diaphragm. *Ha ha ha ha ha ha ha.* Then she moved up a note, so that the sequence began a little higher. The actors sang along. She moved up again, and again. The young voices joined in a beautiful nonsense sound, each repetition a little higher and a little more energized. Then Nu began to move back down the keyboard, and the voices fell with her, growing deeper until she stopped where she began.

"Magic circle," she said.

The cast and the crew, the actors and costume designers and set builders and sound and light specialists, everyone who was not engaged with taking tickets and ushering, crossed their arms in front of them and joined hands in a large circle. Nu drew Henry into the circle beside her, and he looked around at all the young people, some in the costume of the play, and some merely in the costume of the young. They were beautiful, he thought, and thought again how beautiful they were. How beauteous mankind is, Shakespeare had written. And the young believe, and believe that the world is new for them, and believe that they will get away with believing it forever.

Nu began to speak, and said nothing to diminish the feeling within the circle. She spoke of the name of Shakespeare's theater—the Globe—and how fitting it was, as Shakespeare had gathered all the passions of the world within it. She spoke of the first time she had played in Shakespeare, in a festival production in San Diego of

Midsummer's Night Dream. She had only a small part, one of Tita-
nia's attendants, Mistress Peascod. But being within the theater, she
had felt part of something large and joyful, where circles joined,
where beginnings and endings met and made sense. And she told
them what her director had said to the cast before opening.

"For tonight, let there be, a Big, Fat Joy. That's what he said.
And now I'm passing it on to you. For tonight, let there be, a Big,
Fat Joy."

She squeezed Henry's hand, and he squeezed the hand of the
young actor next to him. He thought about the disinfectant he
would put on his hands in just a moment, that precaution of
chemotherapy patients that nobody else in this circle would be
concerned about.

"Break a leg," Nu said. And the circle broke apart, and each one
went back to their role for the evening.

· · · • · · ·

The fuse K. J. had made was so primitive he assumed it would be
untraceable. Two empty tin cans, duct-taped one on top of the
other. He made a pinhole in the bottom of the upper one and a
few tiny holes three-quarters of the way up the sides of the lower
one. He would pour viscous brake fluid into the upper can, and it
would slowly drip into the lower can, filling it. When the fluid in
the lower can reached the holes in its side, it would gradually ooze
through and crawl down the side of the can to the swimming-pool
chemicals. And react with them. And light the fuse to ignite the
pipe bomb.

He had it all in a medium-size box, the size that might be used
to deliver sweaters from a catalog. In the early evening, as *The Tempest* opened, he drove by the house on Catesby Street. The driveway was empty, and the windows were dark except for one light
in the living room picture window. There was no sign of life. He
drove around the block once. The window again, still and square
and illuminated behind drawn curtains.

He drove to a small park that backed up against the Lawrence
Expressway. The grassy field and play structures were deserted,

and he parked under one light near the sign that said that the park closed at dusk. He unscrewed the top from a small metallic can of brake fluid and poured it carefully into the top half of his fuse. The fluid rested, motionless, but he knew that it would eventually seep down into the lower half. Then he covered the top of the can with foil and sealed up the cardboard box with packing tape.

At the house, he parked on the street to keep the box level. And he lifted it from the passenger's side of the car and carried it between two hands to the front porch and placed it delicately under the wooden bench seat filled with terra-cotta pots. Like one of the many gifts to be delivered during the coming season.

He planned to pick up his crew and return to see, if not the explosion itself, the aftermath. See, finally, the satisfaction of the payback.

· · · • · · ·

Henry saw his daughter standing near the ticket window, looking left and right, looking for him. There were people flowing slowly about her, parents and the younger brothers and sisters of the actors and crew, and high school students there to watch their friends. The plaza between the theater building and the other low classroom buildings was illuminated by tall lamps on green poles, each lamp diffusing its light under a cap of white metal, and people walked from light to light to the theater entrance under the broad overhanging eaves. Katherine stood still among them, between the pools of light and the open doorways, and Henry saw beside her the man who must be Heber, and he saw that if Katherine was looking for him, Heber was looking only at Katherine, attentive to her and her varying emotions. Betty was sitting on one of the bench seats around the cement planters, a knowing look of low expectations painted on her face.

Henry greeted Heber with a handshake, and he called Betty to his side for a hug, as he had not seen her for two months. Katherine formally introduced Heber to Henry, and they shook hands again. Then Reverend Nancy appeared with her partner, and Katherine introduced Heber once more. Carter had told them he would be in the play, and they had come to see him. Katherine invited them back to the house for cake and ice cream as well, and they were delighted to come.

Henry looked at his watch. "We should go get seats."

In the theater, they sat together on a row of hard metal folding chairs and looked up to the gilded words: "The Theater of California." Then the house lights dimmed, and the stage curtain hissed up. A pale light showed a painted island, painted on the back wall behind the stage. The island was green and tall and distant, tinged with the dawn's rose light trimming some clouds about the volcanic heights, floating above a sea of impossible blue.

Then the stage went black with a blast of thunder, and sailors shouted as they fought to keep their ship from capsizing in the foretold tempest.

. . . • . . .

Outside the theater, from the far edge of the plaza, Scott had watched his wife greet Henry, introduce the man to him. His daughter was there, and he willed her to be difficult, to disrupt the dumb show taking place before him. To disrupt it on his behalf, knowingly or not. But she did not, and then the reverend showed up. He recognized her, and the spirit of amity that followed seemed to give a blessing to all that was taking place. Scott felt like he was watching a scene from his own life, the life he had in the past, the life he was meant to be living at this moment.

They went in together, through the dark double doors. Scott turned to the Fury in the parking lot, began driving, and without much thought found himself at the house on Catesby Street.

He saw the same lighted window as K. J. The picture window, which was as much about presenting a picture to the neighborhood as it was about allowing the family within the house to look outward. Scott looked at it now, square and curtained and illuminated from inside, the smallish single-pane glass allotted to a postwar ranch, and he wanted to be sitting in the living room, with his family around him. In this house, this subdivision house that sheltered so many of the war's generation, this house that was not even his own childhood dwelling. He believed he belonged to it and in it. And he was as far from it now as he'd been when he first came back from the Arabian Sea. Still sitting outside in an old car that was itself an expression of his nameless nostalgia for his blessed American life.

He left the Fury parked on the street and walked along the side of the garage into the backyard. He still had the key on his ring, and it still fit. Nobody had thought to change the locks, even though someone had been getting in on a regular basis. Scott thought that was dumb, and it made him think again that Katherine needed him.

He prowled the house, as he had done two months ago. His father-in-law's room, dense and warm, his son's room, with a bed and a computer, still looking like a room at a boarding school, something temporary and unsettled about the poster on the wall. Katherine's room with the bunk bed, not a space of intimacy.

On the hutch near the dining room table, he found the book on divorce that Katherine had bought at Borders. He laid it on the table and leafed through it. The underlinings and exclamation points ended after the first chapter.

"Yes!" He made a fist and pulled it down toward himself in triumph. He was quite willing to believe that she had stopped reading after the first chapter because she had realized that she wanted to stay married to him. He looked for clues in the sorts of things she had marked and found, under "Divorce by Marriage Settlement Agreement," a circle around "Good relationship with your ex-spouse, especially important when children are concerned." That clearly pointed to someone who was having second thoughts.

He picked up the book and took it into the sunken den and drew back the black metal curtain from the fireplace. The grate and the ash pan were blackened, and there were fire marks on the bricks at the rear, but he couldn't tell when the last time a fire had been laid. He thought about burning the book, but he didn't want to set the house on fire doing it. Totally counterproductive. It would be more meaningful if Katherine chose to burn it.

He placed the book back on the hutch and decided to wait outside for everyone to come home from the play. He wanted to be invited in. He looked around, made sure that he had not left on any more lights besides the single lamp in the living room near the picture window. And then he went out the front door. He tested the knob, made sure it was locked, and let the screen door close behind him. They hadn't left the porch light on, so he would have to wait in the dark, though he thought they would know he was here once they saw the Fury. Then he settled down on the wooden bench seat and leaned back to wait.

He took no notice of the cardboard box placed innocently beneath him, with viscous brake fluid beginning to drip silently through a pinhole.

· · · • · · ·

The play unscrolled across the stage, gradually revealing the tableau of the happy ending. Father Prospero manipulated the players until, one by one, they fulfilled their appointed roles. The king of Naples, who had helped conspire to rob Prospero of his dukedom, asked for forgiveness while agonizing over the loss of his son. The usurping duke, Prospero's traitorous brother, was required to abdicate and return the rule of Milan to Prospero. The drunken plotters, Caliban, Stephano, and Trinculo, were punished by being dunked in horse piss and harried by hounds. The son of the king of Naples, against all his father's expectations, was miraculously alive. And he had fallen deeply in love with Prospero's daughter, Miranda.

In harmony, the group departed the island to return to Italy, Prospero restored to his realm, the son restored to the father, the lovers' union promising continuation, fair issue, life triumphant.

Did Henry see already the flaws in the happy ending? Did he wonder how the two lovers would feel when they had grown familiar to each other, when they had known each other for more than three hours, when each to the other is as common as an old coat? Did he notice that the traitorous brother is forgiven before asking mercy, and therefore remains unrepentant and malign? Did he consider that Caliban yet lives, half-human and at home nowhere, Prospero's failure left behind to wonder at all he will never possess? Did he think about what the story would be if there were no Italy to set sail for, no happy kingdom to claim, and all had to remain with Caliban on a compromised and flawed island of their own making?

Or did he choose to believe as Prospero might, in the hoped-for peace and reconciliation, in the complete happy ending? When the audience applauded, and the cast came out for a bow, he saw his grandson on the stage, unconquerably happy to be a few paces away from the young Blossom Haven, and next to him he saw his daughter sitting next to Heber, happy in the attenuated happiness she'd found. And they were coming home with him, for cake and ice cream. Believing was foolish, but it was the best he could do.

· · · • · · ·

When K. J. saw the Fury parked under the streetlamp in front of the low ranch house, he knew his plan was working perfectly. He had picked up Mitch and Brownie because he needed witnesses, and now he knew the real villain would be on the scene. Everything was falling into place.

"This is dope," K. J. said. He pulled the Tiburon in behind the Fury and left it idling. "That's it, isn't it? The one you saw Dipshit driving?"

"For sure," Mitch said. "Look at that roof. That's it." The roof of the Fury, flat metal showing through the ripped vinyl top, shone dull under the streetlamp's quiet pool of light.

"Piece-of-shit car." K. J. got out of the Tiburon and hopped around the Fury. He sneered at the dings and scrapes on the long sheet-metal sides, the expansive hood, the chrome bumper pitted with rust. He had no doubt. This was the car that hit him. And its appearance here, on the very night he planted the bomb, convinced him that everything he had planned would work. The drip fuse would ignite at just the right time. Panic and revenge.

He looked at the lighted picture window, the only light on in the house, one of a number of lighted picture windows along the street. Each one signaling to the others a sign of safety, stability, contentment. Each sign gathering power because of its replication in all the others.

He felt like throwing a brick through the window. But his plan was more intelligent and fitting than that. And here was the Fury to confirm it. With Mitch and Brownie watching, he kicked the fender, the one that had struck him, kicked it with his unhurt leg.

"Hey!" A voice came from the darkened porch. K. J. turned to see a man walking down from the porch, right from where he had left the bomb.

"Hey. If you're looking for trouble, look for it with me." Scott strutted down the walk, feeling confident and righteous. He knew these were the boys Carter had told him about, and as he got closer he recognized the skinny one, the one with the leather jacket, the one he had run down with his car. But he didn't feel any guilt for that impulsive gesture at this moment. Now, he felt like he was defending the house, defending it from these young punks who knew nothing about what it meant.

They were backing away from him, backing toward the still idling Tiburon. It was gratifying, the way they fell back, even though one of them was larger than he was. He felt like he was reasserting something, reclaiming something he had lost.

K. J. opened the driver's side door and posed there half in and half out. Scott stood beside the Fury and folded his arms across his chest.

"Is this your house?" K. J. pointed toward the porch where the cardboard box sat.

Scott felt he had some claim. Now more than ever. This street, this landscape of homes, this was his, this was where he belonged.

"Yes. What's it to you?"

"It's perfect." K. J. ducked into the car, and Mitch and Brownie did the same. As Scott watched, the car backed up and then peeled down the blacktop, through the pools of light that fell on alternating sides of the street.

Scott watched it go, pleased with himself. He went back to the porch and wondered how he would tell Katherine about it, modest but still making clear he had done something bravely.

· · · · • · · ·

After the applause peaked and fell for each group of actors who came in from the wings and bowed, the lights gradually rose in the theater building, and all those present gathered their coats and jackets from the backs of the folding chairs and shuffled to the exits. Outside, Henry sat on one of the benches, a little fatigued, and let the others gather around him. Katherine and Heber and Betty stood nearby, and Reverend Nancy. Then Carter, still in makeup and costume, brought Blossom Haven out to introduce her to everyone. Katherine made sure she was coming to the house, and even Betty smiled, though she thought to herself that this was just the kind of girl she would have expected her little brother to hook up with.

Nu came out to be with them a moment. She would be the last one to leave the theater, but she promised to come as soon as she could. Blossom Haven asked if her mother could come. She would soon finish teaching her yoga class. Katherine said of course. Carter left to take off his makeup with cold cream and change clothes, and Henry said he would wait and ride with Carter in the Mustang. Katherine wanted to head home to make sure everything was ready, so she and Heber and Betty left first. Betty told her that of course everything was ready—what could have happened?—but Katherine said she wanted everything to be just right. Betty sighed. Just right was obviously of some higher order than simply ready.

When the Saturn turned onto Catesby Street, Katherine saw the Fury parked under the light and thought that it was good. Everyone was coming home. She pulled into the driveway, and Heber gripped her arm.

"Wait," he said. "There's someone on the porch."

"Don't worry," Katherine said.

"Holy shit!" Betty said. "It's Dad." She began to wish she *had* brought her boyfriend. She was always bitching about her family, and this would have given him a chance to witness it all up close.

Scott walked slowly toward the Saturn. Heber stood up from the passenger's side, tense and watchful. The two men stopped, three feet from each other, while Betty draped herself over her open door, ready for a show. Then Katherine came around the car and touched Scott on the arm.

"Come inside with us," she said. "Cake and ice cream. Everyone will be here in a few minutes."

"Hi, Daddy," Betty said.

"Hi, darling." Scott smiled. "How are you? Still in love?"

"Dad. Honestly . . . ," she said with theatrical exasperation. Scott glanced at Heber, thought he had at least that advantage of him, that he could tease his daughter and call her by a term of endearment.

They all went into the house, and Katherine turned on lights and brought out the cake with "Brave New World" written on it and made the house into a bright and welcoming place. The porch light was turned on, and people came and were welcomed in. The reverend, the choir director, Henry, Carter, Blossom Haven, Nu. Ian, Betty's boyfriend, came after she called him on her cell. When the cake was cut, they had a toast to Shakespeare, to the complete happy ending, to the comedy and continuance of life, to the lovers.

But there was a silence in the room about the world they celebrated and loved. Henry, ripe with the fall of his age, might act as though his friendship with Nu had quickened him, but his body would never let him fool himself for long. In a day, he would be poisoned again, and descend, and never rise as high as he was this night. Carter and Blossom Haven tripped along the cliff edge, still blithe as children about the possibility of stumbling, and Betty, so affectedly wise, had not noticed the unhappiness already growing within from her dependence on her boyfriend's careless charity. Katherine now found herself unwillingly the author of heartsickness when she desired only to do kindness, as two men, each one needy and vain as men can be, waited on her. The reverend might hope that the house is just a figure of where we will all be gathered in, but Nu had not forgotten that this landscape in which we love is stuff and dreams.

The first one to notice the fire was Blossom Haven's mother, the old hippie who cobbled together a living for herself teaching yoga, belly dancing, kripalu, Reiki, being a bar wench at Renaissance Faires, leading meditation retreats to Mount Madonna. She had never been on Catesby Street in her memory and had a general aesthetic disdain for the suburban grid, even though she was living in one of the apartment complexes conceived of as a stepping-stone to these houses. As she turned on to the street, she saw an open flame on the porch of a house, and saw the wooden planks of a bench crackling and burning against the painted siding.

She had no idea that the house catching fire was the one where her daughter was at that moment eating ice cream in the midst of a flawed and makeshift family reunion. She turned into the first driveway on her right and ran to the front door and shouted for someone to call 911. It was the two-story house built over the tear-downs, and nobody answered because it was still an empty shell, unfurnished and unoccupied.

She ran to the house on fire and saw lights on inside and was afraid to run to the front door because the fire was spreading to the soffit above the porch. She took off her shoe and threw it at the kitchen window, but it was a dancer's flat, practically weightless, and it slapped against the window and fell into the fire.

She picked up a landscaping stone, fist-size, and pitched it at the window.

The glass shattered, and the stone thunked through into the kitchen sink. She saw a face appear at the window, at that most everyday place, where a woman washing dishes could look out on the neighborhood.

The face changed from curious to terrified, and a moment later, she saw an old man swing open the front door, stare at the six-foot-tall flames, then slam the door shut.

She ran to the next house over, wearing only one shoe, and hammered on the front door. An older man wearing sweatpants and a cardigan sweater opened the door and gaped at her.

"Fire!" she yelled. "Call 911. Call 911."

Behind her, the pipe bomb popped and showered stones and nails into the flaming front porch.

· · · • · · ·

K. J.'s fuse had worked much better than his pipe bomb. It flashed and caught the cardboard box on fire, which had ignited the varnished boards of the bench. The boards burned hot as kindling, kissed the siding with flames, and spread through the overhang to the roof timbers.

Everyone was in the backyard when the bomb went off. A half hour later, Katherine watches from behind a protective ring of fire trucks and police cars and a minivan from a local news channel. Great canvas hoses, fat and tense, squirm on the asphalt street, and the asphalt is dark and wet under her clogs. It's cool under the purple black sky, November in Northern California, and she pulls her black sweater closer around her.

Several neighbors have invited her in, to wait out whatever would happen, but she wants to stay outside and watch, and say goodbye in that way. She watches streams of water crash onto the siding and fall over the roof of the neighboring house, the two-story house built over the teardowns—she watches the garage burning brightly, all of the family's stagnant artifacts suddenly ripped into combustion and made into the ashen past. She sees that Henry has stayed outside too, with Nu, and Carter with Blossom Haven and her mother, and Betty with Ian. Heber is talking with a police officer, as she will have to do before long.

Scott is no longer present. When they were standing outside, a purple Tiburon nosed into the block, then braked to a stop before the spectacle of people standing in a semicircle on the sidewalk, half their bodies oranged and warm from the light of the fire, half their bodies dark, casting dark stick-figure shadows behind them.

Scott spotted the purple car and ran toward the Fury. He hadn't found the chance, while everyone was eating cake and ice cream, to tell Katherine that he had protected the house, and he was glad he hadn't. Now, as he saw the Tiburon backing out of Catesby Street, he shouted over his shoulder that he would be right back, that he would get them, though it was unclear to anyone who *them* was. And he roared off in pursuit, chasing the Tiburon with his Fury.

He would drive all night, long after he'd lost the other car, long after the chase had proven futile. He would drive, chasing nothing he would ever find, but still chasing, unaware that he was acting out in miniature a figure for his entire life.

Katherine drifts past the newsman combing his hair, past clumps of neighbors, walking slowly over the wet and glary street, keeping her head turned toward the burning house. Heber has finished being questioned and is seeking her out, but she gravitates to her father's side. As she watches the flames that reach high and paint everything around them in lurid yellows and oranges and leave everything outside their scope in black relief, she sees again her father standing on the roof. And that strange new landscape, the plain of roofs humped in shingle-covered peaks stretching forth within the newly platted, newly built-up subdivision, too new for trees to rise up and disrupt the single-story fact of it. She sees again the house as it appears in her dreams, her dream house of the past, with Daddy-protector on the roof, the house proof against all ills.

She finds her father. Neither of them has forsaken the house with their gaze. Nu draws back gracefully, and Katherine puts her arm around her father's waist and he puts his arm over her shoulder.

"All that crap in the garage," he says.

"Yes," she says.

The others slowly gather around them, sons and daughters and friends and lovers, an arc between them and the darkness behind them.

"What are you thinking of?" she asked.

"Your mother. You?"

"I'm thinking of you, on the roof."

Henry shakes his head. "We'll have to call your brothers."

"We'll find someplace together," Katherine says. "Someplace temporary."

Acknowledgments

This novel owes much to my memory of a street in San José where two of my mother's sisters lived with their families and where I visited often. So my first thanks go to my family—my parents, uncles, aunts, brothers, cousins, nieces, nephews, and all.

I'd like to thank the friends and fellow writers who read the manuscript along the way, especially Dorothy Solomon, Linden McNeilly, and Valerie Cohen. And special thanks to Alison Bond, for her many years of support.

My thanks to the Vintage Hams of the '70s. If they read the book, they'll know why.

While writing this novel, I spent time in archives reading about the history of the American suburb. As always, I thank the many librarians who helped point me in the right direction, including the patient professionals who work at the Bancroft Library in Berkeley and in the California Room at the Dr. Martin Luther King Jr. Library in San José. Special gratitude to Lisa Christiansen, of the California History Center at De Anza College.

I am grateful beyond measure for the editing, guidance, and support of Joanne O'Hare and all the staff at the University of Nevada Press.

I would like to thank the Institute for the Study of Culture and Society, at Bowling Green State University, for invaluable support during the writing of the first draft of this book. And my thanks to friends and colleagues in the English Department and Creative Writing Program at BGSU. To the many students I've had the honor of teaching over the years, thanks—your commitment and enthusiasm are inspiring.

Finally, thanks to Kimberly, for everything.